*river reel*

# *river reel*

A NOVEL BY

*Bonnie Laing*

SUMACH PRESS

LIBRARY AND ARCHIVES CANADA CATALOGUING IN PUBLICATION

Laing, Bonnie
River reel : a novel / Bonnie Laing.

ISBN 1-894549-50-3

I. Title.

PS8573.A3795R59 2005     C813'.54     C2005-904725-9

Edited by Lisa Rundle
Designed by Liz Martin

Sumach Press acknowledges the support of the Canada Council
for the Arts and the Ontario Arts Council for our publishing program.
We acknowledge the financial support of the Government of Canada through
the Book Publishing Industry Development Program (BPIDP)
for our publishing activities.

ONTARIO ARTS COUNCIL
CONSEIL DES ARTS DE L'ONTARIO

Printed and bound in Canada

Published by

SUMACH PRESS
1415 Bathurst Street #202
Toronto ON Canada M5R 3H8

sumachpress@on.aibn.com
www.sumachpress.com

*To Greg and Greta,*
*with love and thanks*

## Acknowledgements

I would like to thank the following people who all made valuable contributions to this novel: My writing friends Greg Byers, Sue Chenette, Iris Nowell, Peter Sanders and Joanna Sworn, who read earlier versions of the manuscript and suggested needed changes. As well, Jan Geddes for her eagle eye and great insight. My cousins Jean and James Campbell, who provided details of farming life in Glengarry from the 1930s through to today. Jane Usher, who wrote down her memories of drama school in London in the 1970s. Dane Lanken, who directed me to William Weintraub's wonderful books on Montreal in the bad old days. My editors, Lisa Rundle and Jennifer Day, who helped wrestle the book into shape.

*prologue*

MOTHER AND CHILD. The strongest, longest-lasting bond you will have, like it or not. Images tattooed on the inside of your skull.

Nursery sounds. Watery gurglings followed by "There now. Good girl. Sh-sh-sh." Water sliding on tissue-paper skin. The light fall of talc, like night snow. Pats, small kisses and the shifting of weight from arm to arm, like the balance of love and duty that the relationship requires. A soft nightdress and a diaper to ensure a dry night's sleep. The all-consuming acts of nurture.

Mother and child, child and mother. Annie and Helen, Helen and Annie. Nearly forty years between them.

# chapter 1

"I'm surprised Ewan hasn't called," Annie says from her wheelchair in front of the large living-room window. Outside, a pair of swallows swoops over the river.

Winding the mantle clock, Helen turns and asks, "Ewan who?" The clock, which belonged to Annie's parents, needs to be wound in three places. Annie was very cross that it was allowed to run down while she was in hospital. Helen likes winding it. Turn, turn, turn. Rhythmic, steady, predictable. So unlike my own life, she thinks. Useful, humming, ticking. The way I used to be.

Annie snorts. "Ewan who? Who do you think? Ewan who took me to the dance last night." She snorts again, as she always does in exasperation with Helen's shortcomings which, in her opinion, are many and which have multiplied since Helen came to look after her.

"Oh!" Helen tries to imagine the shrivelled figure in the wheelchair dancing. She can remember her mother in vibrant middle age, glamorously dressed as for a tango. But she can't picture her as young and swaying. Waltzing perhaps. Swing or rock and roll is out of the question — Annie has always seemed to have a rigid spine. That her memory is now loosening is worrying.

"Did you make the rice pudding? The way I like it? With lots of raisins? They're good fibre, you know. Raisins." Annie is poking and slapping at the playdough in her lap, trying to regain the precise use of her left hand.

"It's in the fridge, cooling," Helen replies, relieved that Annie's mind is back in the present, or at least in the future of lunch. Click, click, click. The clock spring is tightening, which helps loosen the tight spring located in the triangle between Helen's shoulder blades and neck. She replaces the clock key. Another duty performed, another step toward the Honour Roll in the Good Daughter Academy. Helen imagines the Good Daughter Academy as a place run by nuns, where the students wear navy blue tunics that end four inches above the knee and have braids tied with white satin bows. The girls are all meek and deeply unhappy, preparing for a lifetime of bridge and Prozac.

"Now I'm going to have my shower and dress. You okay there for a little while? You need anything?" Helen asks.

"I need to get this hand working!" Annie bleats and, with what little strength she has, swats the playdough off her lap and onto the floor. It flaps into a bright orange cow patty.

Helen picks it up and Annie takes it, sheepishly, her chin quivering, her eyelashes blinking back tears. Helen squats in front of her and picks up the historical romance she borrowed from the library for Annie last week. The Empress Josephine, one of Annie's favourites, is a major character. "Why don't you just read, while I get ready?" she says gently.

"I don't like that book. Too many words. And it's too heavy." Annie waves Helen off. "You go do what you have to do. I'm alright. I can look after myself."

I only wish, Helen thinks, taking a deep breath, feeling the spring start to tighten again.

As the hot water hits the back of her neck, where the tension lives, Helen rolls her shoulders and thinks of the curious dance she and Annie are doing. It's a circle dance, the same steps, over and over, with Helen leading. Helen has already spent over an hour in the bathroom this morning, washing Annie, countering the small cries of protest: The water is too hot. Now it's too cold. I don't like that brand of soap. You're washing my back too roughly.

Missing from this dance is the sense of hope, of promise both partners carried when Annie performed this ritual for Helen forty years ago. In its place is love, or what passes as love in adult children — that tattered remnant threaded with habit, guilt and the desire, finally, to be understood, appreciated.

Drying off, Helen catches a glimpse of herself in the bathroom mirror. It has been two months since Annie came home from her three-month stay in rehab, and it shows. Mud circles under her eyes, although usually she's in bed by ten. Grey filaments in her hair. A slope to the shoulders and breasts that reveals how the days have been filled. A gavotte of daily routine, with the Victorian Order of Nurses, the visiting homemakers, the telephone calls from Annie's friends cutting in for a twirl around the floor. The friends want news and dispense gossip about other elderly acquaintances. Doris fell and broke her hip. Harry is awaiting bypass surgery. Again. Margaret's eczema is skin cancer. And there are others who have entered hospital for that most ominous of purposes: tests. Helen has figured out that older people have to retire just so they can find time for their medical appointments, not to mention keeping inventory of their complaints.

In the spare bedroom, Helen picks up the miniature scaffold Bernie made for her, with a perfectly knotted noose and a real trap door that swings down when you pull the matchstick lever at the side. "Hang in there, honey" is burned into the wooden base. Bernie is a stage carpenter who shares Helen's house, a small cottage in a rundown neighbourhood in the East End of Toronto. What I'd give to spend an evening in the kitchen with Bernie, Helen thinks. She smiles as she remembers stuffing herself with his barbecued ribs, ignoring the mess he always leaves, watching as he rolls a toke, listening to disaster stories of the production he's working on, how the lead actor quit one week before the play was due to open because he was offered a bit part on the *X-Files* being filmed in Vancouver. "He has maybe a minute-and-a-half exposure as a yeti!" Bernie reported in amazement.

Helen closes her eyes. It feels like a decade since she's even seen Bernie. She's an actor and director, used to bad gigs, boring gigs, gigs where the play's a turkey, everyone knows it and they still have to play it for six weeks. When this happens, there is an area of her mind she moves into, pretending it isn't happening to her, watching what she does with a kind of detachment, putting it down to a learning experience. She has lived in that airless space for two months now, ever since moving in with her mother to care for her, and there's no end in sight for the run. The part from hell, although she's played plenty of others in that category. Not "best supporting actor" — *only* supporting actor.

"Helen!" Annie shouts. That's enough reflective self-pity for Helen. There is a high degree of panic in Annie's voice. Clutching the towel around her, Helen rushes out to her.

"I'm hungry," Annie announces. "And I need a Kleenex." While Helen goes to fetch one, Annie demands, "And who let that animal in here?"

"There is no animal in here," Helen says evenly, watching Annie fuss with the tissue.

"Don't *hulp* her," the physio has said. He is a slim Swiss whom Helen first glimpsed at the rehab centre, ranging among his geriatric charges on the balls of his feet. Now he visits Annie at home once a week. "She must relearn how to do her daily *tusks*," he said, allowing Helen to see her mother for a brief moment as a stricken walrus. "It vill *hulp* her *self-eshteem.*"

Annie shakes the tissue, wraps it around her nose, blows and misses. I'm sure that did a lot for her self-esteem, Helen thinks as she cleans up the result. Certainly has done a lot for mine.

"I heard an animal, I'm sure of it. And I can smell it," Annie says.

"Here, boy! Here, boy!" Helen calls as she goes back to her room to dress.

Preparing lunch — a tuna sandwich, rice pudding — Helen thinks about the way Annie's mind has become erratic, skipping randomly from stone to stone down the long river of her memory. The doctor says it's an effect of the stroke. But Helen figures that her mother, who has always been very social, has simply moved to the only type of visiting she is now capable of — day trips to people in the past. The imagined animal really puzzles her, though. Perhaps a dog she had down on the farm?

The radio in the kitchen reports that a mass grave with at least 638 bodies in it has been uncovered in Eastern Europe and that a star athlete has been awarded a contract of $56 million over three years. Helen does the math in her head. Probably between $400 and $600 a minute in playing time. She wonders how much those 638 Croats earned for their work.

Lunch is marred by a soft sliver of bone Annie finds in the tuna. "I'm gonna gag!" she announces, and Helen rushes to find a bowl. Annie decides to keep her lunch down. The rice pudding is not sweet enough, and Annie chokes on one of her pills. For a brief second, Helen considers letting her choke, then thumps her on the back, which sends the oblong capsule across the room and into a geranium on the window sill. "Good shot!" Helen praises, while Annie whinnies, "You almost cracked my spine!"

While Annie takes her afternoon nap, Helen escapes to the garden in back of the house. Annie's bungalow sits on a side road, several miles from the nearest town and several hundred feet from her nearest neighbours. The house is about twenty years old, nondescript from the front, with a modest lawn and shrubs. But the back of the property slopes down to the Dominion River and a ramshackle dock, a souvenir of an earlier occupation. The screened porch and picture window in the living room offer a peaceful view of the back garden, the slow-moving river and the pasture land that stretches back from the opposite bank of the river.

In the garden, the weeds become victims of Helen's pent-up energy and frustration. She stabs the earth with the hoe, cutting out the heart of a dandelion root the way Lady Macbeth might. The plot consists of mostly overgrown perennials which, since Annie's illness, have been allowed to get out of hand. She hacks around the hostas, in the way she imagines Lizzie Borden did in her parents. Take that, Creeping Charlie. To give herself a sense of control, she has dug up and replanted many of the flowers, directing them to the places she wants them to occupy. "We're looking for an ensemble performance here," she tells them. The garden doesn't look any better — in fact, it has some embarrassing bald spots — but the effort makes Helen calmer. "I'll whip you into a company yet," she vows, moving a clump of Shasta daisies for the fourth time.

Pushing the wheelbarrow to the compost heap she's created at the side of the property, Helen pauses to look up at the weak clouds streaked across the sky. It has been a nearly perfect summer, and Helen has hardly noticed. She thinks of her Stratford summers, going out to the old limestone quarry at St. Mary's on the afternoons when there wasn't a matinee, diving into the dark clean water, washing away the petty politics, the hissy exchanges of backstage life. Surfacing fresh, ready to take on anything.

"Helen!" Shit, Annie's awake. What did I expect when I came here? Helen wonders, dumping the compost. That Annie would be grateful and recognize that I'm a worthwhile person? That she would make a miraculous recovery, the stroke having altered all her values? That she would stop criticizing me? And why do I still care?

By nine o'clock that night, Helen is aching for a moment to herself, as impatient with Annie as Annie is with her.

"My nightgown's too stiff," Annie pouts.

"You can wear it or you can wear nothing at all," Helen replies, stirring Annie's cup of cocoa into a whirlpool.

"It's too hot," Annie complains of the cocoa as Helen shakes out the evening pills, prepared to overdose her mother into sleep, if necessary.

"Then let it cool. Here," Helen says, handing her the first three pills with a glass of water. Annie looks at them as if they are entrails she has been asked to read. "Just swallow them."

Helen is exhausted, defeated by the waves of details and complaints that have battered her all day and for the past two months. She is barely treading water. Then comes the undertow of guilt. She is old, sick, helpless. She is my mother. She can't help it. Helen makes one last attempt, a stroke toward reconciliation.

"So who was Ewan?" She tucks the bedclothes around her mother, wanting to send her to sleep with a fond memory. "The guy who took you dancing last night?"

"Hunh," mutters Annie, a smile coming to her lips, a dreamy quality in her eyes that has nothing to do with fatigue. "Who was Ewan? Well, the man I almost married." Then she turns her gaze to the wall, locating a spot where the past can be viewed, without the disappointments of the present. As Helen turns out the light, she sees Annie reach out her good hand toward the wall, where shadows from the trees outside slip and slide.

It has become Helen's habit, when Annie is asleep for the night, to pour a cognac and take it with her cigarettes down to the river.

Nine years ago, after she was widowed, Annie moved from Montreal back to the place where she was born, a farming community in Glengarry County, Eastern Ontario, just west of the Quebec border. The bungalow she bought is just a few miles from the farm where she grew up. She joined the local United Church, did volunteer work at the hospital and hooked up with friends she had gone to high school with. She was accepted as if she had never left the community. Until the stroke, Annie's retirement life was a steady hum of bridge, gardening, committee work and excursions to Ottawa for theatre evenings and concerts with the "girls."

Annie did not shrink into widowhood. Instead, with her husband Reg dead, her life seemed to expand, her energy increase, which surprised her children. She took up oil painting and proved to be quite good at it, although far too many of the works were of prettily derelict barns framed by seasonal foliage. Annie announced a love of travel and took several trips with groups of other retired people. In the basement are boxes of fuzzy pictures — Annie on the deck of a boat on the Rhine, halfway up an Aztec pyramid, decked in leis in Hawaii.

There were other surprises. Annie joined a square dance group, even though she claimed to hate the country music and the costumes. A course in Italian cooking was less successful, but a knitting class produced oversized lumpy sweaters for all one Christmas. Whenever Helen came to visit, a new aspect of Annie had opened up, like a lotus blooming. Helen was glad for her and relieved because even her criticism had softened. In short, she seemed happy, as happy as Helen ever remembered her. She was directing her own life instead of everybody else's.

Stepping out onto the old dock down at the river, Helen looks back at the house, its few lights burning through the eerie quiet of the night. She lights a cigarette. She's forbidden to smoke in the house because Annie hates smoking the way only a reformed pack-a-day abuser can. Helen takes a deep draught of Remy Martin, breathing in its richness along with the still night air, the perfect purity of inactivity. She takes a drag on the cigarette and blows a long stream of smoke up to the August sky, where millions of stars blink and shimmer and fly away without warning. The river offers a steady murmur of contentment.

The idea that Annie might have married someone other than Reg had never occurred to Helen. It's strange that she knows every patch of dry skin on her mother's body and every item on her bank statement, but she doesn't know her. She has witnessed Annie's cooings and tirades for years without ever knowing their source. Annie has demanded obedience, attention, affection and fear, but never understanding. That she might have married someone else! Helen thinks back.

\*\*\*

Reg Bannerman is a tall man, with thinning hair, a hearty voice, natty suits and self-confidence to burn. A signet ring on the little finger of one hand. A smile and a handshake you'd reach for when drowning.

It is 1963, and Reg is powering his big burgundy Ford through the slushy streets of Montreal. Little Helen sits beside him in the car, bouncing with excitement. She is proud to be his seat companion today, jealous of the other company he keeps — the poker players, drinking partners and fishermen he entertains in his job as salesman. In the back seat, Sean and Barbara are fighting, or rather Barbara is whining about Sean's aggressive movements that threaten her seat territory.

"Daddy, make him stop!"

"Stop what? I wasn't doing anything!"

"You keep hitting me!"

"I am not! I haven't touched you! Look, Dad, look! My arms are folded."

Reg's joviality is being tested. "One more peep out of either of you and the whole project's off." Reg makes threats like this all the time, even swearing to turn back and go home when they are halfway to Prince Edward Island for a summer vacation. The older kids know Reg's patter as well as his customers do. "Look at Helen," he tells them now. "Only four years old and she can sit still, can't you, honey?" Helen beams with pride as he pats the knee of her snowsuit.

It's the middle of March, and they are on their way to get a dog. No, that is too simple a statement for one of Reg's schemes. Jim, one of Reg's fishing partners, has to get rid of his dog and Reg has offered to take it, even though Annie hates dogs and no one other than Helen wants a second-hand dog. Helen would take a snake, a cockroach, any pet in a pinch.

"What we're going to tell your mother is that Peaches is very valuable," Reg explains as they drive. "That we got her from your Uncle Vic, who couldn't look after her anymore."

Uncle Vic is Reg's uncle, a retired military man the family sees once a year. Even at her age Helen knows Uncle Vic could still look after a regiment if required, as he did in the Second World War, and that he is allergic to dogs.

"Your mother hopes we'll inherit some money from Uncle Vic, so she'll agree to keep it, just to make Vic happy," says Reg. His favourite role with his children is that of conspirator against their mother.

"Why can't we get our own dog?" Barbara wants to know. "A puppy?"

"Your mother would never agree to a pup. And you don't want to be responsible for having a perfectly healthy dog like Peaches put down, do you?" he asks via the rear view mirror. "You want that on your conscience?"

Barbara pouts, uncertain of her moral responsibility toward a dog she has never met. But as in most things, Barbara at fourteen errs on the side of caution and accepts the position her father has placed her in.

"Why can't we get a real dog, like a German shepherd or a Doberman?" Sean demands. At twelve, his hormones are pinballing him into all kinds of macho posturing. He spends far too much time inhaling war comics and watching *Hogan's Heroes*. "Geez! A spaniel! An old lady's dog."

"Spaniels are hunting dogs, you ignorant little sod!" Reg's ability to play benevolent Dad is nearing its limit. "Besides, Jim is a good customer of mine. He'll remember me doing him this favour."

Young as she is, desperate as she is for a pet, Helen sees the basic flaw in this plan. "What if she asks Uncle Vic? What if Mom asks him?" She already anticipates loving the dog then having it taken away when her mother discovers the truth.

"Uncle Vic forgets things at his age," Reg says. Steering with one hand, he fishes in his winter overcoat for a package of Player's and his fliptop Ronson lighter, gets out a cigarette and lights it in one smooth operation, without ever taking his eyes off the road.

He grins, blows a jet of smoke into the frosted windshield and says, "Boy, is she gonna be surprised!"

That's the least of Annie's reactions when Reg and the kids return with Peaches, a placid honey-blond five-year-old with webbed paws that Helen hugs all the way back home. "Give the dog some air, honey," says Reg. "Let your brother and sister play with her."

"She smells," says Barbara.

"She doesn't want to play," adds Sean.

The dog squirms to get out of Helen's constricting grasp. Helen doesn't let her escape, burying her nose in Peaches' fur, patting her big floppy paws. Helen loves with a fierceness that already scares her and that will scare others later in her life.

"Who's going to walk her? And clean up after her?" Annie wants to know, already sponge-mopping the entranceway free of Peaches' slushy tracks.

"I'm not gonna walk a stupid dog," says Sean.

"I'll walk her, Mom, I promise," Helen says. "Every morning and afternoon."

"Hunh! You're too young," Annie counters. She glares at her husband.

"No I'm not, Mommy! Please!" Helen is almost crying now, aware that once more she is in the crossfire between her parents.

"You can just give the dog the run of the backyard," Reg says.

"Oh, yes! And end up with five layers of dog shit when the snow melts," snorts Annie. "How could you do this without even telling me? Kids, go to your room. I need to speak to your father." A shot delivered on two fronts, one to the children, one to Reg.

"No, Mom! Please, please, please!"

"Go!"

Upstairs, Barbara turns on her radio, gets out her *Seventeen* magazine and leafs through the pages. Her room is all done in pink, with big swagging net curtains on the window and a "No animals" sign on the door, a warning to Sean and Helen.

Sean goes into his room, pushing the door against a mound of clothes to gain access. He goes to his desk, the only orderly part of the room, where miniature tanks and other US military equipment are arranged. He organizes yet another battle against the enemy he still refers to as the Gooks.

Only Helen remains on the landing, listening to the loud voices and the sound of slamming pans coming from the kitchen. She cries, certain she has seen Peaches for the last time.

When the children are allowed downstairs again, Peaches is asleep in the living room, dreaming of chasing milk trucks, her paws twitching. Helen's father is seated at the kitchen table, smoking and reading the newspaper.

"One mess in the house and she goes," Annie says. Helen runs to hug her, but Annie stops her with a hand on her shoulder. "Where did you get Peaches?"

"At Uncle Vic's," Helen replies, her mouth drying.

"Don't lie to me!" Annie's voice is worse than a slap. "Especially don't repeat your father's lies. Barbara, where did Peaches come from?"

Barbara shrugs, "Some guy. Dad said he was a customer."

"My best customer," Reg adds.

Annie looks at him. "Why couldn't you just say that? Why the big song and dance?"

Reg gives her one of his sales conference smiles and shrugs. "Why can't the kids have a dog?"

Helen finds her mother upstairs blowing her nose. "I'm sorry, Mommy," she whispers. "I'm sorry I lied. Like Daddy." Guilt is already her most familiar emotion.

Annie pats Helen's head, pockets the Kleenex and says firmly. "You are nothing like your father, you understand? Nothing! One liar in the family is more than enough." Helen nods and Annie pats her again.

\*\*\*

These scenes of discord are repeated over and over again throughout Helen's childhood. On an ordinary weeknight Reg comes in, friendly, overly friendly, overly paternal, a sure sign that he's been drinking. "Hiya, kids! How ya doin'?" To Helen, "How's my little darlin'?"

"You're late," is Annie's greeting.

"Not that late. Is that any way to greet a man who's been working hard all day? Is it kids?"

All three children know better than to say anything.

"Anything exciting happen in school today?"

Sean rolls his eyes and Helen suppresses the urge to report something to the effect that the rest of her Grade 3 class has been killed by the janitor, who was driven mad by the cafeteria's food. At eight, her imagination checks her out of reality as often as it can, always into scenes full of passion and drama. Barbara might announce that her muffins from Home Ec are being put on display for the high school's open house.

"The food's ruined." Annie's voice is a needle.

"Well now, Annie, there are those of us who would say it was no great shakes to start with, right kids?"

None of the children will enter that minefield.

"You don't like it, you can cook it yourself."

"Ah, Annie, I was just teasing."

"No point in cooking good food for a drunk. I don't know why I bother doing anything for any of you." Annie's lower lip is working madly.

"The high school seniors' dance is this Friday," Barbara announces, trying to distract them. "Okay if I stay out past curfew?"

"Are we gonna eat, or what? I'm hungry." Sean has never had any interest in family diplomacy.

"See? You've ruined everyone's dinner." Annie starts slapping the food onto plates, every dish, pan and lid rattling, the oven door slamming. A symphony of barely suppressed rage.

The tension continues throughout dinner. Reg, frozen out of an adult exchange, enquires about school gossip. The three siblings offer monosyllabic replies, their eyes darting to their mother. If Reg comments that it has been warm, Annie claims to have been freezing all day. When she asks if he's paid the gas bill, Reg chuckles, "You worry too much, Annie. You kids wouldn't mind if the heat goes off, would you?"

"I wouldn't like that, Daddy," Barbara pipes up.

Sean fills his mouth with mashed potatoes until his cheeks bulge, then punches both cheeks at once so that potato spurts out of his mouth into the middle of the table. The pimple, he calls it. Helen is no longer hungry even though her stomach churns, digesting something other than food.

The origins of all this friction are a mystery to Helen, especially her mother's rage. She assumes her mother mixes it up at night, after Helen has gone to bed, so that it rises like unbaked bread for the breakfast table. Although Annie's dissatisfaction is constant, it is subject to volcanic eruptions that result in her issuing draconian edicts. Sean telling Annie to "Knock it off!" results in all of the children having to go to their rooms. The one time Helen comes home with a C in math on her report card, none of the children can watch television for a week. Reg making fun of Annie's shepherd's pie means the whole family eats Kraft Dinner for three nights running. This pits the children against each other and drives them to secret acts to undermine each other and their parents. If they are treated as if they are part of a conspiracy, they may as well go underground.

In addition to capricious dictator, Annie assumes the role of domestic martyr. It pains her to see a bed unmade. She is a prisoner to laundry. Why does everyone want to hurt her by leaving food out on the counter? Annie's sighs are as hard to take as her outbursts and most of the family learn to ignore her utterances. Only Helen tries to make her mother happy. It never seems to work, but it does make her Annie's confidante.

In the aftermath of the daily family mini-dramas, Annie takes Helen aside and tells her, "One of these days, I'm just going to leave." Helen nods, panics at the thought of her mother's disappearance, feels guilty about her mother's unhappiness, but loves the attention.

\*\*\*

Reg was over forty and Annie just under when Helen was born. Both had used up their limited parenting skills on their first two children. Annie, never strong on the infant nurturing side of motherhood, had suffered a kind of breakdown before Helen was born. When she recovered, she was impatient, wanting the mothering phase of her life over with.

Luckily for Helen, she is a bright baby, learning things from her older siblings, quite capable of playing on her own. Annie interferes only to tell her what she is doing wrong. Helen was an "afterthought," Reg and Annie tell their friends. Overhearing this at age twelve, Helen will confuse this word with "afterbirth" and imagine herself as bloody waste her parents dragged around after them. By the time Helen was born, Barbara and Sean had fulfilled the fifties ideal of one child of each gender, Barbara decked out in her big-skirted collegiate dresses, Sean intent on what his father refers to as "all-boy" activities — and bullying. Helen is superfluous. There is no role for her, other than as bothersome kid sister, someone who must be babysat and generally coddled in family matters.

So Helen invents her own. Reading is the first thing that rescues her. She's Arriety, the little girl in *The Borrowers*, whose parents adore her, steal things for her. She likes the fact that Arriety lives behind a wall, out of earshot of parental quarrels. As she ploughs her way through the Nancy Drew mysteries, she is Nancy, the girl who drives the action and who also has a red roadster (whatever that is), good friends and a boyfriend, Ned, whom she bosses about. Nancy doesn't have a mother and her father is distant but indulgent. Yet she survives, thrives and solves mysteries. The perfect life. Helen eventually works her way through the family collection of Sir Walter Scott and Dickens, always casting herself as the pure heroine in need of rescue. She is Little Nell, whom everyone will feel sorry for when she's gone. She is the virtuous Rebecca who saves Ivanhoe. The basic dichotomy of her later life is established here — to be independent, yet needed, coddled, loved.

Soon the scenes in her head need a bigger space, and she discovers Reg's workbench at the back of the garage, which is used primarily for collecting unwanted objects. With a small stepladder at one end, she converts it to a stage. She recruits Peaches and unsuspecting younger neighbourhood children, decks them out in cast-off clothing and stages fairy tales, Bible stories, books she's read, always reserving the lead for herself. Peaches gets to play the Big Bad Wolf or Baby Jesus at Christmas. Other neighbourhood children and Mrs. Riley, who occasionally cleans for Annie, make up the audience.

Sometimes there is no one to coerce and even placid Peaches rebels, but still Helen carries on, placing one of Annie's half-slips on her head, covering her hair to become Bernadette of Lourdes, Mary Magdalene or a Walter Scott maiden in distress. At one point, the local librarian, whose career and faith in humankind have been salvaged by the number of books Helen borrows, hands her *The Diary of Anne Frank*. Helen has found the role of her life. A sensitive girl, surrounded by quarrelsome adults, alone in an attic with her thoughts. In adapting Anne's story in her imagination, Helen changes the ending, so that Anne outwits the Nazis and is taken by a handsome stranger to Paris where she sings in a cabaret, eats lobster every day and lives happily ever after.

This is more advanced, herself as playwright, director, actor and audience — complete unto herself. She has carved out a cave in her imagination and equipped it to her specifications, where she rules. But she misses the real-life audience, needs it, and even at this very young age, feels the sense of loss at the end of the performance, when the stage is dark and the theatre silent.

The rest of the family laughs at Helen's airs, with Reg calling her Theda Bara, after the kohl-eyed, stiffly melodramatic silent screen star. Annie declares she is just showing off, taking after the loud-mouthed Reg. The whole family hopes she will outgrow this phase so they can resume storing hockey equipment, dead plants and snow tires on the workbench.

But she doesn't outgrow it. She simply becomes more secretive in her actions — death scenes in the shower, intense dialogues with herself on the way home from school, including arguments with her teachers, which she always wins.

Despite her theatrical flair, Helen, like her siblings, is merely a bit player in the everyday drama of her real family life. The stars are Reg and Annie, finding new sources of conflict to enact, competing for their child audience's attention, clawing each other for top billing. In the walk-on positions are Barbara the conciliator, Sean the indifferent and Helen the penitent.

\*\*\*

That her mother might have married someone else?! To have been raised in peace! Helen can't even imagine how her parents got together, although she knows their marriage was a wartime event and has always assumed it was the result of the passion and uncertainty of the times. They were proof of the adage "Marry in haste, repent at leisure."

Helen takes another draught of brandy. She can never remember her parents talking. They only used words to slice at the thick wad of difference that lay between them. As she leans against the old pilings on the dock, she thinks of her own failed marriage to Guy, the Englishman she met while in theatre school. She reviews her own set of expectations from that time: I was going to have children by now. I would have written a play that appeared at least off-Broadway. A warm, funny, sensitive man would be here helping me cope with my mother. There is irony in the fact that at forty, the dominant role in her life is still that of daughter. For two months, she has had no other identiy.

There are four months to go before the end of the millenium, she thinks. Religious sects are preparing for the end of the world. Computer experts are predicting a total technological meltdown, others see a new start for humankind. And I'm stuck in backwoods Ontario looking after an old lady. Y2K — you're too kind.

Re-entering the house, the only sound is the steady pulse of the mantle clock and a slight snoring from Annie's bedroom. This is a new act for us, Helen realizes. Annie and I are in the wings, waiting to go on. To do what? A breeze has picked up, shivering the leaves on the trees by the river. The mantle clock ticks *keep going, keep going*.

## *chapter 2*

I MIGHT AS WELL BE A CHILD, squeezing rubber balls, moulding play-dough! She gives me this to do whenever she wants to go off on her own, like now. There are times when I think she enjoys seeing me frustrated. But I do have to get my hand and leg working. It's that or the home. They want to put me in the home, and I can't let that happen. Haven't come this far to be stacked away somewhere like last week's newspapers. I can look after myself. Haven't I always? Well, maybe not always.

Home. How can they call such a terrible confining place "home"? Home would be the farm, the place where nothing much happened, but where I was free. Bitter winters and long sunny summers, when even the flies were made stupid with heat. Where there was so little to do after chores that I would go down to the river with my tweezers and pluck the hair on my legs. I had that much time. You always do when you're young. I guess, when you're old, too. It worked. Even now my legs are bald as eggs, although this one is useless.

And here I am living by the river again. The Dominion, the land around it settled by Scots long before anyone thought of that other Dominion, Canada. It's pretty, the river, bent and slow-moving in old age like the rest of us. In the summer, it's cool from the overhanging willows. We'd dangle from their branches before dropping into the sooty water. In the winter, patches of it would be cleared for skating, shinny games taking place every few hundred yards.

Can't swim in it now, of course. And it hardly ever freezes. Too polluted. And mostly from farm chemicals. My folks saw the river as a lifeline, saw themselves as stewards of the land. Now farmers see themselves as businessmen. Spend more time at their computers than they do in the barn, and the river's become a sewer. You know, they don't even let their cows out to pasture between milkings anymore. Just keep them in holding pens, in their stalls, producing milk, the way old-style businessmen used to work their factory hands for all they were worth. Surely the cows must miss the sun and the grass. Farming's changed. Like everything else.

Farming, the river, Ewan. They go together, shift together in memory, like overlapping sheers on a picture window. Seems as though I've always known Ewan, with his family farm just on the next concession to ours. My brother Gordon's best friend. A holy terror when he was young, into trouble all the time. Tipping over outhouses on Halloween. Catching birds and letting them loose in the Presbyterian church during Sunday service. Training his pet pig to fetch turnips for a prize in the dog show at the county fair, then getting mad when they wouldn't give him the prize. Always wanting to be up to something. When I was only eight or so, Ewan dared me to jump from the hayloft onto some hay on the floor of the barn. I stood there swaying with daring and fear for a good fifteen minutes, him and Gordon taunting me. So I jumped, went through the hay, and broke my leg. In a cast for six weeks, the itching under the plaster driving me crazy, scratching with a knitting needle. Should have known then he was a man who'd unsettle me all my life.

Ah, the sweet smell of the hayloft and that feeling of silent satisfaction when it was full at the end of summer. Our farm was a hundred acres, not a bad size for our area. But I never felt I belonged there; always restless to be someplace else. I'd lie awake nights in our house, which was originally log, with other walls built on both sides of the logs, so you couldn't tell it was log except by the small windows and dark rooms. My eyes open in the dark, I'd listen to the rustling of little field mice that came in the house in the fall and built their nests behind the walls, a few of them always managing to avoid the traps my mother set. I liked the idea of those invisible mice. That was the way I saw myself, as having another self no one could see, busy with important things behind the real walls of my life.

Oh, there were things to do. Lordy, yes. Always are on a farm. Looking after the chickens, feeding them, collecting eggs and doing the dishes after meals. Puttering about, dusting the parlour. And of course, during haying or harvesting I'd be out in the fields, as would every other human being who could move for miles around, driving the horses on the wagon while the others would coil, stook and load the hay behind. Every farm kept horses then, and I could ride our Blanche bareback. In the twilight, after the hay was in, along the river in the soft yellow light, Blanche's back so broad I had to ride her shoulders. Farmers kept big horses — Clydesdales, Belgians or Percherons — for the farm chores, a prettier filly for pulling the trap or cutter when going into town, if you were a bit better off but didn't yet own a car.

Better off! Who was better off? It was the thirties, and money had always been scarce in these parts, Depression or no Depression. It's poor farmland, part of the Canadian Shield, just a few inches of topsoil over rock. Rocks were our biggest crop, a new lot of them every year, pushed up by the frost. Glengarry nuggets, we call them. In spring, we'd have to get out there and clear the fields of them before planting, else they'd ruin the machinery. I can still see my brother Gordon heaving those rocks onto the wagon, muttering, "No one ever got rich moving rocks."

Scots seem to love rocks, don't they? Build big castles out of them. Sweep them down the ice in winter and call it a sport, curling. Scots in these parts were either Loyalists from upstate New York, who came after the American Revolution, or crofters from Scotland, forced off their land by the Highland Clearances in the late 1700s to make way for sheep. The fools took one look at the hills and scrub growth around here and thought it looked like home, forgetting that in Scotland, the land was good for sheep and little else. Nice sentiment, but bad judgement, unusual for the grim lot of Scots I grew up amongst.

Grim. That's the word. Life around here was grim. A Presbyterian community, where people believed in hard work and no nonsense, none of what my mother called "frippery," tickling those Rs with her Scots accent. "By their works shall ye know them."

But frippery was always necessary to me. It's what makes life bearable, the lace that makes a plain white cotton nightdress into a princess' gown. I was always looking for the lace.

How often did Maggie and I cruise the shops in Montreal, checking out the lace lingerie, gasping at the price? Maggie, my best friend, who lived in town and had a tongue on her. Poor Maggie, now gone. Back then, we'd devour the weekend papers and movie magazines that showed people who never loaded rocks or trailed a horse around a hayfield all afternoon. There was a war on in Spain, Jean Harlow was shocking Hollywood, bootleg whisky flowed like the Dominion in the New York City we read about. We'd go to the pictures in Alexandria, matinees because they were cheaper, and on the way home discuss whether we would have forced Edward VIII to abdicate the throne of England to marry us, whether Mussolini was good looking or not, and who we would most like to marry, Gary Cooper or John Gilbert? Maggie said she preferred Lord Beaverbrook because he was rich.

Oh, but did Maggie have a knack for making people talk about her! Went out of her way to give them material. "Fast talk is a lot more interesting than that 'Bull struck by train' stuff you read about in *The Glengarry News*," she'd say. People tolerated her ways, forgiving her cheekiness because her mother had died and her father was the village plumber and undertaker, and a drinking man. Did you ever know an undertaker who wasn't a drunk? Must come from having to bury all your friends.

Our farm was near the railway lines and stray men would often show up around dinner time, offering to chop wood or clean out the stables for a meal, most of them tired-looking with little energy to spare. My father would give them some simple chore to do and another plate would be added to the table. Over dinner, we'd hear about shipyard closings in Montreal, of mining towns up north being abandoned and of whole families being driven off their farms out west, with no place to go. Hearing things like that, I'd be grateful for the stew I was eating, but I also wished I could see things like that for myself. To ride atop a boxcar in the sun, with the wind in your hair (I never thought about how it might rain or be cold). Anyone who was anyone was somewhere else. My folks were rooted here, but I wasn't. Swore then that when I moved away, I'd never come back. But here I am, aren't I? Rooted. Felled here by a stroke.

My folks, Angus and Dulcie, had married rather late in life. They never spoke about it, but I know my mother was a mail-order bride, brought over from Scotland after my father advertised in a Western Isles newspaper: "A farm girl, used to hard work, to become wife of a freehold farmer. Passage paid," the advertisement read. Alma, my brother Gordon's wife, found the ad among my mother's things after she died, pressed in a book of poetry called *The Songs of Skye*, along with her marriage certificate, some pictures of strangers who might be my grandparents, aunts and uncles, and a sprig of heather. Alma kept the pictures, even though we'll never know who they were, but then Alma was always a soft touch. Guess my mother brought the book over with her, although I never saw her read anything, except the Bible.

My poor mother. She was a homely woman, which might have been a disappointment to my father, who was quite handsome, with a thick brush of a moustache. He was quiet, very shy, which was probably why he had to advertise for a wife. Was he disappointed with Dulcie's looks? We'll never know. He never let on. They seemed to make a good match. My mother was hard-working, gentle and a decent cook. Though our land was poor, my father was a stubborn worker, and from their beginnings as strangers, they carefully built a life together, having three children, one dying as a baby; putting clapboard on the log house, as well as an additional wing; adding better cattle to the milk herd. They were comfortable with each other and with the slow pace of their lives, God love them, never asking for more. They were rooted.

Even now, I can see them sitting at the kitchen table, within the circle of light from the oil lamp, my mother sewing or counting up her egg money on the oilcloth while my father read to her from the local paper, reporting how a horse-drawn mower had gone over the side of the bridge near Loch Garry and how Willie John MacPhee had drawn two years for setting fire to the bank manager's house. It would make me want to scream to think that this was considered news, but my mother would listen, cluck and comment, taking it all in.

They had a little pact together, my folks. Whenever they wanted to talk about something that we weren't supposed to hear — money or some scandal or gifts for Christmas — they'd switch into Gaelic, my mother's original tongue, which my father spoke haltingly. I envied them that. Their own secret language that shut out everyone else, a touch of the foreign in farmyard Eastern Ontario. And I think I envied the intimacy I heard in those guttural sounds, a closeness to each other I've never found with anyone. Not really.

My mother. Ah, we were close in a funny sort of way, her fussing over me and always taking the hard tasks for herself. Dear Dulcie. No one could ever accuse her of frippery. I suppose it's a common mother–daughter thing, but I'd look at her and be convinced I was adopted, I was that different from her. My mother's hands were never still, and even on the hottest summer afternoons you could hear her humming in the summer kitchen, baking pies, the woodstove turning the room into a forge, despite the breeze blowing through, sweat drizzling down the side of her face. She'd swipe at it with the back of her wrist, leaving a white streak of flour.

We were often at war, my mother and I, although I can't for the life of me remember what it was all about. I can't even remember her ever raising her voice to anyone. Her voice, her soft Scottish purr. She only ever wore plain house dresses, except for a good blue crepe dress she kept for church. She had no interest in how she looked, as if, having been delivered in a plain package, she decided that was her lot in life. I never really understood that, thinking she could have spruced herself up a bit. I remember saying so one time when I was in my teens, all red cupid's-bow lips and rouge-warmed cheeks. She looked at me steady and said, "And *you* could use a little less spr-r-uce."

In spite of this, she spoiled me, possibly because I was the youngest and quite pretty, black-haired like my father but with my mother's sharp brown eyes. She used all her ornamentation on me. She was an excellent seamstress, and whenever I wanted a new dress, she'd squint her eyes at the picture in a magazine that I wanted her to copy, then make up the pattern out of old newspapers. She had a real gift, and two weeks after the fan magazine came out, I'd have a dress that looked like one worn by Mary Pickford. Sometimes she'd look at the picture again and mutter, "I don't think I got the yoke right." But the dresses all looked wonderful.

Some lovely dresses. The white organza one I wore to my high school graduation, the first member of my family to have finished high school, Gordon having been hauled out of school to work on the farm. I took top marks in typing and English, but there was no work to be had around here. A farm community in the middle of the Depression, no one needed typists. The merchants just told the farmers who owed them money to pay up or else, and would often settle for a chicken, a pig or some vegetables. Country-style economics.

Ah, but I almost made a break. My cousin Dorcas and her husband, who worked for the government, offered to board Maggie and me in Ottawa while we went to business college. After that, Dorcas claimed, we could probably get work in the civil service. Maggie's father agreed to the plan, and Maggie and I dreamed for days about sitting in tea shops on Bank Street, wearing hats and gloves, eating cream cakes. But my father said that we couldn't afford it, although the real reason was that he felt no unmarried daughter should be out on her own, especially with a little minx like Maggie, no matter how many cousins were supervising. There were some scenes, I can tell you. I had a temper even then, but it did no good. I stayed home.

Home. That word again. In the home of my youth. The days just tumbling one after the other, with nothing to mark them. Nothing to say "This was a good day" or "That was a bad day" except for the weather. Just a jumble of tasks, one after the other. Make the beds, scrub the floors. It must be like that in that other home they want to send me to. But I'm not going there. I'm not.

Two things kept me going then: Ewan and dancing. I've always loved to dance. Dancing was my escape to my other self, where I was free, part of the music, the equal of whoever held me in his arms. When dancing, you can be carried away — transported, they call it — become someone else without anyone thinking you are putting on airs, or even noticing you, for that matter. You don't need the complications of reality.

Oh, the dances! Back then, there were dances several times a week, though you'd have to go over to Greenfield or Moose Creek to find them, a bunch of us going in a car someone had borrowed from their father, all of us pooling money for gas and the boys drinking home brew in the back seat.

The dance halls were just some old shed or barn outside town in the middle of nowhere, with electric lights strung along the eaves and around a big sign out front. Coming down the road, it looked like Christmas had got stalled in July. You could hear the music before you could even see the place.

Often the car we took was ours, a second-hand Ford, my brother Gordon driving. We'd scoot down the road, picking up Alma MacMillan, who Gordon was sweet on, her cousin Flora who boarded with them, Maggie, Red Alec MacPherson most of the time, and of course, Ewan. There'd be lots of laughing, teasing and smoking, us girls twittering flirtatiously in our summer dresses, hair bobbing around from having been curled in rags all day. Except for me, of course. I had naturally curly hair. Still do. It's one of my best features.

My, but the boys looked good, even Red Alec with that squint of his. Their arms and faces tanned from where the sun caught them. During the summer, Ewan's brown hair would get these golden glints, like light falling on ripe oats. The boys strong from the field work, young enough to dance and drink most of the night and still manage to get up early for chores and a full day in the fields.

Since we couldn't leave until after chores, the dance would usually have started by the time we got there. We travelled as a gang, but once at the dance, we tended to drift apart — Gordon and Alma together, Maggie seizing the first available man, a married one if she thought it would raise eyebrows, Red Alec in search of anyone who'd have him, Ewan, Flora and I left on our own. Ewan, by now a gentleman who didn't like to see anyone left out, waiting, chatting and smoking on the sidelines until someone asked Flora to dance, before he'd ask me. That could take quite awhile, since Flora wasn't about to give Greta Garbo a run for her money. She was a big girl, sad-eyed, with a cowed look and a weak smile that made men protective of her. Her parents had both died, and she had nobody, which is why Alma's folks had taken her in. People felt sorry for her. But pity isn't much of a substitute for affection, is it?

I'd dance with anyone who asked me, imagining Ewan's eyes piercing my back. The band was usually local boys or French Canadians who came over from Hawkesbury. They'd play waltzes, the Lindy and other dances of the day, and Scottish country dances — reels, the Gay Gordons and waltz country-style. Sometimes, they called *The Dashing White Sergeant*. No idea where the dance got that name, but what it involved was a man in the middle, with a woman on either arm. You'd troop back and forth, him twirling each girl in turn. Or it could be a woman and two men. Perhaps it was invented in wartime, when men were scarce at home but too plentiful in army camps. But it suited our dances during the harvest, when the men would work too late or be too tired to dance.

*The Dashing White Sergeant*. I can hear the music now, the military sound of our shoes marching around in a circle. Ewan would take to the floor with Flora and me, dividing his attentions enough to make Flora blush. For a big man, he was a quick dancer, his farm boots skimming the floorboards as if they were dust. After a dance like that, he'd feel comfortable asking me on my own, and we'd drift out onto the floor in a waltz. As a couple. He was much taller than me, and I can still see the triangle on his neck where his shirt opened, the golden hairs that stood looking right back at me. I could read the pulse in his neck.

I often dream about those times now, too often, sometimes even when I'm not asleep. Like now. It's like the Northern Lights, the way they shift down, curtains falling in front of you. One in front of the other, in no apparent pattern. Suddenly, you're there, Ewan, and the dance music is so loud, it confuses me. The scenes keep on shifting, one image falling, your face taking shape, swirling like smoke. Then just as quickly, you're gone, there's this great emptiness and I'm back in this wheelchair, my one good foot keeping time to the dance. Seems awfully warm. And wet. And ... Oh no! Not again!

"Helen!" How long does that girl need to take a shower? "Helen!" Oh, how can this have happened? It's 'cause she's taken so long. It's all her fault. She's bound to notice. "Helen!" I've got to get myself moving. Imagine a grown woman, wetting herself! "Helen!"

## chapter 3

BREAKFAST IS NOT GOING WELL. The oatmeal has lumps in it and the milk is so cold it hurts Annie's teeth. One of the pitted prunes has a pit in it.

"A person could break a tooth on it," Annie says, spitting it out. A string of drool accompanies the pit to her plate. At least the toast is alright. Annie has the appetite of a triathlete.

Helen is just clearing the breakfast dishes when the phone rings.

"Good morning, Ms. Bannerman!" The voice is overly bright, the official cheerful voice of cheerful officialdom. "It's Mrs. MacPherson, from Health Coordination Services. And how are you today?"

"Tired." Helen takes the phone into the living room, out of Annie's hearing range.

"Oh, that's too bad. And how's Mother?" Helen has the impression she's talking to a recording.

"About the same. Any news on vacancies at St. Andrew's?" For the moment, Helen ignores what the term "vacancy" must mean at an old folks' home.

"No, not yet. That's what I'm calling about. It looks like it might be another month."

"You said that last month."

"Well, we have no control over these things, you know. The services are stretched to capacity now."

"I realize that." And there is no way Helen wants the government to take on the job of offing old people in order to create more senior housing spaces. "It's just that I feel stretched to the limit, too."

"Yes, it is hard. I notice in your file, though, that you have a brother and sister. Is there no way they could relieve you for a few days?"

"Good point. But no, there is no way. My sister's too busy giving dinner parties in Toronto and my brother lives in L.A., and has ex-wives to provide for." The bitterness in her voice surprises even Helen.

"Oh, I see. Well!" Mrs. MacPherson's cheer barometer rises again. "Are the VON and the visiting homemakers working out okay?"

"Yes. Yes, they are excellent. Thank you for arranging all this." Helen is grateful, amazed at how quickly the army of efficient individuals moved into action when Annie left the hospital. If only they had a service for aging single daughters whose mothers are inducing homicidal tendencies in them. "I do appreciate all you've done. We'll hang on until there's a space."

"Your mother is very fortunate that you have the type of career that allows you to care for her." Mrs. MacPherson is positively bubbling at this point. "It must be very exciting, working in theatre."

"It can be. When there's work." Even the mention of theatre makes Helen more tired. Or perhaps it's the word "career" or the word "exciting." When was the last time she felt excitement?

"Well, I'll let you know as soon as there's a vacancy," Mrs. MacPherson chirps. "You're at the top of my list."

Top billing at last, Helen thinks. The show from hell, but the billing's good. "Thank you. Yes, please keep us in mind."

As soon as Helen re-enters the kitchen, Annie says, "I'm not going there. There's no point in making arrangements. I don't need them. I can look after myself, and I'm not going."

Annie and Helen have had this conversation many times before. "Ma, you can't look after yourself. You know that. And I can't spend the rest of my life looking after you."

"I've spent most of my life looking after you," Annie counters, a lie. "And worrying about you. You just go. I can look after myself. I expect to have my hand and leg working in no time."

Helen takes a deep breath, reminds herself that this bravado is the result of the stroke, which affected the right side of the brain. Annie has left hemiplegia or paralysis, which leads her to overestimate her abilities.

"Well then, perhaps you could go into the home just until you regain your strength. You'll be able to get daily physio in there."

"Go into the home and the only way you ever come out is in a box," Annie says, her eyes starting to tear.

"Ma, I can't stay here and look after you. I have to work." Helen tries to sound gentle, but firm.

"You could find work around here, if you wanted to. There's openings at the Wal-Mart in Cornwall."

"I work in theatre."

"Well, maybe you could teach drama at the high school. Have you even looked into it?"

"I don't have time to look into anything." Helen's voice has risen. "I'm going for my shower now. We can talk about this later."

By the time Helen is dressed, Marie Lajeunesse, the Franco-Ontarian visiting homemaker, has arrived. Going along the hall, Helen hears Annie saying, "She's very good to me, you know. Yesterday, she made rice pudding. My favourite."

Marie is already folding laundry. "Dat's good," she says, slapping a pile of towels. "Mos' people, dey want to 'ave a son. But a daughter, she looks after you."

"I have two daughters," Annie says. "Both very successful. And artistic. Barbara's an interior decorator. Both she and her husband have their own businesses. Barbara's too busy to come. She has a family."

We all have families, Helen thinks, boiling inside. She wonders when the term "having a family" narrowed down to mean only having children. A stab of regret zigzags through her, then is gone. Breathe deeply, she tells herself and does so.

When Helen comes into the living room, Annie is telling Marie "... acted at Stratford for two seasons but now has more interest in teaching and directing. Maybe you saw her on that CBC series, *Two Solitudes?* It was done in French and English."

Marie confesses that mostly she watches the Sports Network, because of her husband.

It has always amazed Helen to hear her mother describing her to others. At these times, Annie is all praise and self-importance, name-dropping the actors Helen knows and stressing the glamour of theatre. Alone with Helen, she focuses on the uncertainty and Helen's lack of leading lady success.

"I'll never understand why you didn't go back to Stratford after that second year."

"I've told you, Ma. Who wants to play a serving wench with four lines for eight months running? Along with understudying an actress who never gets sick?"

"You got to play her part a few times."

"Matinees, with school audiences. No thanks."

"It's steady work. A paycheque coming in."

"So's garbage collecting."

They've had the same conversation for years. It usually ends with Annie saying, "Do you need some money?"

"No, Ma. I'll ask you if I do."

"Well, you need to get that transmission on your car seen to."

"It'll be alright for a while."

"I do wish you'd find something steady. I worry about you." This is usually accompanied by a sigh of the kind people issue on hearing they're bankrupt.

The most terrible aspect about these recurring conversations is that Helen buys into them. At the end of every job she works, she is convinced that she is not very good, that she will never work again. At some level, she feels Annie is right. She should have sorted herself out by now. At least accepted the uncertainty of working in theatre, not let the lack of money nag at her. Accepted that she will never be a household name, but know that she still does good work that's important.

It still astonishes her how quickly Annie can reduce her to the status of disappointing child. This has always been the case, even when Helen brought home the best grades in school, even though Helen has always been the most attentive of her three children. But then, self-worth never has much to do with fact.

There isn't time for regret. Marie is there, and Helen has the next three hours to do the grocery shopping, pick up Annie's prescriptions, go to the bank and maybe, just maybe, have a half hour to herself. Go to the library, perhaps.

In the supermarket, right near the low-fat, low-salt soups, Helen almost runs down Mrs. Forbes, Annie's old schoolmate and one of her bridge partners.

"And how is your mother?" asks Mrs. Forbes.

"About the same."

"I'll try to get by to see her soon. Any news of St. Andrew's?"

"Nothing yet. No openings for another month, they say."

"Well, let's hope it's soon. You must be worn out. It's good that she has you." Yes, thinks Helen. But is it good that I have her?

Mrs. Forbes is about to push off when something occurs to Helen.

"Mrs. Forbes, did you know a Ewan my mother went out with?"

"Oh my, yes!" says Mrs. Forbes. "They went together for years. They were engaged. Before your mother went off to Montreal to work. Why do you ask?"

"Well, Mom's mind wanders a bit now and again. She mentioned him yesterday, that's all. Said they used to go dancing."

Mrs. Forbes nods. "They say the mind circles back. To better times. Not that they were better times. There was the Depression."

"They were engaged? I never knew that."

"Yes, for a couple of years."

"What happened? Why didn't they marry?"

"Probably couldn't afford to. But you'd have to ask your mother about that."

"It was Mom who broke off the engagement?"

"Now, I don't know that that's the case," Mrs. Forbes says. "Your mother always claimed she went off because he wouldn't marry her."

Her mother as rejected lover. Helen and Mrs. Forbes pause for a moment to consider the strangeness of the universe, before Helen says, "Well, I must hurry. I have to get back before the homemaker leaves. Nice talking to you, Mrs. Forbes. Come by for tea, sometime, will you? Mom and I could both use the company."

"I'll try to make it by the end of the week, dear. Remember me to your mother."

That night it's raining, a hard wild summer storm, with stabs of lightning. Helen is having her brandy and cigarette on the covered porch out back when the phone rings. She runs to get it before it wakes up Annie.

"Hi, Helen! How's Mom?" It's Barbara, calling from Toronto.

"Asleep. At least, I hope she still is."

"Already? Boy, you two are really keeping country hours, aren't you?"

"You make it sound as if I have a choice." Helen is determined that this time Barbara is going to feel her anger.

"Well, how is she doing?"

"About the same. Her mind is wandering a bit, which is worrying."

"Well, I guess we have to expect that, at eighty."

"She's seventy-eight, Barbara."

"Oh, you know what I mean. Any word about St. Andrew's?"

"Yes. They called this morning. At least another month. Any chance you could come down and give me a break?" There! She's said it! Asked for it!

"Oh, sweetie, you know I would love to! But I'm doing a major renovation right now, and Trevor's off to Germany on business at the end of the month. I'm trying to arrange it so I can go with him. We haven't been away since March Break."

Helen hasn't had a holiday in two years, but she refuses to get into a pissing contest. She takes a deep breath. Don't get mad, get even. Get the guilt going. "How's Megan doing?"

"Well, still going to the clinic. She seems better, but she still only weighs eighty-seven pounds. It's worrying."

Megan is Barbara's gymnast daughter, who has a problem with food.

"Is she menstruating yet?"

"Now don't you start, Helen! It's bad enough to listen to Trevor. The doctor says it's not all that abnormal."

"Barbara, a fourteen-year-old who flings her body over bars for five hours a day and vomits up every morsel of food she eats, is already abnormal. Tell her she can't practise till she gains ten pounds."

"Now the doctor says that's precisely the approach we're not supposed to take. No pressure."

No pressure? They've been pressuring that child since she was six months old, thinks Helen. Flash cards when she was two, French immersion daycare, ski lessons, dance lessons, piano lessons, skating lessons and gymnastics. Wherever did she get the idea she had to compete and succeed? But Helen holds her tongue.

"I don't suppose I could talk to Mom?"

"She's asleep, Barbara. And she gets confused easily enough. Try calling earlier."

"This is earlier. I only just got back from my waxing." Barbara sighs. "Tell her I called, will you?"

"I will. Maybe we could call you tomorrow night?"

"No. It's my investment club night. I'll try on the weekend."

"Right! Well, we should be here!" Helen says, too brightly. "'Night, Barbara. Don't buy any shares in the Brooklyn Bridge."

"Good night, Helen. Hang in there."

Hang yourself, she thinks, upset that she's lost her cool. Why is *our* mother only *my* responsibility?

"Helen!"

Shit! Annie's awake. Helen gulps her brandy and heads for the bedroom.

"Ma, what is it?"

Annie is sitting on the edge of the bed, clawing at her nightgown. "Where am I?" she demands.

"You're here, Mom. In your own house. In the bedroom. You must have had a dream." Helen wipes the perspiration that has collected on her forehead. One of the things she's noticed about the elderly is that they seldom sweat. The residue of exertion fades with the ability to exert.

"Was that Ewan on the phone?"

"No, Mom. It was Barbara. I didn't think you were awake."

"Barbara's here?"

"No, Mom. She called. On the phone from Toronto. She'll call again on the weekend."

"Ewan was here. He took me dancing. In the rain. Look! My dress is all wet!" Annie holds out her nightgown in amazement.

Damn! Now Helen will have to change her. She pulls off Annie's nightgown, rough over the ears, and wearily goes to the dresser. "It was a dream, Mom. Only a dream."

"He was here, dammit!" Annie stomps her good foot.

"Okay, Mom. Maybe he was," she soothes, guiding her back so she can put on a new pair of Depends. "But you must try to go back to sleep."

Annie seems confused, but agrees to get back under the covers. "Sleep," she snorts. "I did sleep with him, you know. Ewan. But your father never held it against me." Annie gives a long, loose sigh and her eyelids flutter.

Helen feels a sharp pain that starts in her groin and surges up her spine. For a moment, she can't speak, has trouble breathing. Then she recovers. "It was just a dream, Mom. Go to sleep. Good night."

"Good night, dear," Annie says wearily. "Sorry to be such a bother."

Something inside Helen collapses. She bends over to kiss Annie.

"Sweet dreams, Ma." Annie sighs again.

Helen tops up her brandy and moves into the darkened living room, listening to the last rumbles of the storm as it moves west, dull panes of light in the sky. Another kind of storm is brewing inside of her. That hypocrite! Passing out her prim advice, pretending a cold-blooded attitude to sex!

She stares at the living-room couch, the same one where, at the age of fifteen, she tangled with Serge Lavoie, the house dark, her mother out at cards and not expected for hours. Helen lets herself be carried back.

\*\*\*

Serge is probing the usual prime locations of teenage lust, his touch causing a heady cocktail of desire and a sense of the forbidden to race through Helen. She wants to drink the potion dry.

Suddenly, the lights are on, Annie is there and her voice is shrill above the teens' loud breathing, heaving this time with panic.

"You dirty girl! What are you doing? You!" she says to Serge. "Get out at once."

Serge fumbles with his shirt and pants, searching for his shoes. Helen is limp with shame, unable to look at either of them. Serge stumbles out the door and Annie starts in, all the while pacing the house, polishing surfaces with a dustcloth, her preferred method of stress relief.

"Have you no shame? To just give yourself away to every Tom, Dick and Harry?"

No! No, I don't! Helen wants to scream, because she's been reduced to nothing but shame, even the memory of pleasure evaporating in the heat of her mother's anger. "It wasn't like that! We were only kissing!" she lies, newly awakened nerve endings still alive under her tears.

"And he's French! Do you have that little respect for yourself?"

I have no respect! she wants to answer, knowing that any control she had over herself disappeared the first time Serge slid his hand under her sweater to her breast.

"No man will marry you if you go all the way! Don't you know that? Your virginity is your most precious commodity. Boys will talk!" Annie looks at Helen as if she were mould discovered at the back of the fridge. "You! I knew I had it too easy with Barbara! Why can't you take after your sister?" She noisily rearranges the silver tea service on the buffet. "Have you no sense? If you ask me, sex has always been highly overrated."

Helen can't agree. When she's with Serge, it is as if she has dived into honey. Lust coats her limbs, sweetening every movement. Serge thickens her thoughts and vision; her school lessons are seen and heard through the golden opacity of passion. "H + S = Love," she writes in the margin of her algebra notebook. *Amo Serge,* she conjugates in Latin class. That he is French, and therefore exotic and forbidden, only causes the slow liquid in her veins to stir more often.

They had first quietly eyed each other at the corner grocery store his father ran. Serge went to a Jesuit college in downtown Montreal and helped his father on weekends. The big grocery chains were squeezing out stores like the Lavoies', and the corner shop survived on its beer, cigarette and lottery ticket sales. Small packets of cheese curds on the cash counter were a reminder of an earlier, simpler time in Quebec.

Helen began volunteering to run errands for her parents more often, encouraging their smoking habit. Serge's English was halting, Helen's French worse. They communicated in the language of teenagers — the Beatles, leather jackets and secret cigarettes in back of the store. But they really didn't need much vocabulary. One day Serge offered her a warm bottle of Orange Crush and a week later, with his hand on her breast and his lips on her neck, he whispered *"Tu me plait,"* a phrase she understood. It was the first time Helen was aware of having pleased anyone.

They never dated or were seen together in public, except for one excursion to see *Help!* at the local movie house. Helen's life became a search for opportunities for impassioned gropings that fell short of actual intercourse. On the lawn furniture in the garage and amid the gym mats piled high at the local recreation centre. All gyms smell of sweat and to this day, foot odour reminds Helen of her first passion.

The relationship dissolves in the disgrace of that night. Reg has a word with M. Lavoie and Serge is suddenly a boarder at his college. Helen is sent on no more errands to the store and the matter is never mentioned again. The silence on the subject is harder to bear than her mother's criticism. Helen is further isolated, with no one she can talk to about her great sense of loss and shame. It weighs her down, takes away her natural drive, leaves her spending long hours in her room, crying.

Her sexual explorations are added to the lengthening list of What Helen Does Wrong, which has been building for years. She's too young, too loud, too awkward, too show-offy, too lazy. She is just too, too much.

School sustains her. Although she is completely undisciplined in her studies, Helen still gets good marks, and her cleverness leads to other ways in which she attracts attention — as the gossip columnist on the school newspaper, as debating champion, as the leader of a protest about the amount of time girls have the run of the gym compared to boys, even though she hates gym. The most important recognition comes when she is given the lead in the school play — *Saint Joan*. All her confusion, sorrow and passion find their way through her onto the stage. She has found what Helen Does Right, what even Annie and Reg must applaud on opening night.

\*\*\*

A short bark of a laugh comes out of Helen and she takes another swig of brandy. Her most precious commodity! Perhaps Annie was right. Barbara was better, is still better, at trading commodities.

The night sky is lifting, the storm passing. We're so different, my mother and I, thinks Helen, her anger melting into a lingering sorrow. Why can't parents be honest with their children? Then the answer. It is the child's job to separate; the parent's job to let them. Honesty might slow the process. She switches off the remaining lights in the house, closing the subject down.

*chapter 4*

HELEN. THE MOST STUBBORN OF MY CHILDREN. The one most like me, I suppose, though I'd never tell her that. She insists on these damn exercises, even when I don't feel like it. Weightlifting cans of soup just makes me feel foolish and — oh! There now, I've dropped another one! I'm so mad I could ... "Helen!" Now where is that girl? Where did she say she was going? The laundry? I can't do anything! Useless. Old and useless. The kind of person they send to the home. Oh please! Not the home.

You know, I never used to cry much. Not even when I was a child. Never let anyone see they've had an effect on you or you won't come out ahead. Certainly with Reg, I tried never to show how I felt. Just the ammunition he'd need to coax something more out of me. But I cry a lot now. Tears just bubble up out of me at the slightest provocation. They sort of comfort me — the way you do, Ewan. Why, I never even cried when you suggested we start seeing other people. Or when I heard you had died and how. But I can cry now; now it won't make a difference.

When was it? I suppose it was my last year of high school when I first noticed you in a different way. The loping way you walked, which showed how tall you were. You were always moving, restless. Your hands. Big mitts they were, and I'd shiver every time you cracked your knuckles, which was way too often. Maybe I started to notice you because you began looking at me in a different way, like I was some horse you were planning to buy.

Ah, Ewan. Remember that evening when you came in to play checkers with Gordon and stopped at the kitchen table where I was doing my homework?

"What's that?" you said.

"A book. Ever try reading one of those, Ewan?" I wasn't going to let you get away with anything.

"I know it's a book. What's the language it's written in?"

"Latin."

"Latin? You thinkin' of turning dogan, Annie?"

"I might, if they let women become priests."

"You could always become a nun." Then you bent over closer and I could smell the soap you used. Lifebuoy. "But I think you'd make a terrible nun."

Like Gordon, you'd left school at fifteen to work on the farm, and I think you missed it. You took a real interest in learning. Remember asking me to explain trigonometry? Hunh, I could barely explain trigonometry to myself. But I was clever enough to do well in most courses, and I often saw you pause when you left, fingering my books piled on the chair by the door.

You and Gordon both expected to inherit the family farm as a reward for your lack of education. But you always felt something important had been taken from you, rather than given, didn't you? The Scots were always great believers in education.

That last year in high school. I was chosen to read *In Flanders Fields* on November 11 and give a little speech for the Remembrance Day service. When I got up on the platform, there you were, standing at the back of the auditorium, tossing your cap between your hands. You claimed you had come into town to the feed store, forgetting it was closed for the holiday. But I knew better.

Driving me home in the wagon, you were far away. "That must be something, to fight a war," you said.

"You might get your chance, Ewan. They say there's going to be another one, what with the Germans acting up."

"Yeah. It'd be a good excuse to get away from here." You just kept your eyes on the road.

"Why, I thought you liked it here, Ewan."

You turned and grinned. "I like it right here in this wagon. But I'm not looking forward to spending the next fifty years ploughing rocks."

You saying that felt so strange. Because I myself felt that I couldn't get away fast enough. "I'd be sorry to see you go, Ewan," I said.

And that was it, wasn't it? You pulled the horses to a halt, stopped and turned. "Then I won't go," you said and kissed me for the first time, a quick kiss, light as a petal against my lips. Then, when I didn't pull away, another kiss that started more slowly and lingered longer, my heart knocking like a woodpecker.

"I sure was proud of you up there." Your voice low and a bit bashful. "You have some way with words. And you know how to hold yourself."

Took that with a grain of salt, I can tell you. I didn't quite trust you yet, but I did get a sense of how you admired me. Like trigonometry, you thought that I was something worth having. And I began to believe that myself.

So you came what we called "courting" in those days. To dances or curling. To the pictures in Alexandria. Or just driving in your father's old car. After awhile — how long was it? — you were invited over for Sunday dinner. A new distance between you and Gordon, now that we were courting. You two still talked and argued — you being a Canadiens fan, while Gordon cheered the Leafs — but you spent more time eyeing each other suspiciously, now that girls had entered the picture. Alma and I had separated you, so that you stood on either side of a new field, not knowing how you were going to plant it.

But there was no awkwardness between us, was there, Ewan? Ah! Those times together! It didn't matter what we did, it was just filler until the moment we could be alone. Sort of the way the news and cartoons were the lead-up to the main movie feature. And my, how I loved that main attraction!

It's your voice I remember most clearly. Low, rumbling and smoothed by years of smoking, your laugh starting like the purr of a small motor, rising to the roar of a steam engine, pulling me into its machinery. And you laughed often in those early days, at my weak attempts to keep my distance, at your poor prospects, at the gossipy happenings that were the building materials of the small community we lived in. When you weren't laughing, you spoke in a clipped manner that delivered words like tiny slaps, love pats if you were saying how much you wanted me, stinging smacks if you were telling me what I didn't want to hear, even if it was the truth.

Your eyes, the colour of a winter morning before a snowfall. Your hair, curled when damp. But it's your voice that still haunts me ... singing softly off-key while we danced, sending me away with words you didn't mean.

But we didn't have much use for words then. Restlessness drew us toward each other. My eagerness to see the larger world became focused on exploring you instead. It's funny, but the only thing I knew then about men's bodies had come from Maggie, who filled me in based on seeing the corpses in her father's back-room mortuary. That's about all the sex education I ever got, and that was more than most girls got.

Oh, but I loved the roller coaster rush I felt holding you, running my hands over the parts of your body that were hard where mine were soft, savouring the desperation in your breath at my ear, the heat. I wanted to make love to you — to go all the way — but always stopped short out of fear of the consequences and out of ignorance of how I might prevent them. In our area, there were far too many young women for my liking trapped in rundown farmhouses with small babies. And part of me, I suppose, feared losing that final control over myself.

Everything grows old and stale. I mean, look at me now. And even then. After we'd been going together awhile, the cord between you and me began to chafe, Ewan. Fixated on each other, bored and restless with everything else in our lives, we were tired of going into town and seeing the same people, tired of hearing how the minister's car was seen outside young widow MacRae's one afternoon when everyone thought she shouldn't need any more consolation since her husband had been dead for fourteen months. Or how Black Rory MacGregor had gotten drunk and thrown a bottle at the train passing through town, smashing a window. How Myrtle Dewar's new baby was sickly and likely to go the way of her other four dead children. It seemed nothing ever changed, only multiplied.

Nothing was new except for one thing. You and I had explored most of the ways you can express your desire and still claim to be intact. You were pressuring me to enter that last new zone.

"Not till we're married," I said, pushing your hand away even though my skin was on fire. How often had I said that? We were on an old horse blanket, under the willows by the river.

"We'll be too old to do it then," you said, sitting up, lighting a cigarette and taking a pull on the moonshine you'd brought. You'd been drinking more, as things grew more tense between us. The summer sky crowded with stars and a bright moon.

"Unless, of course, you'd agree to live with my folks." You looked at me hard, but you knew I wouldn't agree to that. Your farm! Barely produced enough for one family to live on, let alone two. Building another house was out of the question. It was wartime now, and there were building supply shortages.

Your father was a quiet man who'd recently lost a leg in a mowing accident. A nice man with a sly smile. But your mother! A witch of a woman, strict and church-going, never allowing guests or family to even smoke in the house. Didn't approve of most people, and she certainly didn't approve of me, saying I was frivolous. I suppose I was. And then there were your two younger sisters, still at home, although your brother had moved to Ottawa.

"I could never live with your mother and you know it. And she'd never have me."

I moved to the edge of the blanket.

"She'd have to accept it if we just went away and were married quietly."

Well, I wasn't about to miss the most glorious, most dramatic moment of a young woman's life, was I? The fuss, the satin and crepe de Chine, the flowers and presents. Not for me, the wedding that Gordon and Alma had, a little church service with the Reverend Watkinson and his stutter, only thirty guests filling the front pews, the women wearing the only hat they owned, some of the men not even in suits, wildflowers on the altar. Everyone back out to the farm for punch and tea, Gordon and Alma going off to Massena for three days on a honeymoon before moving into the room over the summer kitchen. Sneak away to be married and people would think you were in a family way, counting on their fingers till your first child was born.

Maybe if we ran away to someplace interesting, like New York or Paris. Or if marriage meant a home of my own, polished furniture with antimacassars on the arms and back of the stuffed sofa. Where we'd eat in the dining room all the time and you wouldn't have dirt under your fingernails. Daydreams.

Truth was, I didn't really want marriage. Not then. I wanted you, and I wanted excitement, and I was beginning to realize I wasn't likely to get them together. You were stuck, Ewan, but I wasn't, not if I could imagine my life without you. But I couldn't then.

"I'm thinking of sneaking away anyway," you said, flicking your ash. "Join up somewheres else."

You had enlisted, but your mother had gone to the recruiting office, pointing out that because of your father's accident, you were the only working male on the farm. The army dismissed you outright and that night, you got very drunk.

"Don't say 'somewheres.' It makes you sound like a farmer."

You grabbed my arm. "I am a fuckin' farmer! And I wish to hell I had some fuckin' choice about it!" You let go of my arm and blew out all the air in your lungs.

"Ewan, be sensible. Who'll look after the farm if you go?"

"I dunno. And I don't care. I really don't. Maybe Jim can quit his fancy job in the War Ministry and come down and help." You took another drag on your cigarette. "I'm twenty-one years old, and my life is over," you said quietly and with such bitterness. "I know everything that's going to happen."

I was all softness and cooing then, trying to win you back, stroking your neck and pushing my nose up against your sleeve. But the ardour had left you. I knew you meant it. If you weren't leaving for the army, you were leaving me, seeing in me all that trapped you. And I wasn't about to let you get away before I did. I had to do something.

That night I was wearing my blue dress, the one with the tucks going down the front. I just stood up and took it off, the way you would for a medical. Then my slip and underwear. Your mouth fell open, but you didn't say a thing. I went down to the river and pushed off doing a gentle breast stroke toward the middle, then turned over and floated until I heard you splash into the water. The moon pale on our skin, so we looked like two ghosts moving toward each other, the shadows slicing us into segments of arms, shoulders, buttocks, thighs. Half faces.

Everything was liquid, like now, when one memory floods over into another. The river, our mouths, our hands sliding over each other, the slippery way you entered me, smoothing the awkwardness of our efforts. It hurt, but I cried out more from release than from pain, knowing I'd moved us beyond our stalemate. We floated into another dimension, of pleasure and wonder, the only kind of new experience available to us. The only kind we could afford. I'd drawn you closer to me, not realizing that it would add to the claustrophobia I felt.

Afterwards, we lay on the blanket, astonished that everything else in the world still seemed to be the same. The stars still shining, the moon giving imperfect light. We drove home in near silence, coming into the kitchen, where my father was leaning toward the radio, listening to a report about heavy Canadian casualties in an attempted landing at a French seaside village called Dieppe. The announcer reading the names of the regiments involved.

My father looked up. "That's the regiment Johnny Mac's boy is in," he said quietly, getting up to go to bed.

Where am I? I can't be remembering that foolishness. Must keep these cans moving. Cream of mushroom. Cream of tomato. Must be time for lunch soon. Yes! Try lifting them. Can't quite get my hand around ... There! Now up ... up ... Damn! Another one on the floor. "Helen!" Oh what's the use! What's the use of any of it?

*chapter 5*


ANOTHER DAY DOESN'T BEGIN so much as come back to the loop it was on yesterday. Breakfast. Juice to wash down the small mound of pills Annie takes. Stewed rhubarb for regularity. An egg to sooth a delicate stomach, poached to minimize the cholesterol. Dry toast, no butter to further clog the arteries. Coffee for Helen, but not for Annie, not in her condition.

Helen takes advantage of the calm. She swallows another mouthful of coffee and says, "This Ewan who took you dancing, did he live around here?"

"Who?" Annie is moving her pills around on the table, putting them into patterns.

"Yesterday you mentioned a Ewan, who took you dancing. Said he was almost my father." Helen pushes a water glass toward Annie, urging her to swallow the pills, not just play with them.

"Ah, Ewan. Poor man. Died a long time ago." Annie pushes away the pills and the memory in one gesture.

"So he was your beau. Did he live around here?"

"Next concession down from our farm. He farmed, too." Annie carefully moves her pills from one side of the plate to the other with her right hand. "And he was a wonderful dancer." She pauses, spinning a golden oval capsule around on the table. "Is today Wednesday?"

"No, it's Thursday. The day the nurse comes."

"'Cause if it's Wednesday, it's garbage day."

"I took the garbage out yesterday. Today's Thursday."

"Oh." Annie looks around the room, refusing to look at Helen. The subject of Ewan is closed. On the radio, the announcer reports that the Pope has condemned poverty and abortion. "C'mon!" Helen retorts, clearing the dishes. "One or the other! You can't have it both ways." The announcer ignores her, finishing the news with an upbeat item about a Hollywood star who has just married her seventh husband, a dry cleaner, thirty-six years younger than she is. "I wonder how they met," Helen ponders.

The VON nurse arrives, a large farm woman named Susan. Helen has an hour free while the nurse checks on Annie and bathes her. She hotfoots it to town. She buys cigarettes and more brandy, then has a precious half hour in which to read the newspaper and have coffee in the local donut shop. In the arts pages of the *Globe & Mail* is the announcement that John Fitzgerald, former head of the Garrick Theatre School, founder of the Atlantic Regional Theatre Centre, director and actor who once shared the stage with Olivier, Geilgud and Richardson (not in the same production, mind you), has died of a heart attack at the age of sixty-eight. As she reads these words, a sharp bolt of pain hits Helen in the gut and her throat thickens. Scenes start fluttering in her mind.

\*\*\*

She's a student at the University of Toronto, with John Fitzgerald pacing in front of the class. "Look for the spine of your character, the driving motivation, the force that blinds him to all other aspects of his character. Start with your spine."

Helen feels he is looking straight at her, that he recognizes that she has no spine to speak of. She doesn't realize that everyone else in the class feels the same way. I am a tabula rasa, she thinks. A blank slate that any character can be imprinted on. It is all I have to offer as an actor.

He stands before Helen. "Have you ever felt something so strongly that it blinded you to everything else?" His smile is almost a sneer.

Helen can't look at him. She knows she has felt this way, but she also knows she could never articulate it. "No. Can't say that I have."

"Ha! Thought not!" He turns to the class. "Isn't it strange the way virgins carry this aura about them?" Helen lowers her head, but hears the titter of confirmation going around the class. "Catholics think only the Virgin Mary possesses this halo. But only because it's difficult to find another adult virgin in the Catholic Church." Guffaws for that one.

Despite this and other humiliations, it is John who will take Helen's fierce need and use it to build her skill. He transforms it into an intensity that can be felt fifty rows from the stage. He begins the work but never finishes it. It is unfinished yet.

One evening Helen watches as he strides about the huge main room of the converted coach house he lives in, the fireplace roaring, John roaring louder, playing Sir Harry Lauder, falling about as he does "Just a Wee Dock-An-Dorris."

His students are falling about, too, giggling, too much cheap Spanish wine in their veins, too much marijuana smoke in the air. He is old enough to be their father, but the key distinction is, he isn't. It's the late seventies, and John is still questioning all authority, including that of the cops who come to the door to say that the neighbours have complained of the noise. In those days, all Toronto policemen seemed to be Scottish. Hearing Harry Lauder on the stereo, they decide to overlook the fact that the only air available in the room is illegal.

John mocks everyone constantly, including Helen on the night he undresses her for the first time, using his teeth, an exercise that becomes difficult when he reaches the zipper on her jeans. In retrospect, Helen recognizes that she didn't so much desire him as what he stood for. In losing her virginity to him, she hoped to receive by osmosis some of his qualities — recklessness, self-confidence, immunity to guilt.

It doesn't quite work like that, of course. The morning after, Helen wakes up madly in love, convinced that she has found her life partner, that no one else has felt as intensely as she does. John fills every cell in her body, crowds out any other thought. She can look at the garbage piled outside the back of her building and think: John would say it makes a perfect set for *The Threepenny Opera*.

Having given herself over to the power of infatuation, her entire emotional structure tilts dangerously. Feeling she has freed herself in this relationship, she assumes John feels the same way. Worse, she feels that all of John's negative characteristics — his cynicism and condescension — can be redeemed by love.

Never mind that John doesn't want to be redeemed, that he's having quite a good time just as he is, thank you very much. Helen knows he has seduced practically every other woman in the class, and as it turns out, most of the women working in Canadian theatre. A few of the men, as well. But it doesn't matter. This time it is different. Helen is different. She has found a focus for her need and a vocation to boot. She has found her spine.

Of course, it ends badly. Very badly. He continues to mock her in class, then ignores her after she protests. She can't bear not to be with him, sits around her room biting her fingernails when he goes to some social engagement without her, then questions him relentlessly when he comes back. There are grand histrionic scenes in which she threatens to do him damage and he tells her to grow up. She ignores all of her classes that aren't theatre and her grades slip. John tries to end the relationship immediately, but his ego and Helen's neediness, her eagerness to explore all the hidden crevices of sex, keep him sleeping with her, on and off, for two months. When he finally does dump her, tells her to stay away from him, she ends up at his coach house while other people are there, screaming and trying to hit him with a statue of a Peruvian saint. The other students in the theatre program whisper about her behind her back. She may have found her spine, but the rest of her is extremely fragile. She babbles incoherently about the difference between ethics and mores in her philosophy class. When the dean intervenes and suggests she drop out for one term, she has a complete breakdown, taking a razor to her body, making over two hundred cuts, then swallowing forty aspirin to kill the pain. She is treated in emergency, then sent back to Montreal to be hospitalized.

Helen's memories of that time in the psychiatric ward are both sharp and vague. The woman in the next bed who thought she had cancer but who was really bulimic. The window in the ward that overlooked the door where hearses collected the hospital's dead. Drugs blurring the difference between waking and sleeping. Standing behind a window with a nurse, watching a man twitching as he is given electro-shock, a sight meant to prepare her for her own treatment, to reassure her.

She is silent, unable to give voice to her pain, words being inadequate to describe the confusion of guilt, fear and self-loathing she feels. Drugs, group therapy and electro-shock are tried to draw her out. The shock treatments eliminate her short-term memory so that she wakes up unable to remember where she is, but dimly conscious that she is in deep trouble.

Though her desire to act has contributed to her downfall, acting becomes her salvation. The second month she is in hospital, a smart young resident called Dr. Glickstein is assigned to her case. He learns that she has studied drama and so asks her to improvise for him. She does a reasonable mime of a woman packing a suitcase and someone gardening. But when he asks her to mime a sword fight, she finds she can defend herself but not thrust. Asked to do a woman frantically searching for her child in a supermarket, she starts shaking. Dr. Glickstein is onto something. Helen starts to speak, mostly telling him that she doesn't know what's wrong with her.

He calls in her parents. Helen is there when Reg explains to the doctor that Annie comes from Eastern Ontario, a part of the country where there is a great deal of in-breeding, which naturally leads to weakness in the mind. He cites Annie's cousin Douglas, who is a "fruit," as an example of this. As usual, Annie fights back, naming off the number of Reg's family who are alcoholics and citing his "retarded" aunt. Both parents point out that their other two children are fine, skating over Sean's bouts of juvenile delinquency. Dr. Glickstein smiles.

After her parents have gone, still arguing as to who has damaged Helen the most, Dr. Glickstein asks, "Do you like opera?"

Helen shrugs. "I haven't seen much of it. The acting is usually pretty hammy. I like the music though."

"Your parents are very Wagnerian. Lots of Sturm und Drang, no?"

Helen has to smile. "Actually, most nights it was more like Verdi or Puccini. Great histrionics." The scenes where she sat helpless on the sidelines march through her mind and she feels a familiar self-loathing. She realizes that John Fitzgerald was the first outsider to have confirmed her worthlessness.

"They aren't going to change, you know," Dr. Glickstein says softly. "And you are not responsible for the way they are." Helen starts to cry, something she can do if her tea cools before she has had a chance to drink it. "So!" the doctor says cheerily. "We have to change the way you cope with it."

Helen falls in love with the doctor, even though he is chubby, prematurely balding and wears polka dot bow ties. Dr. Glickstein tells her it's okay, it's called transference, it's normal and not permanent. He guides Helen back into her life, moving her out of hospital into a residence for young women, reducing, then eliminating the number of anti-depressants she takes, finding an old college mate who can get her an audition for the Webber Douglas Academy of Dramatic Art in England. Not only is she accepted, she even wins a bursary for special needs students, although her mental state doesn't feel "special." It feels more like an anvil hanging off her heart. Dr. Glickstein even persuades Annie and Reg that it is in their best interests to cough up the money to send Helen abroad, even though Reg protests that she's not nearly pretty enough to be a success as an actress.

"Ethel Barrymore, Edith Evans, Marie Dressler, Marjorie Main, Agnes Moorehead," Dr. Glickstein tells him. "None of them *Playboy* centrefolds. All of them successful actresses."

In her last session with Dr. Glickstein before she takes off for London, Helen is in agony about leaving, terrified of being on her own in a strange country. Dr. Glickstein gives her the name of a therapist in London she can check in with. He takes her hand.

"You know, what you are doing is called a geographic cure," he says. "It's only a partial cure. It takes you away from the source of your pain, but the habit of pain travels with you. You still have to work on that." Helen blubbers and nods. "And if in three years you are still in love with me, I promise to divorce my wife and marry you." Helen has to laugh. Dr. Glickstein continues, "And I still think you should read less Dostoevsky. Enjoy your new life."

\*\*\*

In the donut shop, Helen looks down at the few spidery lines that remain on her arm where the razor cut. It was a very sharp razor, slicing cleanly, leaving few scars. Most of them are on her genitals. A familiar shame and self-loathing washes over her, then goes. It was a long time ago. She is someone else, now. John was a stranger, now he's dead.

She shudders, shaking off the last remnant of pain, then jumps up, drops the *Globe & Mail* and stubs out her cigarette. She's late. She'll be holding back Susan. Indeed, the VON is standing by her Honda when Helen turns into the drive.

"I'm so sorry, I got reading something," Helen says.

"Oh, don't worry. I only just finished. Her blood pressure is up a bit," Susan says. "Not too serious, mind, but up." Susan is a strong, placid woman who can lift Annie with one arm, while straightening the bed clothes beneath her. She could announce the Second Coming so that it sounded like a mail delivery.

"That's not good," Helen says, gathering her purchases. "And her mind seems to be wandering more."

"Ah! Poor soul!" Susan says, getting into her car. "Not much to look forward to, is there? I'll tell Dr. Fisher about the blood pressure. See you next week!" And she's gone, her tires spinning gravel.

Helen goes in to see Annie, who's lying on her bed. The nurse has bathed her, washed her hair, rubbed her with lotion and poked her for vital signs, all of which has tired her. She looks and smells like a newborn, wrinkled and helpless.

"How about chicken noodle soup for lunch?" Helen suggests. "There's some frozen from what I made last week."

"Whatever you want, dear," says Annie. "I'm not too hungry."

## chapter 6

HOW CAN A BODY BE SO TIRED just from taking a bath? I used to have energy to burn, racing after one or another of our horses in a field. Now it tires me more to be washed than it tires Susan to wash me. That Susan! Lifts me as if I were a laying hen. Does a much better job of washing me than Helen does. That girl's impatience shows in every movement she makes. Never can do anything calmly. Always restless, always looking to how she can change things. Doesn't realize things change by themselves, don't they, Ewan? Fancy you sneaking into my bedroom while my daughter's off making lunch. What if she caught us? What a scandal that would make!

Well, we did almost get caught the once. And it certainly led to a change, didn't it? Everything was changing then, mostly because of the war. The war changed everything.

It's funny, war. It can benefit those it doesn't actually kill or harm. Opens things up. People drop their reserve, live in the moment, because in a moment, things can change. The war needed planes, the plane manufacturers needed workers and too many men were overseas. So they had to advertise for women, and Maggie was right up off the mark to apply. "Montreal! We'll get to live in Montreal!"

Montreal. Sin City. But even my father had to agree I was leaving home for a noble cause. And you, Ewan, you were almost relieved, weren't you? We were in a sort of groove, going to a dance, leaving early to make love in a bush or a barn or on the seat of your truck, fumbling with wartime rubbers, trying to remain passionate while a branch or a gear shift prodded us, finding each other's bodies under layers of clothing in the winter. Could have never imagined we'd ever be alone in a bedroom like we are now.

Me working in Montreal and coming back on weekends broke up the routine. And Montreal in those days! Maggie and I got off the train and thought we'd landed on Mars. We'd travelled less than a hundred miles, but it might have been a million, with everything so different. The big grey buildings towering over streets that were always filled with traffic, even at three o'clock in the morning. Churches everywhere with the office towers in between just as solemn. Religious and financial altars. Streetcars swaying along, making the streets seem even narrower than they already were. Ste. Catherine Street, its neon lights, shops and nightclubs, glittering like a Christmas tree. Sherbrooke Street, the pricy shops, the mansions, the canopy of trees, McGill University and the art gallery — all oozing money and class.

Even though the war was on, the shops were filled with chic clothing. And the department stores! Acres of goods, including row on row of perfume and cosmetic counters, promising any woman the power to become enticing. I was like one of those people, archeologists I think they call them, who'd come across a civilization I'd heard about but could never prove existed.

One of the first Saturday afternoons we had off from the factory, Maggie insisted that we take a gander at the Canadian version of Sodom and Gomorrah — the Main, St. Laurent Boulevard, the street that cut the city in half. It was notorious across Canada, even in the States, for its sailors, bars and brothels. No respectable woman would be caught dead on it, but as Maggie pointed out, nobody in Montreal knew us. A little timidly at first, we started our expedition down below Dorchester Boulevard, where the Main ran up from the docks. Sailors, longshoremen, smoke and noise and bars. Lots of bars. Then Chinatown with its flashy red signs, noisy restaurants, ducks and slabs of pork hanging in the windows, gambling rooms at the top of smoky staircases. Chinese in pyjama-like clothing, with pigtails down their backs, right out of the elementary school geography books back home. The smell of sandalwood and fresh fish in the shops, the Chinese signs as much a mystery to us as the French ones everywhere else.

Where did we go from there? Up the street, wolf whistles as we passed the tattoo parlours and bars, men in uniform looking for what they couldn't find in Moose Jaw, Gimli or Wawa. At the street corners, you could look over onto de Bullion Street, where the prostitutes would be hanging out the windows, advertising their wares, with rates posted beside the doors as if they were selling slabs of cheese, like the cheese factories back home. My! How innocent our quiet passion was then, Ewan.

Up the hill past Sherbrooke Street, the Main changed into yet another country — rundown stores with dry goods in the windows, Hebrew signs outside and men in long black overcoats, ringlets beside each ear, scurrying across the road. A large public bath, butcher shops with huge sides of smoked meat in the window, bakeries with braided breads and fragrant smells drifting out into the air. What intense joy I felt then, seeing things that no one else I knew had seen, a special knowledge I would always carry with me.

Ah, but the French. Montreal was really about the French, the people whose culture made the city the great bazaar that it was. Back home, the French were thought of as some sorry, second-rate lot who had too many children and paid too much attention to their priests. They were thought to be able to speak English if they really tried. Weighed down by the Church, by poverty, by the fact that they had lost on the Plains of Abraham and had been losing ever since. There was plenty of evidence of poverty and loss in the East End of Montreal, but I wasn't ready for the smartly dressed, perfectly made up trim women who clicked along the streets in their high heels, their small hats tilted at a flirty angle. The laughter, the hand gestures and the enthusiasm you heard when the French greeted each other. I couldn't understand a word, but I felt that their lives must be more exciting than ours; they seemed to be enjoying it so much more. The men smoked too much, gave you a good going over with their eyes and winked at you, as if letting you in on a secret. So kind if you couldn't speak French and they couldn't speak English, whereas back home, we regarded a person as stupid if they couldn't understand us.

And of course, the servicemen crowded the sidewalks, filling up the bars, looking so cocky in their uniforms. Soldiers, sailors and airmen from almost any country you could think of except Germany, and there were even some of them in a POW camp on St. Helen's Island. British airmen over here to train on bombers, free Norwegian sailors stranded by the invasion of their homeland, prairie boys who'd joined the navy just to see that much water. Big Yankee soldiers eager to get into the action in Europe and Gurkhas on their way to England, all adding to the thrum of the city. Anyone with money was guaranteed a good time, and more money floated around then than there had been in a long time. There was a war on, but Montreal thought it was a party.

And poor Maggie and I, only wallflowers at that party, at least in the beginning. Even though we were in our twenties, we were boarded under the strict supervision of Elsie and Hector MacKinnon. Elsie had grown up on a farm down the road from ours and everyone thought she had done rather well, marrying Hector, who wore a suit to work and was an elder in the Presbyterian Church. Poor Elsie, a birdlike woman with a tendency to talk too much in a nervous way, but so kind. Hector was the opposite, countering her chattiness and fluttery movements by saying little and looking stern. Maggie and I nicknamed him "Tombstone." The MacKinnons — over forty, childless, in a comfortable house in the west end — had lives empty as gourds and plenty of room to take in boarders. Frankly, I think Elsie wanted someone to talk to or, at least, someone who'd pretend to listen.

God, but they were strict! No socializing except with church groups, or at wartime fundraisers, service clubs or Masonic dos. Maggie and I managed one night a week at the movies, but we weren't to be turned loose to explore the fleshpots of Montreal.

Ah, but there was work. We worked five and a half days a week at a huge aircraft plant in the north end of the city, the plant bigger than the whole village where we'd gone to school. Putting together aircraft parts, on an assembly line. Boring work, but work that gave us as much time as we wanted to talk and gossip over the noise of the welding guns and machinery. Poor Mr. ... now what was his name? Maggie would know ... Wheeler, that was it! Mr. Wheeler, our supervisor, driven mad by our chat and our ways, barely able to cope with his wife, let alone three hundred young women. Oh but Maggie could be brazen, getting up to go to the washroom every half hour when she wanted a cigarette, telling Mr. Wheeler when he protested that she had this "female problem," sidling up to him and offering to sketch out the details. He turned red, all three hundred of us got the giggles, and for the next three years, he never spoke to Maggie again.

The women on the line. A lot of them were married, many of them with husbands overseas. Doris, from Verdun, whose husband had fathered a child in England. Angela, her mother collecting her at the factory gate every night so she wouldn't go astray. Talking amongst themselves mostly, but occasionally giving us single gals the lowdown on men. And on sex. I never imagined that respectable women could talk about men like that. The French Canadians tended to keep to themselves, except for Denise, who became friends with Maggie, teaching her French in between Maggie's cigarette breaks. I can still hear Maggie murmuring *"Je te trouve sympatique,"* to Mr. Wheeler, her laugh becoming a cackle that ignited laughter all down the line. Maggie learned quite a lot of French, which stood her in good stead later on.

The days were long and the work boring, but the money was good and we were on our own. Me and Maggie. Earning our own way. Making our own lives. Waking each morning feeling more worldly than we'd been the day before, despite the watchful MacKinnons.

Of course, we went back home. Every second Saturday afternoon we returned, taking the train, Maggie shocking the patrons of Stewart's General Store with her stories of married women on the assembly line having affairs, telling them about the amount of dog poop on the sidewalks, how Montreal had more bars than churches and how all the women wore skirts above their knees.

And what did we talk about, Ewan? I remember cuddling in your truck, going on about all the iron grillwork in Montreal, about buying a silk slip with my wages and giving away the plots of movies that wouldn't come to Alexandria for months. I would mostly talk and you would mostly listen, sometimes irritated, weren't you? I thought you should have been more interested because not much was happening in your life, except the odd set of twin calves being born.

Sundays, dinner at your place, your mother sucking in her breath at the shortness of my skirt or at that sweet black hat I had with the little veil that shadowed my eyes. Tired, going back on the train Sunday nights, Maggie and I would talk about the long journey we had taken from where we'd grown up, and how foreign it seemed to return there.

Other weekends, when we stayed in the city, Maggie and I would head downtown at noon, finally sitting in a tea shop in hats and gloves, talking about the future course of our lives. We no longer wanted to marry movie stars. We wanted officers. At least Maggie did. I wasn't sure, locked as I was to you, Ewan. We walked endlessly through the shops, selecting items we couldn't afford, occasionally buying something — a charmeuse nightgown for my hope chest, for the time when you and I could make love in a bed and wake up together.

Murray's. That's where Maggie and I usually went, splurging on a late lunch of chicken pot pie, overlooking Ste. CatherineStreet, imagining what life might be like if we were as free as the streams of people who passed below us. It was there that I finally told Maggie the way things were between you and me. For all her fast talk, she whistled.

"Well, I suppose it's all right since you plan on getting married."

"We don't talk about that any more."

"Well, it's not the big prize it seemed a few years ago, is it?" said Maggie, blowing out smoke rings.

"No," I had to admit. "I do love him. I just wish ..."

"You wish he had more gumption. That he could see a little farther than Alexandria." Out the window, fat snowflakes were jigging around people's feet. "Now there's what I'm after," Maggie said, nodding toward a group of servicemen who had stopped to light their cigarettes. She turned back to me.

"Just make sure you don't get in the family way, Annie. Nothing kills romance faster than that."

How well we knew that, Ewan. Remember the scare? Me coming home for Christmas fearing I was bearing one little present no one wanted. Not much of a way to celebrate the holiday. I'd bought myself this new red crepe dress, and I had my hair coiled into a roll in the back of my head. So sophisticated, somewhat like the Duchess of Windsor, I thought. It almost made up for the unease I felt whenever I thought about how late I was.

Do you remember meeting the afternoon train that Christmas Eve? Going into Claire's Tea Room to warm up, a group of farmers in the corner obviously drinking more than tea out of their cups? The pale look on your face when I said, "I didn't get the Curse last month."

"Well, that's it, then. We'll marry," you said, after a long minute.

The anger I felt. "You might ask me!"

"Not a time for niceties, is it?"

"I don't know about you, but I've got all the time in the world." I rose to put on my coat as if to leave, but you grabbed my hand.

"Alright then, Lady Muck. Will you marry me?"

"No!" I said loudly, and moved away. But I sat down again right quick when all the farmers turned to look at me, and I realized I meant it. I didn't want to marry you at that moment, didn't want a baby, was unsure I ever wanted babies. I just desperately wanted to be out of that

Tea Room, out of Glengarry forever. I didn't want you or any bean of a baby to dictate what happened to me.

"Perhaps you're just late," you said softly, taking my hand once again.

"What do you know about it?"

"Not much. I'm sorry." Almost whispering. "I'll see you right, Annie, whatever happens, whatever you want." Well! All my fear and anger went back into that corral where they lived, ready to ride at any moment. The only thing left was the old tenderness toward you. I think I knew then I'd never find a better man.

Christmas Day. Cold as a harlot's heart, steam coming off Gordon and my father as they stamped their feet, back from chores, ready for our special Christmas breakfast of kedgeree. You arriving before the table was cleared with a little necklace of seed pearls you'd bought in Alexandria. I still have it, you know.

"I'll trade this in on a ring if you want," you whispered. No time to talk before Christmas dinner at your house at noon, another dinner at my parents' place at suppertime. I'll never forget how your mother looked, as if she had an outbreak of boils, at the sight of my new red dress.

The morning of Boxing Day I began to bleed, just before the usual big do at our place that afternoon. You came in the door, I kissed you and whispered "You don't have to trade in the necklace." Well, you looked at me as if I were Santa Claus, having brought you this big gift, your smile was that wide, your relief shining out of every pore. You drank more that afternoon than I'd ever seen you, and with each drink, you became more relaxed and happy. Willy Billy sawing a reel on his fiddle in the corner, you dancing me around our kitchen table, planting wet kisses on my face and neck. Then at one point, your face red and moist, you pulled me in and said, "We were ready to marry. Why don't we just do it, eh?"

You were too drunk to talk to sensibly, and I guess I was a little hurt that you'd been so relieved at my news. "Not till you're able to keep me," I said smartly. "And in my own house." You looked as if I'd slapped you. I swallowed a drink and said, "Let's dance."

Maggie and I stumbled onto the train back to Montreal that evening, still giggling. So I didn't see or talk to you again until New Year's Eve

— Hogmanay, as my mother called it. A big holiday in Scotland. You showed up to take me to a dance in Alexandria, sober and subdued, as if someone had given you a good talking to. You were quiet all the way to the dance, but in that we were travelling with Gordon and Alma, it didn't seem strange.

The dance. I always remember the dances, although sometimes they run one into the other in my mind, like spilled paint. But that New Year's dance is clear. Hot and noisy, smoke from cigarettes and the old woodstove at the back fogging the air, steam billowing out into the night every time someone opened the door. We found a table, you and I, Gordon and Alma, Maggie and that soldier we'd met on the train, who she had persuaded to get off with us rather than travel on to see his aunt in Ottawa. A few others. Glen MacPherson and the Royal Stewarts, a trio of musical brothers from Cornwall, were playing. I was ready for a new year, so much being new — Montreal, my job, the small freedoms that earning your own money brought. Snuggling up to your shoulder I said, "Let's dance the year out."

You smiled wanly and led me out on the dance floor for a waltz, then a reel, but your mind was busy with something outside the hall. A second reel, me pulling on your hand, you saying, "Let's go outside. I want to talk."

It didn't seem a surprising idea. The dance was dry, Glengarry still being under prohibition. The good Presbyterians, who equated alcohol with Hitler, saw to it that it remained dry into the sixties. Below zero temperatures and a light dusting of snow, but a great deal of activity in the parking lot, as the men and a few couples sneaked out for a tot. I thought that was what we were going for, so I lightly draped my coat over my shoulders, teetering out to the car in my high heels.

Everything about the next moments in the car are clear, as if it were yesterday, as if someone switched the channels and I am watching myself starring in my own program. The frost on one of the car windows made a pattern that looked like a castle on a hill. Snow had fallen on my red crepe dress. You pulled out the little flask I had given you for Christmas. It was silver, from Birks. You took a drink, then passed it to me. Homemade rye that burned the back of your throat. You saying very quietly, "I think maybe we should stop seeing each other for awhile. Maybe see other people. See if what we really want is each other."

I couldn't speak. Even now the memory causes my blood to rage. Something collapsed in my stomach, allowing hot liquid to flow into every vein. Not only could I see my breath, I could hear the sound it made when it hit the cold air, the surprise I felt that I was still breathing when, for a few seconds, everything had stopped. When I could speak, I asked as bravely as I could manage, "You want to go out with other girls?"

"No." You finally looked at me. "Not really. But we seem to be stuck here somehow, and I think maybe some time apart will help us know if we really are right for each other."

"You don't mean it." My voice quavering.

"I think it might be best. Don't you?"

How did it happen next? The bile moving around my entrails now rose into my throat, moved into my arms and hands. I remember attacking you, knocking the flask out of your hand, tearing at your face and hair with my nails. I even remember that my nails were stylishly painted Oriental Red. All of the growth I'd experienced since I went to Montreal evaporated and I screamed, "You've ruined me, and now you want me to find someone else?"

I kept slapping at you, trying to tear your shirt, feeling that nothing less than your ripped flesh would satisfy my rage.

"Don't, Annie! Stop! Let's talk about this!" You tried to grab my hands, push me away, and I fell against the car door, unable to breathe, flailing and falling out of the car into the slush. I think you scrambled after me. Picking myself up, I began to run, sliding on the ice in the parking lot in my heels, you after me, yelling at me to stop. I didn't, until I was well out onto the road, staggering along the tire ruts, suddenly aware of how cold it was and how I was out without my boots, hat, scarf and gloves, hugging my purse inside my wrapped coat.

How long was it? Maybe ten minutes, until Gordon drove up alongside me and ordered me into the car. "You must be drunk. Or mad. Maybe both."

"I'm mad all right," I answered, my voice as watery as my stomach.

"Get in the car," he ordered, flinging open the door. "Ewan said you had a bit of a fight. Here, have a fag, and calm down." I got in the car and he shook his cigarette pack at me.

"It wasn't a fight." I remember I felt calm and still, the way a pond is after you've drained most of it away. But my hand shook when I lit the cigarette.

"You'll catch your death of cold, you little fool. Let's get you back to the dance, warm you up a bit."

"Take me home, Gordon. I'm not going back to the dance."

"Are you daft? Half your stuff is still there and Alma's waiting for me. It's only forty minutes to midnight."

"Take me home or I'm going to get out and walk the rest of the way."

Gordon had never been a match for my will, and I guess he sensed that something important had happened. So he drove me home, dropping me at the kitchen door, then skidding around in the yard so he could get back to the dance as quickly as possible. I remember my folks sitting at the kitchen table, in the mellow circle of the lamplight, listening to Guy Lombardo on the radio, live from New York City, my mother knitting socks for the troops overseas. She rose as I came in the door.

My father's reaction to any display of emotion had always been the same: avoid it at all costs. He quickly folded his newspaper and scooted upstairs, believing he shouldn't be party to "women's things." I couldn't say much, and my mother was never one for words. When I finally told her what had happened, she murmured "Well, now, we don't know that maybe it's for the best." Her response to any crisis, God love her, whether it was a weasel in the hen house or the invasion of Poland. She rubbed my back, made me tea.

You shouldn't have done it, Ewan. You said what we both were thinking and that was fatal. If you'd learned anything living in these parts, it's that once the truth is spoken, it's out there, and can never again be fenced back in. It might have unfolded that I left you, not the other way around, but it wasn't just my hurt pride. I felt you were rejecting me because I had grown, and that's a terrible judgement to hand down on anyone.

You won't answer. Well, it was a long time ago. And lunch will be ready pretty soon. I can smell that chicken broth. It smells like home. My home. I still have my appetite. I'm grateful for that. It'll help me get stronger, so I can get moving again. So I can stay home and look after myself, like I've always done, haven't I?

*chapter 7*


EVENINGS ARE ALL THE SAME. Dinner, then TV, starting with the news, Annie commenting, "Now why would those Palestinians want to blow themselves up? There'll be none of them left if they keep that up." When a child has been killed, "Poor wee thing," followed by, "And where were the parents?" Then, "I don't see why there's all this fuss about taxes. There've always been taxes." After the news, a series of sitcoms with predictable laugh tracks, Annie laughing right along with them, Helen becoming depressed.

Annie's still tired at bedtime, a good sign, Helen thinks. Maybe she'll sleep through the night. Annie's left arm is deadweight as Helen tries to manoeuver her into her nightdress. It's like trying to get a wrench sideways down the sleeve.

"Relax, Mom. Relax your arm and let me guide it," she coaxes.

Annie sighs, "I don't know how much more relaxed I could be. I'm that tired." Nevertheless, her arm repeats little boxing jabs into the fabric of the nightdress. The phone rings. It's Sean, calling from Los Angeles.

"How's the old girl?" he asks. Sean speaks with the charm he uses to assure nervous air travellers over the intercom as he criss-crosses America, bringing Japanese tourists to Florida and New York, transporting deal-making executives and Disney-crazed Easterners to California. He's an airline pilot with three ex-wives and assorted children scattered across the US.

"She's doing alright," Helen says cautiously, then takes a deep breath. "Why don't you come and see for yourself? The air ticket can't be too much of a problem."

"Is that Sean?" Annie roars from the bedroom. "Let me speak to him!"

"In a minute, Ma!" Helen shouts back. To the receiver she says, "Sean?"

"You better let me talk to her," he chuckles. "Don't want her having another stroke."

She takes the phone in to Annie, who's rocking on the side of the bed with excitement, only half in her nightgown, a wide grin on her face. Helen listens to Annie's side of the conversation:

"Not too bad ... I'll be walking soon, the way I'm going ... Oh, I don't need to go into any home. I'm fine here!"

Helen thinks of the lies Annie and Sean have always shared, almost another language, foreign to reality. Sean is not lazy in school, merely "unchallenged." Annie doesn't favour Sean, it's just that a boy needs more looking after than girls. Sean never beat up Emilio down the block; Emilio and his friends ambushed Sean, who fought his way clear. Sean's marriages have failed because he is too generous with his wives, not firm enough. Of course Sean doesn't see his children often enough. How can he with his busy flight schedule?

The only one who seriously tried to break down this speaking in tongues was Reg. And he got nowhere.

\*\*\*

Helen is twelve, huddled at the top of the stairs, hugging the senile Peaches who is now too old to protest her fondling. Downstairs is raging a battle royal.

"He's been arrested, Annie! For dealing drugs! He hasn't just been caught stealing jujubes at the corner store!" Reg is pacing the living room, waving the paper the police delivered an hour ago.

"I'm sure it's not his fault! It's probably a mistake! We owe him the benefit of the doubt." Annie's voice, though shrill, sounds unconvinced.

"I am not posting bail. He can rot in jail. It might teach him a lesson." Reg goes to the liquor cabinet and hauls out the Scotch.

"Sure! Just look at the lessons he got at home. If his father thinks it's okay to get drunk, why shouldn't he think it's okay to take drugs?" The toss of Annie's head indicates she's assumed the high ground.

"He wasn't just taking drugs, Annie, he was dealing them, like the Mafia. Like the biker gangs. And to an undercover cop, the stupid, dumb bastard!" Sean's stupidity irritates Reg even more than the crime.

"So you're going to let him go to jail, when we could post bail for him and he'd probably get probation, since it's his first offence? Reg!

What are you thinking?"

Reg considers this for a moment. "I'm thinking it's time you stopped protecting that spoiled little shit and let him grow up. He's twenty years old. He's technically a man. He should know better."

"Oh yes! Take a hard line now! Now that he's an adult! When you wouldn't do any of the things a father is supposed to do when he was growing up!"

"I took him fishing," Reg says, as if it were the acme of parenting. "I'm not posting bail and that's final." To provide a fitting ending, he drains the Scotch in his glass.

"You have to!" Annie pleads.

"No I don't, " Reg replies, and he takes out his lighter, flicks it and sets fire to the police notice. Annie lunges at him, but she is too short to reach the flaming paper he holds high.

Annie sobs. "You bastard, Reg. You bastard!"

In the end, Annie borrows the money from her brother Gordon, who has done quite well since the Ontario Milk Marketing Board was set up. The following month, she persuades their family doctor to hire her as a part-time receptionist so that she will never again have to beg Reg for anything. Sean gets off with a conditional discharge and enlists in the air force the day the conditions are removed, to take up training in Alberta. Annie is appalled. Reg is proud.

"Whattya know? Maybe he does take after the old man after all!" he says, and launches into details of his wartime exploits that they've all heard before.

Lost in all this is Helen. Annie doesn't speak to Reg for several weeks, and she says little to Helen, either, except, "Now don't you start trouble. I've got enough on my hands." Reg merely spends more time out of the house with his clients. Peaches is put down.

\*\*\*

"Oh, I understand. Summer must be a busy time, what with everyone taking vacations." Annie is nodding brightly. "Okay, dear. I'll hand you back to Helen."

"She really walking?" Sean asks when Helen comes back on the line.

"No. Of course not." Helen walks the phone into the kitchen.

"She doesn't want to go into the home."

"I know. But there's no other option. Unless you want to come and take care of her." Helen finds she's getting quite good at sharing guilt.

"Well, if you stuck around she could manage. It's not as if Hollywood's beating down your door, is it?"

"Hollywood couldn't even find my door, Sean. It's too busy looking at its own navel. But I am scheduled to teach a course at the National Theatre School in October, and I'm going to do it." Helen's voice has turned to ice. "Good night, Sean."

"Hey! You know, you take yourself a little too seriously, you know that, Helen?" Sean's voice has turned from Beach Boy to Big Brother.

"Maybe because no one else does, Sean." Helen wants to cry.

"Listen, I wouldn't be any good with her, if I were there. You know that." Helen murmurs agreement, because what he says is true. But she would appreciate him making the gesture. "I'll come up around Thanksgiving. See if I can get any of the highly subsidized grandchildren to come, too. Okay?"

Now Helen is crying. "Okay, Sean. Bye now."

"Bye. And cut yourself some slack."

Helen dries her eyes and goes back to the bedroom where she finally wrestles Annie into her nightgown and puts her to bed. "It was nice of Sean to call," Annie says, sighing. "He says he'll come soon."

Helen kisses her lightly. "I'm sure he will. 'Night, Mom."

"'Night, dear. Now don't you stay up too late."

"I won't."

Helen puts the last of the supper dishes in the dishwasher and pours herself a brandy, feeling a slight twinge that perhaps she's a little too fond of this nightly ritual. She takes her first sip.

Why do I still care? she thinks. Her mind quickly reviews her years of therapy, after her marriage ended, after her father died. She thinks of her years of living abroad, of the other people she has found to replace her family. And still she cares what her family thinks of her. One phone call from Sean can get her going and she's back in her childhood, futilely trying to find where she fits in the family, knowing that no one fits in this family.

"Find your inner child," she tells her students. "You must have access to the you who is eager to grow, to change, to learn. You must be open to all of the possibilities within your personality." If I can help *them* to grow and expand, why can't I do that for myself? she thinks. The brandy isn't working. She'll call Bernie.

"Hello." The richness of his baritone voice saying that one word is enough to calm her.

"I thought I'd share with you the fact that my mother has a new beau," she says, trying to sound as light as possible.

"How the hell are you? I was going to call you, but we've been working late every night this week on the set, and I didn't want to wake your mother. What about this new beau?"

"She's reliving a romance from her youth with a guy who used to take her dancing and is now dead."

"Bummer. She going a little AWOL?"

"A little, but most of the time she's okay."

"And are you okay?"

"I'm alright. Just tired and very eager to get my life back. Tell me how my life is doing."

"Well, your contract arrived from the school, and I've forwarded it on to you. The tomatoes this year are sensational, ditto the basil, so I've been making tomato sauce at all hours of the morning. Your roses are great, too, and we've had a good crop of raspberries. I ate most of them, though."

"You're welcome to them. What about the bills?"

"Hey! I'm working, and I'm paying them. Well, I pay them when the envelope says 'Final Notice.' And I'm keeping track. We'll settle up when you're back."

"God! It feels as if I'll never get back."

Helen feels a wave of affection for the squat storey-and-a-half house with its sagging front porch that she bought using the money she earned doing the *Two Solitudes* series. She played the rich lead's private secretary, who had always been in love with the rich lead. While the down payment on the house was simple, the arrangements she has had to make to pay the mortgage each month have been baroque.

There was the schizophrenic housemate who neglected to take her medication, and an attempt by Helen to sell Amway, which wasn't too successful but which left her with a lifetime supply of cleaning materials.

There was the housemate with a small child who used a Magic Marker on Helen's only good dress and drove her tricycle into the living-room wall. The stereo system now covers the hole. There have been all the part-time jobs Helen has taken between gigs — dog walking, house-sitting, temp office work, telemarketing for a charity, temporary gardener in a greenhouse, pizza delivery, night clerk in a convenience store, home sewing for a garment manufacturer and a pyramid scheme to sell a range of "natural" vitamins. She now has a lifetime supply of those, too.

Helen met Bernie while doing a small experimental piece of theatre. She was trying to balance her rehearsal schedule with her contractual obligation with a language school toward a Korean student she was boarding. The boarding arrangements, generous in terms of money, required her to provide three meals a day of typical Canadian food, as well as Canadian conversation and Canadian experience for the young student.

When she explained to Bernie the reason for one of her flying exits, he said, "That's easy. Leave him a frozen TV dinner or the number to Pizza Pizza. Experience doesn't get more Canadian than that."

She and Bernie became friends, and at the end of the production run, Bernie said, "Look, I have to move. The house I'm living in is being sold. Why don't I become your boarder when the Korean leaves?"

For once luck was with Helen. Bernie's carpentry skills have helped keep the house from falling down. He has replaced the roof and the eavestroughs and built a deck on the back. He has also remodelled the kitchen, using the framework of a set from a television cooking show acquired for a song when the show was cancelled. His curries are unequalled, in Helen's experience. He could use a few tips on housecleaning, but Helen doesn't mind.

Helen is in awe of Bernie — his self-reliance, his calmness, even in the hysterical moments before a theatre opening. He's from Nova Scotia, a Black man whose mother was a cleaner and whose father died in a steel-plant accident when Bernie was four. Raised to fight poverty, racism and the effects of his mother's fundamentalist religion, Bernie's survival skills are amazing, even in the shaky world of Canadian theatre. Of his failed marriage to a white woman, the mother of his only child, Bernie says, "She was making a social statement. I wasn't."

"No word from the home?" he asks now.

"The word from the home is that it's at least another month."

"Can't Barbara give you a break?"

Helen sucks on her teeth and says, "No. She's too busy planning *herself* a break. In Germany."

"You're not okay, are you?"

"Bernie, I can't believe that I still fall into this game. Of obeying my mother. Of feeling I must explain myself to her. Of feeling that it is right that I take a back seat to my brother and sister, that it's perfectly okay for them to just dump all this responsibility on me." Her tears can be heard in the last few words.

"Shit! If only there wasn't this production ..."

"No. No, Bernie. It's okay. I know you have work to do."

"Well, I don't like you going through all this shit by yourself."

"I'm okay."

"You don't sound okay."

"Tell me what you're doing. How are my cats?"

"Oh, yeah. That's big news. Cato caught a mole. Brought it in for me to see. Wanted to mail it to you, but I wouldn't let him."

"He couldn't afford the postage anyway."

"True. Cassandra is still eating as if the Martians had landed in Mississauga."

"God, I miss them. You, too."

"How come the neutered cat gets precedence over the unneutered human?"

Helen laughs. "You haven't been neutered? I thought two years of living with me did that to any man."

Bernie's turn to laugh. "Anytime you want to check it out, honey, you let me know."

"Yeah, I will."

Up until six months ago, Bernie and Helen's relationship was one of warm companionship. Hugs, laughs, no sexual stuff. Then came the phone call that Annie had suffered a stroke. Helen cancelled a class for the following day, and Bernie drove her down to Union Station to catch the late train, which deposited her in Ottawa at five a.m. For two days she lived at the hospital, sleeping on a vinyl bench in the visitor's lounge, while she waited to see if Annie would make it, to see how much damage the stroke had done. Barbara drove down on the Saturday to relieve her.

Helen took the train back to Toronto, exhausted.

Bernie met the train, took her home, placed a strong martini in her hand while he prepared the meal, coquilles St. Jacques. While he cooked and throughout dinner, Helen talked about her mother, about the war zone she had grown up in, how she always felt she could change things, but couldn't. The details, served up with a good bottle of chardonnay, left her in tears. "You know that Czech satire, *The Good Soldier Schweik* who always does his duty?" she blubbered. "Well, I've been the Good Daughter Schweik. And I hate the role."

Bernie stood behind her, massaging her neck. "You never got what you needed," he said.

Helen said nothing, just leaned into his hands, gave herself over to the truth. Bernie kissed the nape of her neck, and she reached back for him.

There is a moment at the height of desire when everything seems clear, and everything is possible. The clarity of singular purpose. It occurred while they were busy removing each other's clothing in the kitchen, only what was clear to Helen had nothing to do with sex. Helen stopped and pulled away.

"No," she muttered. "It's not right."

"Feels all right," Bernie said, trying to retrieve the moment.

"Right for all the wrong reasons."

If Helen has learned anything over the years it's to recognize the difference between need and love, and she tried explaining this to Bernie. "Yeah, sure," he said, then left the room.

The moment had passed and never occurred again, although a certain physical awkwardness has marked their relationship since. Helen remembers the intense betrayal she felt a month later when Bernie didn't come home for two days while working on a show.

"A dancer," he explained when he came back. "They sure know the moves."

"I was worried, worried sick that something had happened to you," Helen accused, trying to stir up a scene.

Bernie said quietly, "Don't give me that shit. If you were worried, you only had to call the theatre."

\*\*\*

"Tell me about your show, " Helen says, to get her mind off Bernie's sensational rear end.

"Oh! It's awful! Fucking awful. And I'm building this post-apocalyptic castle sort of set, so we've got gothic everywhere and menace and the whole thing weighs a ton. The stage manager is threatening to quit."

"I thought it was supposed to be a comedy."

"Aha! You think that because you've read the script. But Axel, the director says it's ironic, not comic. The actors are tearing their hair out. And Axel is still demanding rewrites from Harold, who's got AIDS and can't work long hours."

"Suddenly, I feel better being here."

"Oh, yes, my darling. You don't want to be involved with this number. Even the box office people are on Prozac."

"God, I miss you Bernie."

"Me too." There is silence in which both of them consider the transitional state of their relationship.

"How's Jed doing?" A reference to Bernie's son.

"Pretty good, I guess. He hasn't borrowed any money off me this month, yet."

Helen laughs. What she wouldn't give to be at her own kitchen table, opposite Bernie, sharing a joint with Jed, talking about Jed's latest gig with his band, Jed's latest girlfriend, Jed's latest day job. All of Jed's endeavours seem to end in disaster — the band not paid and stranded at a bar in Wawa, a girlfriend giving him up on the advice of her therapist, the job of dishwasher ending when the restaurant suddenly shuts down, under order of the health inspector. Helen and Bernie sit there amazed, transfixed by Jed's perpetual optimism. He is always on the brink of a recording contract, of acquiring the most desirable woman in the Western Hemisphere, of landing the perfect waiting job where he will only have to work four nights a week for amazing wages, plus tips. "It's happening, man," he says, a grin as wide as the equator.

"Maybe he's smoking too much of that stuff," Bernie says after Jed's gone, shaking his head.

"I don't think he makes enough money to be able to smoke too much of that stuff," Helen says, emptying the ashtrays.

"Where does he get all that positive energy from? His mother is nothing if not earnest, and I come from a long line of downtrodden people. Where'd he get those upbeat genes?"

"His father is pretty good at making the best of things," Helen says slyly. "Or maybe he's just always up with you so you won't worry about him."

"You always worry about kids," Bernie sighs, and Helen pauses. Maybe that's it. Maybe she's taken the wrong tack with Annie all these years. Why do I tell her the truth? she asks herself, then answers her own question: Because I think *one* of her children should.

"Say hello to him from me," she says quietly into the phone.

"I will. He's coming to mooch a meal on Sunday. But I could cancel if you want me to come down there."

Relief! For a moment, Helen is elated. Then she tries to picture Bernie and her mother together and the different ways she relates to each. It is a formula for schizophrenia. "No, don't," Helen says. "I'll be alright. We're in a routine now. I'd want to go running out to bars with you if you arrived."

"Afraid the locals might join the Klan? That what you're worried about?"

"Oh, Bernie! It has nothing to do with your colour. You know that." She pauses for a second, sorting out why exactly she doesn't want him here. She does not want her relationship with Bernie to be … what is the word? … *contaminated* by her mother. "This … she … my mother, it's something I've got to sort through for myself. I need to understand the power she has over me, and get rid of it. Or at least put it in its place."

"Okay," Bernie says. "But if you change your mind, I'm here."

"Yeah, thanks. Good night."

"Good night, Schweik."

*chapter 8*

HELEN'S DOWN IN THE BASEMENT rooting about in my things, and I
don't want her to. There are things there I should have thrown out years
ago. Those are my things. I'll decide what to do with them.

Oh, she pretends we're doing this cleanup together. Plops me down
in front of Oprah and gives me a box of photographs to go through.
Says she's just trying to get me organized. But I know what she's up
to. Clearing out stuff so I can just be whisked away to the home at a
moment's notice. Well, it's not going to happen. I only wish I could get
downstairs and stop her, but ... if wishes were horses, eh?

Listen to that woman! Always jabbering on about relationships!
Getting people to tell her things on national TV that they'd blush to
tell a priest. Of course, she's more powerful than the Church, Oprah is.
Probably richer, too. But all that touchy-feely claptrap! Why doesn't she
just tell people to get on with their lives? Most people have to.

Relationships! In my day you were either friends or you weren't, you
were being courted by a boy or you weren't. I've always found it easy
to let people go. Easier than letting go of my possessions. Oh, I'm too
fond of them, I know. I've kept far too much stuff. I think it was my
upbringing. Practical. Nothing just for the fun of it. Well, I've always
found that beautiful things have their own purpose. The point of knick-
knacks is that they have no point, and that can be very refreshing in a
life devoted to basics and hard work. Style is important. It's what gives
substance meaning. The way silver gives you back a shining reflection
of yourself.

Objects are always the same, while people change and disappoint
you. Men especially have a habit of changing, of slipping their best
qualities into their back pockets, no matter how well you treat them.
But things — beautiful things — can quiet you, assure you. They are
... what's that word? Constant! Sometimes men prove themselves to be
constant, too. Like you, Ewan. You proved yourself constant ...

How long was it? A month, two months later? Don't remember much of the month of January that year. Moved in slow motion. Caught a cold, spent far too much time in bed asleep, trying to wipe out my own thoughts. At work, a small piece of hot steel fired into my arm when I wasn't paying attention. Funny — it hurt, but I remember looking at my arm as if it belonged to someone else. Didn't go back home weekends anymore, but Maggie did, coming back at the end of the month to report that you were seen going to the movies in Alexandria with Flora.

"I'll bet his mother likes her," Maggie reported, snorting delicately.

"She would. She'd be able to boss her around, just like the other cows in the barn."

Maggie made a lowing sound and imitated the way Flora would twist her hands when she was nervous. I had to laugh. Maggie. Always good at getting you out of yourself. It was she who made me to go to the Valentine's Dance put on by the St. Andrew's Society of Montreal. Mr. MacKinnon was secretary of the Society.

"It'll do you good," she said. "Mr. MacKinnon says there'll be some servicemen there, 'decent servicemen, mind you,'" she added in Hector's boring baritone.

"I don't feel like it, Maggie. Honestly. I don't care if I ever dance again."

"Well I care! You don't go, I can't go. So says Fuhrer MacKinnon. Please? You can wear your red dress. Please?"

Funny the way things turn out. At times I think life should come with its own laugh track. It was at that dance that I met Reg. He and his buddies at the dance thinking there might be some genuine Scotch to be found there, it being in short supply on this side of the Atlantic during the war.

"I hope your heart isn't as black as your hair," were the first words he said, standing in front of me. Tall, not very handsome, but very, very sure of himself.

"You'll have to stick around to find out," I said back, bold as anything, so that Maggie, seated next to me, gawked. Guess those weeks of feeling sorry for myself had made me bolder.

He asked me to dance, a waltz, I remember. Now what was that song? Everyone was humming it at the time. "A Nightingale Sang in

Berkeley Square," that's it! Funny how I can remember that, but not the name of the woman who comes here three times a week to look after me. It's like my memory is solid at the core, but around the edges, where new information arrives, it's tatted, like a doily.

"I've actually been there. Before the war," Reg said, as we slipped across the floor.

"Been where?"

"Berkeley Square. It's in Mayfair, in London. If it hasn't been bombed already," he said and pulled me closer to hum into my hair.

Well! You can just imagine what that did to me, with my craving for adventure! Montreal was the only city I'd ever been to, other than Ottawa, so I was pretty impressed. I knew boring old Dominion Square posed no threat to Berkeley Square. And he looked so fine in his uniform. But doesn't every man? I guess that's why they design them that way.

"Are you one of those black Celts?" he asked when the music stopped, lightly touching my hair. It's my best feature, really. Naturally curly. Have I mentioned that?

"No, though my mother is Scottish. Born there. A black Celt is someone who's dour all the time. That's not me."

"I guessed that," he said with a grin, then looked around. "I can see why some of them might be dour. This dance is as dry as the Sahara Desert. Whoever heard of a Scottish do without Scotch?" He looked around the room to see who might be enjoying themselves. The music changed.

"Presbyterians," I informed him. "There's prohibition in the county I come from."

"A county? You come from a county?"

"Glengarry County. In Eastern Ontario. My family owns a farm there."

"A farmer's daughter!" he hooted, while I blushed. "Well, I'm a travelling salesman. At least I was before the war. Together, we make a dirty joke!"

Giggling, I followed him back to the table. When the band took a break, he bought us both ginger ales, then winked. "I could use a little fresh air, and these drinks could use a little personality. Care to step outside for a bit?"

I wasn't sure. Things seemed to be moving along rather quickly. I looked over to where Maggie was biting her nails and having her ear talked off by Elsie. Hector MacKinnon looked as if his piles were bothering him again. "Sure," I said.

Outside, it was bitterly cold, I remember. Reg pulled out his smokes, a flashy Zippo lighter and a silver hip flask with his initials on it. He took a slug from the flask, poured another into his ginger ale and a third shot into mine.

"Whoa!" I hissed, looking around to see if anyone was looking. "None for me. The MacKinnons will kick me out of the house."

Reg winked. "Then you'll have to stay with me. Of course, it might be a bit crowded, since four of us are sharing a room at the Windsor. Cigarette?"

How would you describe it? A Cinderella moment, I suppose, me lighter than the smoke I blew delicately out of my nose. Shivering in the cold, feeling as glamorous as any movie star Maggie and I had mooned over on a Wednesday night. Illicitly drinking with a stranger, about whom I knew nothing and who knew nothing about me. Reinventing myself. This was why I had come to Montreal, to experience what I knew was out there. Not just drinking rough rye on a fire escape outside a church hall with a flirtatious airforce officer, but moving into a new part of the world, a new part of myself.

Ah, Ewan, I wanted you to see me then! To see what I was capable of being. A sophisticated woman of the world, heading off in new directions. Any thought of you still caused a stab of pain, but I knew then I would never go back to Glengarry again. Not in any real sense. Not even if you came to get me.

When was it? A week or two later, I think. I know it was a Saturday. Maggie and I came back from the shops, and Elsie said I had a visitor. You were on one of the chairs in the parlour, twirling your cap between your knees. Those big hands of yours, always restless. When I came in you stood up, and you seemed taller than you had been, too big for the room. And shabbier, your coat worn at the elbows, your cap stained around the rim.

All you said was "Hello Annie," as if you'd only been away a few hours. I remember Elsie came in, twittering about what awful weather and about tea. We said "yes" to tea, just to get rid of her. You twisted your neck and got right to the point.

"I've been thinking, Annie. I miss you. Miss you a lot. It's been a long couple of months."

"Yes." How well I knew that.

"I'm sorry for what I said New Year's. I didn't mean it. It's just that we seemed sort of stuck." I can still see you fiddling with your cap. "I don't need time. I know how I feel about you."

I remember my heart tap dancing. How many times had I imagined a scene like this, how I would handle it? And here it was, here I was. "That still doesn't change things, does it? We'd still be stuck."

You nodded. "Maybe, but I've done something else. I've taken a job at the Lefevre factory in Alexandria. They've got this big war contract, and they're taking on extra help."

What a jolt that was! I couldn't imagine you in a factory or anywhere but on your own farm.

"What about the farm?"

"Well, I do the milking before I leave for work and again when I come home. My sisters help, too. It makes for a long day, but it means some good extra money. To save to build a house."

"But what about the summer? The crops?"

"Well, I might quit the factory if I have to and find another job in the fall. There's a lot of work around now, with the war. As you know."

I can still see you. A haggard look, dark stains under your eyes, as if you hadn't slept in months. What would it be like on weekends when I came up, after your sixteen-hour days? Not much left of you. And for what? A little bungalow stuck in a corner of the farm. I thought of the fine mansions on Sherbrooke Street Maggie and I had passed on our way home. And tonight, Reg had promised to take me to a night club, although the MacKinnons thought it was to be a church concert. It would be my first time ever in a club.

I suppose everyone has moments like that. When you make a choice and your life shifts direction, although you don't know it at the time. I only knew he'd hurt me a great deal and I wanted to hurt him back. And I wanted to keep my options open because I didn't really know what I wanted. So I did that "spit in your eye" trick that Barbara Stanwyck does so well in the movies, not realizing that my life wasn't a movie, only an accumulating pile of events, the happy ending nowhere in sight.

How did I put it? I can't recall, but I told you I now thought your suggestion of seeing other people was a good one. I think I said, "In fact, I have a date in two hours, and I'd better get ready for it." I remember looking at my nails, the blood-red polish, and flicking them casually.

You didn't say anything for a moment, then said, "Fine," and stood up. I suppose I was hoping for some greater reaction from you, some argument or passion, for you to say you loved me. Something more suited to my dramatic new life. But when I followed you to the front door, you were pulling on your boots.

"Ewan, maybe what we need, what I need, is a little more time." Trying to sound all adult, trying to get the scene to play my way.

I remember the look on your face, your tired smile. "We've known each other all of our lives, Annie. If there is one thing we don't need, it's more time." You straightened, flipped the cap back on your head. "You know what you want. Bye Annie, and good luck."

And that was that. The great love affair of my life over, not with any high emotion, but with the quiet closing of a door, shutting in great layers of feeling. How long was it before you moved on entirely? I think you married Flora about a year and half later, and a year after that your father died, leaving you the farm. You quit the factory job, built a small bungalow for your mother and Carol, the sister who never married. You and Flora took over the farmhouse. That's the way life works sometimes. Had I known that in two years we'd have had a life of our own, would it have made a difference?

Ah! What's the point of going over all that now? At least I never had to live in that rambling wreck of a house. I've lived in better houses. I never would have known what Royal Doulton was, let alone been able to collect it. They've provided me with some comfort, my things. Oh, I know they're old, cold objects, nothing that can touch you inside. But they are proof that I led a different life, that I got somewhere, made something of myself. They were the things I turned to when I felt low, when living with Reg got to be too much. They reminded me of who I thought I was. That's why I don't want Helen messing about down there. She might decide to throw out something I really want. Something I really want. Now that's been hard to come by, hasn't it?

Listen to that! Oprah's got this Buddhist monk on, and they're still talking about relationships. Now what would a monk know about relationships? He sure giggles a lot. Maybe there's more to a monkish life than meets the eye! Oh, enough of this rubbish!

What is that girl doing down there? It's time for my tea. And I need the bathroom. We certainly don't want another accident, do we? "Helen! Helen, help me!" There! That ought to get her up here in a hurry.

# chapter 9

HELEN HAS LEFT ANNIE IN THE LIVING ROOM, the television on, a box of photographs on her lap and an empty box on either side of her — one for the photos she wants to keep and one for discards. She has sternly told Annie that any photo whose occupants she can't identify should be in the discard pile.

"Since when can you boss me around?" says Annie, the photo box listing dangerously on her lap.

"I'm not bossing you around. I'm trying to be sensible." Helen breathes loudly.

"If you were sensible, you'd be married with a couple of kids by now," says Annie, dropping the first of the keepers into its box.

How do I always end up on the defensive, even when I'm in charge? Helen wonders as she heads down to the basement, keeping herself calm through yogic breathing.

She faces an army of garment bags, stretching across one wall. The number of them almost defeats her. She opens one. There is a cocktail dress, empire-style, with a white lace bodice and a slim black crepe skirt. A rhinestone pin marks the spot in front where the two colours and the two fabrics meet, just below where the bodice is cut to reveal cleavage.

Helen remembers sitting on the floor of the living room in their old house in Montreal as Annie sashays down the stairs wearing that dress. Annie holds her head back in a haughty manner, small clip-on rhinestone earrings sending signals out on either side of her head, a sleek bouffant cap of glossy black hair. Annie is very grateful that Jackie Kennedy has made this haircut popular.

Annie is ready for her audience, dressed for another Ad and Sales Club dinner. Reg, having his obligatory whisky before leaving, says, "Annie, my girl, you look sensational. Doesn't she kids?"

For once, the family is united. Helen and Barbara clap and ooh and aahh, while Annie arranges a small vial of perfume, a handkerchief, her silver cigarette case and other items in her dainty beaded evening bag. She smiles at them, even at Reg.

Helen blinks, seeing herself coming down the stairs on Stratford's apron stage, her head held high, playing Lady Anne in *Richard III* in front of five hundred bored high school students. It's a matinee, too warm outside, the students have been on the bus too long and they are now making spitballs by chewing up bits of the program. Helen ignores them. The costume is a heavy brocade, a little tight on Helen since it was made for the actor who regularly plays Lady Anne, not her understudy. Helen ignores this too, blanking out the fidgeting in the stalls, the jewelled bracelets weighing down her wrists. She is Anne — proud, grieving, convinced she will have her vengeance on the crab-like man at the bottom of the stairs.

As she descends, there is a slight hush in the cavity, a pause in the boredom. She looks at the actor playing Richard and he's suddenly more alive. Unseen by the audience, his face has tensed, ready to engage. All eyes are looking for her weakness, the reason she is only an understudy. She tosses her head, flicking her veil, signalling that the expectation will be disappointed, that the audience is about to witness a performance of a lifetime. The spitballs stop flying. The afternoon is suspended and for a few seconds, she is the centre of the universe, the woman Shakespeare had in mind when he wrote the role. This, she remembers, this is why I became an actor, the moment burning through the intervening years.

I learned it from her! Helen realizes, amazed. She has always assumed her extroversion came from the hearty salesman Reg, who could sell sand to the Bedouin. But fingering the white lace, she realizes she is in greater measure Annie's daughter. The rest of the scene of that long ago night falls into place. The way Reg drapes the mink stole over Annie's shoulders, his finger drifting down her neck. Annie flicking an invisible piece of lint off Reg's lapel. Both of them smiling, both ignoring the scuffed up children on the floor in front of the TV. An act, a magnificent act, as they prepare to please and seduce others, having failed to win each other's hearts. Both knowing the script and the role they will play. A professional, polished performance.

Later, when they come in, Helen will hear them whispering so as to not wake the children. Stage whispers and giggles worthy of the best sound effects technician. She pretends to be asleep when her mother bends over her to kiss her good night, her mouth a light moth smelling of garlic and stale wine. Her eyes closed tightly, Helen imagines it is Susan Hayward or Lana Turner kissing her which, in a sense, it is.

That's what held them together, Helen recognizes, passing her hand over a red taffeta dress with a V-neck and a slash up one leg, a sequinned pantsuit, a ball gown of dark grey tulle illusion over a pale grey underskirt. Costumed for marriage, fulfilling to the letter their contract. Annie's ambition and Reg's glad-handing salesmanship, both of them working any party like veteran politicians. Helen smiles as she sifts through the other dresses. They are all in excellent condition, fresh from the dry cleaners, waiting for the next invitation.

I wonder why she kept them all? Helen thinks as she opens another bag, this one full of tailored suits. A theatre costume department could probably use the cocktail numbers, especially if they did a lot of Noel Coward or Terence Rattigan. But who does Noel Coward or Terence Rattigan any more? Maybe a vintage clothing store would take them on consignment. At any rate, Helen decides that they're too exotic for the local Goodwill shop. She turns to the boxes.

There is a set of demi-tasse cups, delicately etched with gold, Wedgwood! never even removed from their tissue paper. Why would she buy these? Helen wonders, knowing her mother rarely drinks coffee. She finds the sales slip at the bottom of the box, with the words "Final Sale" stamped across it. Mystery solved. Annie never could resist a sale. She puts them aside, thinking she might take them back to Toronto, how nicely they'll go with the espresso machine Bernie and she bought each other last Christmas. A little exotic for the pine kitchen table, but what the hell.

Helen recalls how Annie, constantly at war with Reg, transferred all her energy onto new objects of desire. Her new dates were shopping trips, which she looked forward to and for which she dressed with flair. Not for Annie, comfortable shoes for walking long distances along Ste. CatherineStreet or in airport-sized suburban malls. No. She wore high heels that showed her smooth, slim legs to advantage, for heavy, middle-aged shoe salesmen to admire. On winter shopping sprees, she wore her fur coat, a muskrat with a mink collar, that showed that she was a woman of means, even though as the day wore on, it felt like bricks had been hung from her shoulders. But she was, after all, engaged in a courtship dance, not a plodding routine.

Her purest moments of surrender, of release and pleasure, came during sales, when she sparkled with the possibility of conquest, of acquiring the love object totally. The object — a new lamp, a pair of pearl earrings — would appear irresistible due to the reduced price. That others wanted an item, would try to elbow her aside in their pursuit of it, only made the consummation, the purchase, that much more delicious. Coming home from a sale, she would place her hand inside the bag with its soft folds of tissue paper and stroke the cashmere skin of a sale sweater with post–coital-like dreaminess. In the course of a year, she would celebrate anniversaries with these new loves — the January sales, end of season clearances, Record-Breaking Days, Scratch-and-Save Days and the much longed-for Warehouse Sale. Having acquired her new lovers, she took care to keep the relationship going, pouring specialist lemon oil like wine on a new Sheraton-style hall table, keeping the glow alive in her relationship with new candlesticks by means of soft caresses with Goddard's silver gloves.

Annie gave herself over so completely to these new passions, Helen recalls, that she would neglect the real needs of her family — a new vacuum cleaner or a pair of gym shoes for one of the kids — in favour of the remarkable value of a discontinued line of crystal or the siren song of a pair of deeply discounted Italian leather shoes. And Reg never minded. He prided himself on being a good provider, provided material goods were what you needed. Having failed to win Annie's love, he settled for feeding her greed. After all, the decked out house on the West Island was a monument to his prosperity.

From the second box Helen takes a damask tablecloth, never used, a ribbon enclosing the crisp folds. As she undoes the ribbon, it disintegrates and falls to the floor as dust. When she shakes out the tablecloth, the fabric breaks along most of the stiffly ironed folds, cracking into stiff squares. This is like entering a mummy's tomb, thinks Helen, then smiles at the pun, wondering how Annie could be so attached to things when she herself cares about them so little. She does a mental inventory of the garage sale and Sally Ann furniture she has equipped her own house with. The slightly battered wicker chairs that cost only ten dollars each. The pine washstand that had been put out as garbage in Rosedale.

The link to Annie has evaporated. They have exited on opposite sides of the stage. Upstairs, Annie is calling her name.

When Helen comes back into the living room, there are discarded photos fanned out in a skirt around Annie, in no particular pattern. None are in the discard box. Oprah is hugging an Oriental man in saffron robes.

"There you are! Isn't it time for a cup of tea? Maybe one of those cookies that the Church women sent over." Annie tosses another photo on the floor.

"Uh, what are you doing ? You're throwing out all those photos?" Helen asks, gesturing to the collection on the floor. There are only a few in the keeper box.

Annie snorts. "Of course not! I'm only sorting them."

"Uh, how?" The pictures overlap each other for a radius of three feet.

"Well, now." Annie looks down at the mess. "Some of them, I think those over there are from the cottage at St. Sauveur before we sold it, and then there's some of the house on Chamberlain Avenue ..." She drifts off, unable to locate them. "Well, where did I put the ones of Barbara's wedding?" She looks around quite frantically. "They were right here!" Agitated, she shuffles a handful still in her lap.

"Never mind, Mom, I'll sort through them later." Helen starts collecting the ones on the floor.

"They were right here, I tell you. Did you move them?"

"Don't you need to go to the bathroom?" Helen has cleared a path for the wheelchair.

"Well, someone moved them! I know where I put them."

"Maybe so. What about the bathroom?"

"You don't believe me!"

"I do, Ma. I do. We'll sort them out later."

"I don't know." Annie's lip is quivering in frustration. "What about tea?"

"Right after the bathroom."

Over tea, Helen puts a handful of old photographs, whose occupants she can't identify, in front of Annie. "Do you know who these people are?"

Annie fingers them awkwardly with her bad hand. "They were the parents of our neighbours, I think. The MacRaes."

"Well, if you're not sure, maybe we should just get rid of them."

"Get rid of them?" Annie is indignant. "The Pioneer Museum collects photos like these!"

"Umh, I don't think these photos are old enough for that." Helen holds up one of two young men in front of an old tractor, squinting into the sun. "What about these two?"

Annie shakily places the picture in the talons of her left hand. "That's your Uncle Gordon and the first tractor he bought. Second-hand." She trails a finger of her good hand over the surface. "And that's Ewan with him."

Helen takes the photo back with new interest. She sees a tall man, taller than her Uncle Gordon, his hair tousled, with strong arms streaked with dirt, mid-laugh, having slapped the wheel guard as if it were a horse's flank. "He was a handsome man, your Ewan."

Annie takes the photo again. "Yes, he was. A good man, too." Annie has forgotten her cookie and tea.

"I'm surprised you let a man like that get away," Helen says, only half-teasingly.

"Ah!" Annie tosses down the photo. "It was he who let me get away." She looks toward the wall.

Helen is intrigued. There is none of the impatience she hears in Annie's voice when she speaks about Reg. "Is that why you broke up, Mom? Because you went away? To Montreal?"

Annie's eyes have narrowed when she turns back to Helen. "Actually, we both wanted to get away from here. From the farm. I was the only one who made it."

"And that changed your relationship?"

"Yes and no." Annie sighs and then says clearly, "You're old enough to know, Helen, that it's never that simple. A relationship can never stay the same. If it's going to last, it's got to change and move, become a living thing. And I think women, especially, spend far too much energy trying to resist change. Trying to hold on to the perfect moment. And you never can. I know that now." Annie has tears in her eyes.

Helen has never witnessed such reflection in her mother. She reaches across the table to squeeze her hand. "You think perhaps you made a mistake? Chose the wrong man?" she asks tenderly.

Annie pulls her hand away. "No! No! I would have made a terrible farmer's wife." She looks to Helen for reassurance. "Well, can you see me milking cows morning and night every day for forty years?"

Helen recognizes that her mother needs reinforcement. Now is not the time to question her judgement. She leans back. "No, of course not. And besides, it would have wrecked your nails."

"And then I met Reg," Annie adds.

Helen nods. "And then you met Reg." She rises from the table. "Now what about the rest of those photos? Who are those old people beside the windmill?"

"I've had enough of looking at old pictures," Annie announces, pushing her wheelchair away. "Old pictures, old times. What's the use of recalling all that? What's on TV? It must be nearly time for Jeopardy."

The TV is announcing a new reality-based game show in which several pairs of ex-lovers describe their former partner's intimate body flaws, and based on this information the audience has to guess which of the group was the partner. The news headlines are that the Toronto Stock Exchange and the American Southwest have set records for being hot.

Helen gathers the photos together, glancing once more at her uncle looking impossibly young, and his cocky, happy friend. She can see why you'd remember a man like that when you're feeling low, when you're feeling your life is over. His smile has that confidence that says he will handle things, no matter what happens. He conveys it even to Helen, who smiles back at him, feeling she knows him a little. She thinks about who in her past she might turn to when her life is over. John Fitzgerald? No comfort there. Guy? She can't even remember why she married him. Bernie. Bernie would come calling. She shakes herself. Ghosts are collecting in this house, she thinks. I must try to dust more.

It's a beautiful night when Helen walks out with her brandy and cigarette, still sifting through the cast list of the men in her life. A milky cloud washes the moon, but otherwise the sky is dark and brilliant with stars. She breathes deeply to bring her mind to the same level of stillness as the night. It seems to pause for a moment, the frogs and crickets silent. Leaning against the dock at the river, she sees a pinpoint of light moving erratically along the shore, coming toward her. It turns out to be a cigarette — soon she can make out a figure attached to it.

"Good evening," a warm voice says from the shadows. A tall, rangy man comes through the wall of dark leaves.

"Good evening. Lovely night, isn't it?"

"Sure is." The man nods toward the bungalow. "You live here?"

"Temporarily. My mother lives here, but she's been ill. I've come down to look after her."

"Duncan Urquart," the man says, offering his hand.

Helen takes his hand, aware of strong forearms, calloused fingers. "How do you do? I'm Helen Bannerman."

"You look familiar. You from around here?"

"No. My mother is, but I was raised in Montreal."

"Funny, I could swear."

This has happened to Helen before, people mistaking a face on TV for someone they knew in kindergarten. "You might have seen me on TV," she says as modestly as she can.

"You an actress?" He stands back with new respect.

"Sometimes. I also teach and direct. I had a small continuing role on CBC a few years back. A lot of people remember my face from then."

Duncan lets out a low whistle. "Holy shit. A TV star in Glengarry County!"

Helen takes a sip of brandy. "Hardly a star. I had about ten words a show. But I did do a TV commercial about toilet bowl cleaners a couple of years back that got me a lot of recognition. Little kids would stop their mothers in the supermarket and say, 'Look! There's the Saniscrub lady!'"

Duncan chuckles. "Must be quite a change for you, nursing your Ma down here."

"Yes, it is. I'm overdue for another change."

Duncan offers Helen a cigarette. "It ain't easy, I know. I helped take care of my mother before she passed away. From cancer. It was a full-time job, even though there were others who helped. You feel torn all the time, wanting to do what's right by her, but at the same time, wishing she'd get it over with, so you can get on with your own life."

"Exactly! You've got it exactly!" Helen takes a cigarette from him, and they give each other a conspiratorial smile. The recognition of a kindred spirit. There is something very familiar about Duncan that relaxes Helen.

"Your mother was lucky to have you," Helen says. "Usually it's the women who get stuck." Duncan lights her cigarette." Do you live nearby?"

"Used to. I'm just back visiting. I've been working overseas for the past few years. Got into a boat-building business out in Malaysia."

"Malaysia! How exotic! So you are just here on holiday?"

"Wouldn't call it a holiday. My brother's got me doing chores on the farm while I try to decide whether or not to go back. My partner's offered to buy me out. And it's a good offer. Could buy me a nice property here."

Helen sips her brandy. "Nice to have that option. But Canada must seem awfully dull after the Far East. Not much happening around here."

"You're right there. Not much else to do at night but take a long walk by the river. I miss water." Duncan nods toward the river. "Any body of water'll do."

Helen takes in his looks, a man her own age, maybe older, with pale cool eyes and a tanned pliant face that folds easily into a smile. "The boats you build, they're sailboats?"

"Only kind of boat there is. Made of teak and built for ocean sailing. Do you sail?"

"I used to a bit. When I was married. It's a marvellous sensation, feeling the wind carrying you away." Helen pauses a moment, trying to remember the last time she felt carried away.

"Best feeling in the world. When she's heeled over and racing with the wind. The rush, the excitement of it. It's almost better than sex." Duncan catches himself. "Almost. Don't wish to be crude. "

Helen laughs. "That's alright. I can't remember that far back."

"Now, that's a shame. I hope you don't mind me saying, but it's a lonely task, looking after your Ma, isn't it? I've seen you come down here before at night. Just smoke and have a quiet moment to yourself."

This piece of information surprises Helen and disturbs her. How come she's never noticed him? How long has he been there? "You've seen me before? I never saw you."

Duncan's turn to feel awkward. "Well, you looked like you were enjoying the time to yourself. Didn't want to butt in."

He gives her a soft smile that almost makes his eyes disappear. Her first reaction dissipates. She's always liked the idea of being watched, onstage or off. She swallows a large slug of brandy.

"I'd best keep moving. I usually follow the tow path along to the bridge down there and come back by the road. Nice to meet you."

"My pleasure," says Helen, rising. "Time to look in on Mama."

Duncan seems reluctant to go. "Maybe see you again some other night."

"Yes. If you do, please speak up."

As she takes the path up to the house, a thought occurs to her and she turns. "Do you like brandy?" But she's speaking to the darkness, Duncan already gone. Her mood and step are lighter as she heads up to the house.

# chapter 10

THE DARK. AMAZING WHAT YOU can see in it. Slips of light and shadows. Like now. With just the light from the hall I can see you leaning on that Massey Harris tractor, telling Gordon he should trade it in on a Rolls Royce. "They both got two names, Gordon," you said. Ah, you could make me laugh, Ewan. But then, so could Reg, in those early days, before he was shipped overseas. You never met him. I wonder what you would have thought of him, what you would have seen. Whatever did I see?

Reg. Not classically handsome, but definitely attractive, with a grin that could move a rock. Always on. Him at the door that evening after Ewan left, trailing snowflakes, with a small nosegay of violets for Elsie, she twittering more than usual at the sight of them. Told me later he stole them from a funeral hearse he'd passed that afternoon. Me in my only other good dress, a purple wool crepe with mauve appliqués. What was it he said? "You look delish." That was it.

Reg, the super salesman, eager to win everyone's favour. Never happy unless he'd charmed everyone in the room. Sitting at the kitchen table, sipping tea, he tells Hector and Elsie that we're headed for a benefit concert for Polish refugees. He listens to Hector ranting on about conscription and the cowardly French-Canadians who are resisting it. Reg's contribution? "Of course, as a man in uniform, prepared to give my life for my country, I have to agree with you."

For a moment, Hector almost looks content. Elsie burbles on about how no mother wants to send her son to war, Hector silencing her with, "What would *you* know? You have no son."

What a grand night that turned out to be! At last we escape the MacKinnons and once outside, Reg tucks his hand under my elbow and tells me we're heading for the Bellevue Casino, to meet up with some buddies of his. The Bellevue Casino! Montreal's swankiest night club!

At the door, he slips the maitre d' a dollar, and like magic, we have a table right near the railing upstairs. Tall women, gauzy and sequinned, are doing a synchronized dance on the stage. Small lamps on every table give off their own gauzy light.

Out of nowhere, Reg's airforce mates and their girls join us, and suddenly, we are a party. One of the girls uses a cigarette holder, I remember. Another has a real gold compact. When the waiter comes to take our order, Reg nods toward me and says, "She'll have a Whisky Sour, won't you, Annie?"

Whatever possessed him to say that? I'd never had a real cocktail in my life but I'd memorized a menu of them from the movies. And so soon after breaking up with Ewan, I wasn't about to let any man tell me what to do.

"I'll have a Daiquiri," I say to the waiter, not knowing what is in one. I guess that's when I discovered I don't like rum. Still don't. Reg just chuckled.

How did the rest of the evening go? Very noisy, very sophisticated, especially when a blond stripper comes on. As she peels off her clothes, trained white doves flutter onto her to cover up the naughty bits. I'm embarrassed, of course, don't know where to look, but I wouldn't show it.

Reg leaning over and whispering, "They got anything like that where you come from, Annie?"

Trying to hold my own, eager to fit in, I blow out a stream of smoke and say, "We have birds like that. Only they're called chickens." Ha! I thought he'd never stop laughing.

There were many evenings like that over the next six weeks, I think it would have been. The movies on Wednesday, nightclubs or officers' parties on the weekends. Reg and his mates coming into the city from the airfield on the South Shore where they were training, taking a room together and piling as much fun into twenty-four hours as they could. The MacKinnons never objected to me being out late, thinking Reg was like Leslie Howard in *Gone With The Wind* — serious, noble and well-intentioned. When I think back, it seems as though we were never alone. Always party time, except when Reg wanted something more, and he'd do his best to find out what fabric the appliqués on my dress were made of, until I made him stop. Even those caresses were different from what

I knew — hurried, breathless, stolen from a lively party. Different from you, Ewan. Nothing to linger over or moon about, a quick rush. It was all a game, a silly game. Exactly what I needed then.

With Reg, the talk was mostly chit-chat, but somewhere along the line I picked up a few things about him. His family was from Kingston, his father a lawyer, and they were quite well off. But all Reg inherited from his barrister father was the smooth talk. He was the black sheep of the family, the one who'd been kicked out of boarding school for sneaking a local girl into the dorm one night. Later, he'd gone to university at Western but flunked out his first year, having majored in frat parties. I suppose you could say Reg was a man of action — always restless, on the move, the way I wanted to be then. He'd toured all over the States in a rodeo and once worked on a millionaire's yacht off the coast of California. He'd visited Europe and even the Middle East before the war. His grandmother had left him a small legacy, which allowed him to be the one buying drinks for everyone.

His uncle had finally got him a job in sales in Montreal, which he proved to be quite good at, until the war offered the promise of more excitement. It did that for all of us.

I guess it was the end of March when Reg arrived one night and announced to Hector, Elsie and me that his air training was over, that they were shipping out to England within the month. My mind went blank, flashes of panic stabbing through it. I hadn't allowed myself to think of the future since New Year's Eve. Between the factory work and Reg, I was totally operating in the present. Like now, the future wasn't something I wanted to think about. I was happy that nothing was the same as it had been on the farm, nothing was familiar. All that newness was like a drug, energizing me. Then, all of a sudden, I was facing withdrawal.

There wasn't too much time to think about Reg's leaving because we were on our way to a party at the Berkeley Hotel. In the cab, Reg leaned over to me, nuzzling, and said, "I took a room by myself tonight. At the Windsor. I was hoping you might join me there," and he squeezed my knee.

Ewan, I thought of you then, and I remember the anger that found its way through me. "I'm not the kind of farmer's daughter you think I am," I said, moving over to the other side of the seat, looking anxiously at the cab driver to see if he'd heard, if he might understand English.

4

Reg just laughed softly. "Oh, I know that, Annie. I've known that since I met you." He moved over to me, and with his lips brushing my neck, he added, "Think it over."

That night comes through so clearly now, just like that light in the hall. I think I danced with every man in the room, straightening my spine every time Reg came close. Every time he passed me a drink, I flashed him a brittle smile. The last thing I wanted was to think it over. When he suggested we leave the dance early, I agreed. As we stood in the snow on Sherbrooke Street, in a cloud of smoke and warm breath, I announced, "I'm not going back to your room with you, Reg."

You see, the truth was, I didn't desire Reg. I wanted what I already had: parties, laughs, excitement. I didn't want any kind of intimacy with him, already suspecting that if I delved beneath the surface, there wouldn't be much there.

Reg just nodded. "I didn't think you were that conventional, Annie. Thought I spied a streak of rebellion in there. But I guess at heart you're a country virgin."

Oh! How that line got to me! "No, I'm not," I said hotly. "Which is why I'll never trust another man. And I hope you're not going to give me that 'I'm shipping overseas, I might be killed' line." Wherever did I get the courage to say that? I'd been gone from Glengarry less than a year.

By that time, I was trembling, from cold and the mix of emotions inside me.

"Let's get you some coffee," he said and steered me down the street to an all-night diner.

So I told him about you, Ewan, how trapped I had felt, how sex hadn't eased anything, only tangled it so that I couldn't see my way clear. I don't know how I could say such things to him, given that we'd never talked seriously before. Anyway, I ended with, "So I guess that's it, between us. I hope to God you don't tell anyone about this."

Reg simply took my hand, "Why would you think it's over between us?"

"Well, I'm a fallen women, who refuses to fall again," I said, as bravely as I could.

Reg just gave one of his little laughs. "I always believe in trying things out. I wouldn't want a woman no one else wanted."

And that was it. God! How I loved him at that moment! The freedom that gave me! How everything seemed to just fall into place. Here was someone who accepted me just as I was, warts and all. My reinvention had taken place: I had become someone else, and everything that had happened before then was over and gone. What we so often long for — a kind of rebirth.

Where was I? Oh, yes. Reg came to pick me up for the pictures on Wednesday, bringing two train tickets for Maxville, the village nearest our farm, for Saturday. "Why in heaven's name would you want to go there?" I asked.

"So I can ask your father for your hand in marriage," he said matter-of-factly. I was speechless, so he added. "Time I settled down. You, too. Can't have you traipsing out to dances on your own while I'm in England."

My blood was racing in all directions. "You might at least ask me!"

"Okay, will you marry me, Annie, the farmer's daughter?"

What to say? I was flattered, it was exciting, we had so little time left to be together before he shipped overseas. There was no time to think about it. No time to consider that married life was not going to be a stream of non-stop parties. I said "yes" because of the drama of it all.

Now I can't say Reg totally charmed my parents or Gordon. But he certainly discombobulated them. I remember he brought flowers for my mother, who had never received flowers out of season in her life. She stood there, smiling and wondering at roses in April, before I led her off to put them in a vase. He presented my father with a bottle of Scotch, which my father examined for far too long, before Gordon took it from him and suggested a drink all around. The drink broke the ice and Reg asked to be shown the farm, slapping the haunches of our cattle, asking how much horsepower the tractor had, wondering what return on investment the farm might yield. At dinner, he went into ecstasies over the thick chicken gravy and the lemon meringue pie. Then he asked to have a private word with my father, while my mother and I washed the dishes, my mother murmuring, "You might want to start learning a bit about cooking yourself, Annie." I won't say my folks really took to him, but they were intrigued. Any doubts they had they put down to Reg being a man of the world.

The wedding. Not the wedding I'd dreamed of with you, Ewan. A wartime affair, me in a short dress because of the material shortage, and a broad picture hat, not a veil, Reg in his uniform; an afternoon wedding in Montreal, with Reg's side of the church filled with a few stylish people from Kingston and servicemen, and my side filled with farmers tugging at their uncomfortable collars. I was uneasy about my guests, ashamed, even though my mother wore a new blue dress and hat. Looking back, I suppose I was ill at ease because, with my marriage, I was moving beyond the farm, but toward what, I was not quite sure. I was in the middle, no longer belonging to the community I had grown up in, not yet belonging anywhere else. Just not belonging. I've always wanted to fit in, wherever I was, and this was my wedding.

What else? Meeting Reg's mother for the first time, a reserved woman in a pale grey suit, there without her husband, who'd disowned Reg. Nice enough to me, but still cool. Later, I discovered that was the only temperature Reg's whole family operated in. Maggie as maid of honour, looking smart as ever in a pink print dress and hat larger than mine. There's a picture of us all somewhere in that box I was sorting through today.

The reception, if you could call it that, was back at the MacKinnon's, all the food homemade, even the wedding cake that Dorcas MacKay had made. I'd have preferred a tall, store-bought one, but I didn't have a choice. The differences in the guests! My folks sipping fruit punch and tea in the parlour, Reg and his mates out on the front porch, tipping the contents of their hip flasks into their punch, smoking, making coarse comments and flirting with Maggie, one of three women out there with them. I kept smiling, making small talk with the visitors from Glengarry, trying to win over Reg's mother. But I felt cheated, Ewan, let down, feeling that on this, the first day of my new life, I should be happy or at least at ease. Ha! You would say I'd *never* been at ease, wouldn't you Ewan?

Mercifully, everyone from back home had to leave to catch the last train back and we trooped down to Windsor Station to see them off. As the train pulled away, Reg lit a cigarette and announced to his cronies, "Let's continue this shindig down at Rockhead's," which we did. Reg in a hurry, never lingering for the moment, as I found out later that night.

Ah, the revelations that come to you at night, just before sleep so you can't act on them. Our "honeymoon." One night at the Windsor Hotel, before Reg reported back to base. After a quick and somewhat drunken consummation of our marriage, when Reg had fallen asleep, I lay awake, realizing that neither one of us had ever used the word "love" with the other. It was only then that I allowed myself to slip from the present into the past. Alone on my wedding night, I thought of you, Ewan, and I slipped into sleep with your hands on me.

The dark. The lights that go on in the dark. I can still see those dark-skinned musicians down at Rockhead's, clear as glass. Hear their music, too. The melancholy sound of a saxophone, wishing for better times, better things. Making love for the first time as a married woman, in a bed, with your husband who is about to be shipped overseas, perhaps never to return. And you're glad that it's dark. That he can't see your face or worse, your sad thoughts.

What's that? Ah! Helen's going to bed. I must have drifted off. I can hear her rinsing the brandy glass so I won't know she drinks every night after she's put me to bed. The soft click as she checks the doors. It's good she's having an early night. Shut off that hall light and leave me to the true dark. We've a lot to do tomorrow.

# *chapter 11*

HELEN AND ANNIE ARE OFF on a big adventure, Annie's first outing since she's come home from hospital. They are off to the mall in Cornwall to buy Annie some looser-fitting clothes that she might be able to put on by herself. Fashion dictated by the travelling physio.

It starts off badly. There is a lot of fussing about what Annie wants to wear on the excursion — a blouse with ruffles that Helen has not ironed to Annie's satisfaction. Annie insists on lipstick and mascara, which results in a rather piratical look to one eye and unfortunate slashes on her chin. Helen's offer to help doesn't help.

Once out of the house, Helen tries to help Annie swing from the wheelchair into the car. But halfway out of the chair, Annie lacks the strength to continue, so Helen grabs her under both arms and heaves her, accidentally hitting Annie's head on the door frame. Annie howls.

"I'm sorry, Ma! You moved just as I was lifting you. You okay?"

"How can you be so clumsy? I don't need you to lift me. I can look after myself! My poor head." Annie sits on the edge of the car seat, with her feet dangling outside, crying. "You could have knocked me out! My poor head!"

"I'm sorry, Ma! I said I'm sorry! And it wasn't a hard enough bump to knock you out, was it? Let me see." Helen goes to part Annie's hair, but Annie swats her away.

"Leave me alone!"

Helen turns and walks back into the house, already at the end of her patience and they haven't even left the driveway yet. This was a lousy idea. She'll go without Annie.

"Helen!" Helen looks out the window where Annie sits half in and half out of the car, rocking, trying to lift herself up. She has never seemed so small nor so helpless. "Helen!"

Guilt and pity win over Helen, and she hurries back outside. "Sit still, Ma! You'll end up on the ground."

"Well then, help me into the car!"

"You sure you want to go? You think this is a good idea? Maybe you're not ready yet." Helen asks because she has her own doubts.

"You promised you'd take me! Now let's go!" Annie is too agitated for her own good.

Helen eases Annie back onto the seat, swings her legs into the car, reaches over and fastens the seat belt, arranging Annie's purse, Kleenex and bag of pills on her lap. Annie sinks back, exhausted, her mouth open, nothing but her will keeping her going. Helen tangles with the wheelchair, taking off the seat cushion, the foot pads and the arm rests, folding it up, hefting it into the trunk, where one stubborn wheel sticks out over the edge. A couple more shoves and shifts and she finally gets it in. She is covered in sweat, her breath heaving. For what seems like a very long moment, they sit side by side in the car in the driveway, while Helen summons up the energy to go further. What in God's name are we doing? she asks herself.

There are other problems along the way. Annie notes that Helen's car isn't as clean as she'd like it, and she hates the caterwauling on the radio.

"Do we have to listen to that noise?"

"It's Mozart, not noise," corrects Helen.

"A lot of seesawing fiddles, if you ask me. Gets on my nerves."

"Yeah, I know what that's like," mutters Helen, trying to find another station.

"I like music with words," Annie pronounces.

"Opera, then?"

"English words."

The ride to Cornwall takes half an hour, during which the seat belt is too tight, the lack of air conditioning is mentioned, the window is opened because it's too stuffy, then shut because it's too breezy. Several cars that pass them are going too fast, several cars in front are going too slow and Helen herself is going too fast. Helen begins to contemplate the maximum jail term for matricide.

But once they arrive at the mall, gliding into a spot reserved for the handicapped, the journey changes direction. As Helen is hauling the wheelchair out of the trunk, a burly man in a tractor cap offers to help, lifting the wheelchair as if it were made of paper. Annie goes all twittery and girlish as the man lifts her out of her seat and places her in the chair in one smooth graceful gesture. He even tips his cap and calls Annie "Ma'am," which unbalances even Helen. She wheels Annie into the mall as if she were participating in a royal procession.

Annie hates the wheelchair, hates to have anyone see her in it, but today her attitude softens, as does Helen's. A young mother with a toddler holds the door open to the mall and gives Helen a sympathetic smile. Salespeople, who normally can't be found even to take your money, materialize beside the chair and ask Annie in voices that are too loud and enunciating too precisely, the way kindergarten teachers speak, "And how are you today?" Kids come up to the chair and make eye contact with Annie, who's right at their level, older women nod at Helen knowingly and the mall crowds part to let them pass. Deference is paid to the old, the weak and those who care for them. It amazes both women and their spirits lift.

The physio has given them the fashion rules. No zippers or buttons. Velcro closures are good. Clothing must be loose, washable, elasticized at the waist. No trailing scarves, tabs, belts or other paraphenalia that might get caught in the wheelchair or a walker. In the first store they pick out a blue outfit with loose-legged pants, an elasticized waist and a generous top.

"I want to try it on," Annie declares.

"You sure?" Helen is checking out whether the aisle to the change room will be wide enough.

"I'm not buying an outfit without trying it on first!" Annie says, as if Helen has suggested participation in a marathon.

In the fitting room, Helen manages to get Annie's blouse off, but when Helen tries to pull on the blue top, it gets stuck on one elbow and over Annie's ears.

"Keep your arm straight, Ma!"

"I can't! It's stuck! Pull it the other way."

"Okay, but I'm going to try to get it off, so we can put it over your head first."

The top won't budge past Annie's ears. She snorts. "What are you doing now?" Helen smothers a giggle. She can't help it. "What are you laughing at?"

Helen blurts, "We're going to have to buy this one. I can't get it off."

And then she laughs out loud.

Annie snorts again. "If we have to go back through the store like this, am I decent?"

Helen looks at the tiny body with its arms in the air, encased in blue fleece. "You look like a blue popsicle. A very fashionable blue popsicle, mind you," and laughs loud enough to bring tears to her eyes. "A Smurf!"

Annie can't help but laugh herself, and the large saleswoman coming to check their progress finds both of them considering scissors as a solution. Together, the saleswoman and Helen manage to get the top around the elbow and down off Annie's ears.

"Well, how does it look?" Annie wants to know.

"Perfect. Colour suits you. But we better try a bigger top. Now you don't want to try on the pants, do you?" Annie agrees that maybe they can forego that. They look big enough and the saleswoman assures Helen that they can be exchanged if they're not satisfactory.

Back out in the mall, fortified by the fact that they have accomplished something for all this effort, the women contemplate the rest of the stores. Annie's eyes light up at the acres of goods to buy. She wants to see it all, asking Helen to stop so she can examine clocks, electronic equipment, scented candles, office furniture, souvenir mugs, orthopaedic shoes, towels, mixmasters, Tickle Me Elmos, cassette players, picture frames, even snow tires.

At a display of electronic games, she asks, "What's that?"

The salesman explains that it is a computer game.

"Can it play euchre?"

"Ah, no," the salesman acknowledges.

"Is there a seniors' discount?" At this point Helen wheels her away to a luxury lingerie shop across the aisle. Annie fingers a cerise silk caftan with her good hand.

"This would look good on you, Helen."

The comment takes Helen aback. "Why do you think that?" She looks at the price tag on it and inwardly gasps.

"It's a good strong colour. Go well with your hair. And you being an actress and all, it would suit you. Do you like it?"

"It's ... nice. I think the pearl grey would be more my style, though." Helen assumes Annie's playing a game, a new game, which is refreshing.

"Too boring. What about the dark green then?"

"The dark green is very sophisticated."

"Good. I'm going to buy it for you." Annie pushes herself off in the direction of the cashier, trailing green silk behind her, before Helen can finish asking herself when she would ever be likely to wear a silk caftan. She is surprised, but pleased, trying to remember the last time her mother complimented her or spontaneously gave her anything.

Catching up with Annie at the cashier, she says, "It's very expensive. And I'm not sure when I might wear it."

"I'm going to ask if they give a seniors' discount," Annie says. "It's the kind of thing actresses wear backstage, isn't it?"

Helen thinks of the tiny dingy dressing rooms attached to the small theatres she usually performs in, which often house the theatre's cleaning supplies and double as the only backstage toilet. "Maybe Hollywood actresses."

"You should spoil yourself a bit," Annie says, clawing for her Visa card in her purse. "And it might make that fellow who lives in your house take notice."

Helen tries to imagine Bernie's reaction if she came downstairs in the caftan one morning instead of her normal tartan flannel dressing gown. Then another thought slides in.

"Uh, Ma?"

"It sure is taking them a while to wrap up that thing."

"Ma? Bernie? The guy who rents from me? Have I told you he's Black?"

"Black? I don't know why they can't use a perfectly good word like 'negro' or 'coloured.'"

"Maybe it's because we are all coloured, only some of us are coloured beige." The women wait while the saleswoman carefully folds tissue paper, then the gown, then applies the stickers to hold the tissue in place. "So it doesn't bother you then, that a Black man is living in my house?"

"Well, it would bother some I could mention at the Women's Institute. But I thought you said he came from Nova Scotia?"

"He does."

Annie snorts. "Must be one of those Black Celts they used to talk about. Oh my! What is that girl going to do next? Iron it?"

"Almost ready, Ma." Helen has avoided telling Annie that Bernie's Black for nearly two years now, fearing her disapproval. And it isn't there. She wonders what other difficulties she has manufactured. Phantom worries, like phantom pain. Real enough if you're living them.

Taking charge of the exquisitely packaged caftan, Annie pronounces, "A person should always have an outfit that makes them feel better about themselves, don't you think? Good clothes can make you feel special."

Special. What Helen has always wanted to feel, but could never quite manage on her own. She thinks about the gauzy cotton dress she bought on the west coast when she was touring schools in a production of *Peter Pan*, how she wore it for years until it was just wisps of multicoloured soft cloth she would fold herself in when she felt most vulnerable. "Absolutely," she says and grins. She even manages to maintain the grin throughout Annie's protest about the store's lack of a seniors' discount. They wheel out with the bags piled on Annie's lap, almost rising to her chin.

They barrel through the mall, delighting in their brief liberation from routine. Annie explains to Helen how to tell if gloves are hand-stitched and illustrates the difference between china and porcelain by shakily holding up a Belleek cup to the light, which glows through the thin china. For once, Helen listens, hearing something other than greed in Annie's evaluation of things. They have lunch in the food court, selecting from a wall of franchises offering indigestible fried food in the guise of ethnic delicacies. "Chinese," Annie decides.

Helen watches Annie slowly picking the nuts out of her Almond Chicken Guy Ding and temporarily loses what's left of her appetite. Then she notices the occupants of other tables around them. Young blue-jean mothers smoking while their children fuss, a few old men staring blankly around while they nurse a cup of coffee, teenagers with bad complexions drinking pop and experimenting with mating rituals. At least Annie is enjoying her food. Helen takes another stab at her egg roll.

"We should have done this more often," Annie announces.

"Done what?"

"Gone shopping together. Barbara and I often went together, but not you and I." Annie is attempting to get some bean sprouts off the top shopping bag next to her.

"I hate shopping, Ma. You know that."

"You don't seem to be having that bad a time today."

Helen has to agree. This has been one of their better times together. But what shopping requires is enough time and enough money, neither of which she has. She tells Annie this.

"When I was young," Annie says, her eyes looking over Helen's shoulder, "Maggie and I would go shopping, even when we had no money at all. It was just a way of dreaming or wishing. It was how we plotted our future."

Helen recognizes that she has never had a close woman friend like Annie had in Maggie. A confidante. She's always just tried to figure things out for herself, with the help of the odd therapist.

"That sounds nice." Helen helps Annie deal with the last of the bean sprouts. "But you sure made up for it once you got some money."

Annie nods. "I never lost that sense of possibility when I shopped," and again she has a far-off look.

Helen worries that Annie might be too tired, but she insists on buying more clothes before the expedition is over. They find another outfit, a skirt with an elasticized waist and a matching buttonless blouse, before Annie begins to fade, her chin falling to her chest, her good hand becoming agitated. Helen gets her back to the car and Annie sleeps the whole way home while Helen explores in her head what Annie might have been thinking in buying her the caftan. As she tucks Annie in that night, early because the trip has worn her out, she says, "Thank you for the caftan, Ma. It's beautiful. I've never owned such a luxurious garment."

"Not even when you were married to Guy?"

"Not even then. I've never been as stylish as you, Ma."

"No. Well, you had other things to think about. Other than clothes. I didn't."

Helen takes a step back. "Now of course you had other things to think about, Ma. Don't sell yourself short."

"I was never as clever as my children. I went for what was obvious."

"What do you mean by that, Ma?"

"Oh, I'm tired, dear. But thanks for taking me shopping. It gave me quite a lift."

"Me, too," Helen says softly, and as she kisses her mother's forehead, she hears the deeper breathing that tells her Annie is already asleep. "Thanks for seeing me in a different light," she whispers.

The colour is draining from the sky when she goes into the living room for her cigarettes. The last streaks of the sunset stain the west, and she notices a dot of the same colour down by the water. Duncan's cigarette. She can barely see the outline of him. He seems part of the shadows. She picks up the brandy bottle and two glasses on the way out.

"Good evening," she says, then realizes it's her stage voice she's using. Down girl, she tells herself.

"You're earlier than usual. How's Mom?"

"Exhausted. We went into Cornwall today, shopping. First time she's been out. She was pretty excited."

"She has to be the only person in the world who'd get excited shopping in Cornwall. What did you buy? Pulp and paper or contraband cigarettes?" Duncan shifts as he speaks.

"Actually, she bought me a lovely green silk caftan. Care for a brandy?"

"You bet."

Helen pours the brown liquid into two glasses and notices her movements are a bit jerky. Down girl, she says to herself again.

"So why aren't you wearing the caftan?" Duncan hoists his glass to her.

"It's a bit fancy for an assignation on a tow path. But you might be interested. It's made of Thai silk."

"Best in the world."

Helen is conscious of how easy it is to talk to Duncan, as if they've known each other for ages. A sign of her loneliness or a real connection? "We had a good day, actually," she says. "I hate shopping, but to my mother it's almost a religion. And it was great to see her light up like that."

"Ha! If it's a religion, it's the most popular one in the world and spreading like crazy. Peasants in Bangladesh want Mickey Mouse T-shirts. Tibetan nomads crave Coke. The Church of the Latter Day Consumer." Duncan shifts again and takes a swig of brandy.

"Well, I think it's her background. For her generation, there was the Depression and the war, and I think they had it pretty tough. It made her hunger for pretty things."

"Things!" barks Duncan. "Did they make her happy?"

"Hell, no. Oh, for a few minutes, an hour maybe. I don't think she's ever been happy. Especially in her marriage." Helen can't believe how much she's telling this near stranger.

"A happy marriage is an oxymoron."

Helen laughs. "You're pretty cynical. But my parents were up for the Nobel Prize for unhappy marriage, fighting all the time. Around them, it was like UN peacekeeping. You concentrated on dodging the bullets."

"You've been married, right?"

"Yes, briefly. Not briefly enough. You?"

"No, never. But at least you learned something from their experience. Get out early on."

For more than ten years, Helen has attributed her unmarried, uncoupled status to not having found the right man; never has she considered it a conscious choice. She has had moments when her ovaries have fluttered and she's pondered whether or not she wants to have a child. These moments passed. Her desire to mate has never been very strong, and she's put it down to her painful experience with Guy. A reaction, not a choice. Now she's not so sure.

"Maybe your parents just liked fighting," Duncan offers.

Helen scoffs. "Nonsense! No one would choose to live like that!"

"You sure? Different strokes for different folks and all that? Some of us, a lot of people, need something to rub up against, something to fight in order to feel really alive. Take me. I like sailing in tropical storms. Scares the shit out of me, and I love that rush."

Helen dives at the chance to talk about something other than her mother. "Tell me about it."

"It's funny, but, like, when you see a wall of water thirty metres high coming at you, time seems both to stand still and to hurry, at the same time."

"Your life flashing in front of you? That sort of thing?"

"That ain't it. It's that survival kinda has its own time frame. You will do anything to survive, and you lose track of how short or long a time it is." He pauses, then adds, "Being scared has a life of its own."

"You've felt that way more than once?"

"Yeah, once too often." Duncan gets up and paces.

"So you must be pretty bored here."

He laughs. "Not bored. Impatient. Waiting for a sign. Life must be pretty exciting in your line of work."

Helen thinks of the boredom of backstage life. Playing cards, waiting to go on again in the second act. The endless wait for the lighting and sound people to finish before filming a scene. But she knows that's not what's required here. People want to hear about the glamour, the fun of theatre life. So she launches into descriptions of some of the gigs she's worked, peppering the account with anecdotes of life on the theatrical fringe. How, in a summer theatre murder mystery, when she was to open a closet door to fetch a gun, the doorknob fell off and she ended up bludgeoning the victim to death with it instead of shooting him. About a student Romeo who got a visible erection when caressed by Juliet — after he was supposed to be dead. About the time the entire cast fell through the floorboards while dancing in the Donnelly trilogy. She spins a magical web, making theatre life appear larger than life.

They have another Remy Martin and Helen asks more about Duncan's daring on the high seas, eager for any kind of adventure. He doesn't disappoint, describing how he once outran an approaching typhoon and how his boat was once boarded by pirates in the Philippines. His stories make Helen gasp and laugh.

Duncan moves about. Restlessness seems to be his trademark. "Ah! But it ain't all like that, is it?" he says. "There are those moments when the darkness swoops in like fog. Scrambling your thoughts, shaking your certainty that you've made the right choices."

An invisible hand has gripped Helen's throat. "Yes," she croaks and pauses a moment. "Sometimes I worry about what's in store for me when I'm my mother's age."

"Well, for starters, you won't be your mother, will you?"

"That's for sure."

Duncan drains his glass. "Well, I'd best be going. Thanks for the brandy."

"Thank *you*."

"For what?"

"Never mind. See you again, I hope?"

"You bet. Good night to you," and Duncan is gone down the tow path, the darkness absorbing him.

Helen is momentarily stunned, her body heated. *Why in God's name did I have to mention my mother again?* She carefully picks up the glasses, the bottle and her cigarettes and slowly climbs the path back to the house. It's as if there is a warm current beneath her feet, at her back, gently coaxing her toward the kitchen lights. The weight of Annie has been lightened, by today's outing and by an attraction to a man who is pulling her in another direction.

## chapter 12

AH! A LOVELY TIME OF DAY. Swaying between waking and sleeping, sleeping and waking with the morning light soft as a pillow. When you can't tell if you're awake or dreaming. In my dreams, I can still walk and run and dance and it seems foolish to wake up and realize that all that has gone.

A quiet time of day except for that distant noise. What is it? A tractor. That would be Gordon, finished the milking and already in the fields. I must have slept late, although I can't hear anyone in the kitchen. Maybe they've forgotten about me. Not as if I'm needed for anything important. The work of a farm goes on with or without a useless daughter who sleeps late. I'll lie here in the shadows of sleep and wakefulness, till they find me.

I didn't think about you much back then, Ewan, in the early days of my marriage. Not like now. Oh, occasionally I would see a plaid shirt down at Eaton's that I thought would look handsome on you. But I kept busy, at what I can't remember, but I was focused on the future, not on the past, chiselling it out every time I hung a new set of curtains. Curtains, floors, towels, canisters for the kitchen. The bricks and mortar of married life. Married life! Wasn't what I imagined it would be, was it?

Of course, it didn't really get started until Reg was demobbed and came home. Early in 1946, I guess it was. What a do that was! I'd planned a little party at the flat I'd rented us, where Maggie and I had been living. Maggie had married Patrick, another airman, about a year after Reg and I were married. But Reg invited everyone in his squadron, the party soon overflowed the flat and we moved on to the Chez Parée and a few other clubs. A wild night it was. The next day, my head throbbing, I got the first glimpse of how my life was about to change. Reg had been up, made the coffee, and came back into the bedroom where I was still in bed, hoping a couple of aspirin would soon start to work on my hangover.

He threw off the covers, slapped my bottom and said, "Time you cooked your husband a good breakfast. I've waited two years for this."

Hunh! You can imagine how I took that suggestion. My first instinct was to tell him to cook his own damn breakfast, that he was the reason I felt so bad, but I didn't. I couldn't. He was a war hero, a man who'd fought for his country and who'd come home to me. I had no choice but to get up and start frying bacon, which turned over my already queasy stomach. Back then, everyone knew that was what a wife did. There was some sort of code, never written down, but acknowledged by all: wives got up and cooked their husbands' breakfast. No one had told me quite like that, but I knew.

So many surprises in store. As I was preparing to go back into work the next day, having taken a few days off, he gave me a squeeze and said, "You can go in and tell them you're quitting. You don't have to work any more." Like he was doing me a favour.

They'd already been letting women go at the factory, but I was a forewoman now, with some seniority, and the demand for commercial aircraft was picking up. They'd kept me on, as well as Maggie, who was now a widow and needed the work. Mind you, I was never wild about the type of work — I figure you could train monkeys to do what we did on the assembly line — but I did like the idea of earning my own way. And, for the first time in my life, I had been useful. It's important, that. My little flat, which I had furnished with my own money, was a testament to my usefulness. A tidy savings account, which I thought we might spend on a proper honeymoon, in Niagara Falls.

I remember trying to hang on to that part of my life. I said, as casually as I could, "I can't imagine what I'll do all day, if I don't go to work."

Reg took me on his knee. "Well, for starters, you can learn how to cook. You could definitely use some improvement in that department. And you can start making babies."

Just like that. It was as close as Reg and I ever came to talking things over. Reg didn't believe in planning or consulting or even giving prior notice. He just said he was going to do something and then he did it, regardless of what I or anyone else might think. My first reaction was to say, "No!" or "Why so fast?" but I kept up my little wife front and said nothing. It was at that moment that I first felt something stirring in my blood, something that could be whipped into rage at a moment's notice from then on. At the oddest times, it would come bursting out, at Reg or something he might say, or at the kids, with their perpetual questions and perpetual demands. And sometimes it would spill out onto a chair that was in my way or the top of a jar that wouldn't come off. It all seems so silly now.

Where was I? Oh yes. I did convince Reg that I should keep my job until he found work, but through the influence of his squadron leader, he was soon hired on, selling industrial cable at a plant in the East End. And whatever else, Reg could sell.

The end of my career. Celebrated with the person I'd started it with, Maggie. On the last day of work, Maggie and I went for lunch at Murray's downtown, for old time's sake. Chicken pot pie, as usual, looking out over Ste. Catherine Street at Eaton's across the road. Maggie announcing she was taking her widow's pension and finally going to business college. How did she put it? "So I can wear more than a pair of overalls to work." She had a small apartment in lower Westmount, on her own.

"Well, things have certainly changed, haven't they?" I said, thinking back to the two naive girls who had giggled their way to Montreal four years earlier.

Maggie nodded. "Never dreamed I'd even be married by twenty-five, let alone widowed."

"Do you still miss Patrick?" I asked softly. Close as we were, this had been delicate territory since the awful night when we'd received the telegram that his plane had been shot down over Germany. A week of hoping he might be a prisoner of war, before an officer showed up at the door to say he was dead. She never seemed to want to talk about it.

Maggie shook her head, not in denial but as if to clear it. "Yes, I suppose so. But we never had enough time together. So I miss more the idea of him."

An odd thing to say, but I understood what she meant.

"You know what the worst part is?" She was looking at me squarely, then. "I can't remember him."

I was shocked but said nothing as she continued. "Oh, I have photographs, and I remember the scar he had in one eyebrow, and I remember how his body felt, but I don't really have a sense of him, of who he was.

I never really got to know him. So it's like he was never real." She was crying now. "And if I, his wife, can't remember him, then who will? Can you tell me what purpose his life served? Can you tell me that?"

Both of us were crying then, hugging, right there at the table, with others looking away. I think I said something stupid, trying to help. "There will be someone else. You'll marry again, Maggie."

Not the right thing to say. She straightened up and blew her nose. "I'm not sure I want to. I don't seem to have the right instincts for marriage."

And she never did remarry. Strange how things work out, isn't it? Poor Maggie — the Merry Widow, the lone outsider among all us couples, showing up for Christmas and anniversaries, always dressed to the nines, the indulgent aunt to my children, the world traveller. But always, always removed, as if she were standing outside the room we were in, never wanting to enter it again.

\*\*\*

There's that hum again. The tractor's moving down the road. And there's someone up, now, moving about the kitchen, coming down the hall. I can smell coffee. They've just noticed I'm still asleep and my mother's coming to get me out of bed. But no. It's not her. Someone very familiar, but not her.

"How did you sleep, Ma? Ready to get up?"

She's very familiar, a little too familiar, if you ask me, pulling back the covers, placing her arm under my back. She moves in a much sharper way than my mother did.

"Where am I?"

"At home. In your own bed. You must have been sleeping well."

"Helen?"

"Who else were you expecting? Not that beau again?"

"No, not him. Not right now."

Helen is my daughter. My youngest daughter. Why is she here? Why is she ... ? Ah, I remember, I remember.

"C'mon, Ma. We've got to get you up."

"Quit pulling at me! I'll get up in my own good time."

## chapter 13

HELEN AND ANNIE ARE SEATED at the kitchen table. In front of them, a plastic box with twenty-one compartments, marked for morning, noon and night, and the seven days of the week. To one side is a small herd of bottles and vials of tablets — Annie's lifeline. This is another of the physio's ideas, to let Annie sort her own pills. "It vill improve her annual dexterity," he claims.

"Pink, pink, pink, pink," Annie says, dropping small pills into each morning section. Even using her good hand, she accidentally drops two into one box. Helen fishes out the extra.

"What are you taking?" Annie is instantly flustered.

"You dropped two into the same box. I'm just taking one out. Here." She gives it back to Annie.

"Now you've got me all confused! Where was I?"

"Start with Thursday. Small pink pill in each morning compartment."

Annie seems to take forever to shake the pills onto the table, claw up three more and drop them into the box. "Pink, pink, pink," she says, then sighs as if she has just carried in boulders from the garden.

"Now these ones," Helen says, easing a larger vial toward Annie.

"What are these for?"

Helen reads the label. "Cardizem. No idea. Probably to do with your heart."

Annie pushes the bottle away. "If I don't know what it's for, I'm not going to take it."

Helen pushes the bottle back. "Ma, all of these were prescribed by Dr. Fisher because you need them, to prevent another stroke. Now I'll check when the nurse comes to see what this one is for, specifically. But in the meantime, you'll take them, and you'll put them in the box." Helen can't believe the stern parental tone in her own voice.

Annie shakes the bottle hard, so that the large capsules spill out onto the table and over onto the floor. As Helen gets down to pick them up, she hears, "Monday, Tuesday, damn! Where did that go?" as another one falls to the floor. Only eight more bottles to go, thinks Helen, wondering what she can do to bring her fraying nerves under control. Her fingernails are already bitten to the quick. Maybe she should bake something, to keep herself occupied while Annie sorts the pills. But, no. She needs to keep an eye on what Annie's doing.

"What colour do you call this?" Annie is holding up a dark red pill.

"Burgundy. Wine-coloured. Maroon. I don't know. What colour do you call it?"

Annie looks at the pill as if it has just dropped from another galaxy. "Most of my pills are white. Or yellow. Only vitamin pills come in this colour."

Helen takes a deep breath. "Just put them in the box, Ma."

"Red, red ... red, red, red, red, red! There!"

"Seven more, Ma! You take these guys morning and night."

"Where does it say that?" Annie picks up the bottle, squints at the label.

"Just put them in the box, Ma!" Helen's patience has reached its limit.

"Wait a minute! How many of these do I take morning and night?"

Helen grabs the bottle from her, shakes out seven and drops them in each of the night compartments. She slams the bottle to one side, picks up the next and says, "One in each noon compartment. Now!" She is suddenly aware that it is not her own voice she is using, but Annie's. Annie going ballistic when someone has left the mayonnaise on the counter. Annie insisting that the house plants be watered on a Tuesday, never on a Wednesday. The barbecue overturned on the patio when the briquettes didn't catch fire fast enough. Annie's war with the way things worked.

"You should do something about that temper of yours," Annie says calmly and quietly, picking up another vial of pills.

Helen can't speak because of the thick wad of rage in her throat. When she does, her voice is shrill. "I should do something about my temper? Are you kidding? You've never had the patience of a gnat!" A silent pause and another deep breath that allows guilt to flood in. "I'm sorry. I know you can't do these things as quickly as you used to. I think I've inherited my short fuse from you."

Annie pauses over Wednesday, pill in hand. "What 'short fuse'?"

Helen gives a short bark of exasperation. The extent of Annie's self-awareness is to check her look in a mirror. "Ma! The way you became angry if the dog didn't eat her food fast enough. If the traffic light didn't change fast enough. Stamping your foot if the garage door didn't open as soon as you pressed the button. I repeat, you've never had the patience of a gnat."

Annie's lower lip quivers. "Well, I've certainly had to learn it now." Her hand trembles as she drops the pills into the remaining compartments. She pushes the bottle aside and shakily reaches for another. Helen puts her hand over Annie's.

"I'm sorry, Ma! I didn't mean to get at you. I'm sorry you were angry for so many years. And I'm sorry you've had a stroke and can't do things the way you used to."

Annie pushes Helen's hand away. "I know I've never had any patience. Patience is something that you have when you're content. When you're doing what you want to do, when you have a purpose. You should have patience. You've found work that you like, that you think is worthwhile. I just had housework, and I never could see much point in it. Just doing the same dumb beast tasks over and over again, like milking cows. Without the money you got from the milk."

Helen nods. "When I'm working, I am patient. It's when I'm not working that the anxiety steps in. Wondering if I'm ever going to work again. Wondering if I've ever been any good. Thinking I have some talent, but perhaps, not enough. And wondering where the next mortgage payment is coming from. It's not conducive to serenity of mind."

"You know I've always offered to help you with that." Annie shakes the bottle and the pills dance out across the table.

Helen feels the knot in her stomach tighten further. Here we go again. "I appreciate the offer of help, Ma. It's the way in which you do it. Reinforcing my sense of failure. And I suppose I am a failure, having the lousiest house in the family and still struggling to keep it going."

Annie stops and looks over Helen's shoulder, to where a sunbeam is playing on the wall. "Having your own place is important. Especially to a woman. I know." She continues gazing for what seems like a long while, so that Helen is reluctant to intrude. "Sometimes, it costs you a lot more than money."

Helen sees a rare opening to her mother's frame of mind. "What do you mean, Ma? You mean, the price you paid in anger?"

"I wasn't angry!" Annie waves away the idea with her good hand. "I know I was sometimes strict."

You can say that again, thinks Helen, but she says nothing. She lines up another pill bottle. Annie pauses.

"My mother was never still. She was always doing something, working. Even in the evening, beside the stove, she'd be darning socks or knitting."

Helen is intrigued by the memory of this grandmother she never knew. Annie continues.

"And she never complained. Never wanted more. She was so ... accepting." Annie sighs. "I wish I'd inherited that from her."

Helen doesn't know what to say. "Maybe she was just happy. She lived as she wanted to live."

"Happy!" Annie snorts. "Now there's a word that's overused. Where was I? What are these?" She shakes a vial.

"Digoxin. One in every noon space."

\*\*\*

It is almost dark, and Helen is just picking up her cigarettes and brandy when she notices a diffuse light on the river headed for Annie's sagging dock. Mist is rising from the water so that the light shifts. But through the haze, Duncan noses a canoe in to the dock and lifts his oil lantern onto it.

"I guess the lure of the sea has reclaimed you," says Helen as she comes down the path.

"I've been on my brother's tractor, going around in circles all afternoon," Duncan says. "I just had to do something different. God! How he can stand to do that year after year is beyond me."

"Harvesting already?"

"Yup. Barley's ready. Care to climb aboard?"

Helen glances back to the silent house. "Don't think I can. My mother might wake up."

"Ten minutes. Fifteen at most. Just up past the bridge, then back the same distance the other way. You can listen as we go by."

Helen still hesitates.

"What's going to happen in fifteen minutes?"

He's right, thinks Helen. Nothing has happened in two and a half months. Duncan extends his hand, and Helen awkwardly steps down. She grabs the gunnels and gropes her way to the front of the canoe, conscious of her rear end waggling in front of Duncan.

"I brought a pillow there. Sit on the bottom and lean back. You'll be more comfortable." Helen does as she's told. The canoe steadies and Duncan pushes off, sending the craft almost to the middle of the river in one strong stroke.

Helen leans back and looks at the streaky moon rising behind the trees. The only sounds are provided by the frogs and the lapping of the paddle. Duncan and Helen say nothing for a few minutes as they glide past willows and a cluster of cows that have come down to the fence to check them out. They receive a lowing murmur of approval. Helen closes her eyes, trailing her fingers in the water, feeling its tug. She thinks: This is peaceful. I am at peace.

Duncan breaks the silence. "I can't stand routine. Never could. I've only been home a few weeks and already the routine of farm living is driving me crazy."

Helen nods. "Try the routine of looking after a stroke victim for more than two months. I'm surprised I haven't murdered her, cut her into little pieces and stored her in the freezer."

"A guy on the next concession did that to his wife."

Helen shudders. "I didn't mean it literally."

"I know. But you can see how someone could be driven to do that, can't you?"

They glide under the low bridge that supports the county road, suddenly in total darkness, and emerge on the other side to see bats beating their way out from under the struts.

"We've just emerged from the underworld," Helen says. "We're on the River Styx."

"And that makes me, what's his name? The guy who guides the boat?"

"Charon. You're delivering me."

"Yeah, but then I'm also taking you to hell. And I think we're both dead."

"Not hell, the underworld. Where you get to be your alter ego," Helen says.

"And who would your alter ego be?"

"An insurance adjuster or an accountant. Someone who's normal, like everyone else."

"Who the hell wants to be like everyone else?" Duncan scoffs.

"I do, when the house insurance is due and I have $34.75 in my bank account. If I was an adjuster, whatever that is, I could maybe fudge the files, to make it look like I've paid."

Duncan deftly eases the paddle wide to turn the canoe. The boat glides into the current, then stops. For a second, nothing moves.

"They're gonna put that on your tombstone, are they? When you hit the underworld? 'She paid the house insurance'?"

"You're right. It ought to read, 'She defined the role of serving wench in *Henry IV, Part Two.*'"

Duncan chuckles. "You know though, one thing I've learned from sailing is that when you're on the edge, you're most alive. The unexpected, the near miss, hits you with what you really are. And all you're not. Listen to your mast crack in half in a storm, your heart in your throat, and you'll know you weren't cut out for a tractor."

"Mmm," murmurs Helen, thinking of her own experience. If anyone offered her a full-time job teaching or directing drama, she'd panic. The constraint! Not knowing what is going to happen *is* her routine. She needs the unexpected. It's just that she hasn't reconciled it to the way she was raised, to be a good, dependable worker bee.

They glide back under the bridge.

\*\*\*

Helen thinks of the summer she spent as artistic director of a theatre in the Muskokas. The board of directors dictated the season's lineup: one Agatha Christie, one Neil Simon and a musical, provided it didn't require more than seven actors. But Helen talked them into another British mystery, *Sleuth;* a comedy on homelessness written by a cooperative in Saskatchewan; and a revue of Noel Coward songs, which at least would put to use the costumes normally reserved for the Miss Marple mystery.

Her lean salary was to be supplemented by accommodation provided by the Playhouse — a cottage on a lake outside of town, which sounded idyllic. Helen drove up from Toronto, arriving to find that the porch collapsed as soon as she set foot on it, a doubly unfortunate incident since a skunk and its family lived under it. It was early May, the night air was cold, and she quickly unloaded the car, only to discover that the sole source of heat was a rusted wood stove, the chimney of which obviously had not been cleaned in several seasons. The damp air was heavy with mould and the smell of mouse droppings, only one of the wall plugs worked, the sink faucet dripped constantly and, as she found out later that night during a torrential thunderstorm, the roof leaked in several places.

At the Playhouse, things were in worse shape. The stage manager drank heavily, and one of the four actors hired for the season was the granddaughter of the board's vice-chair, a laconic young woman whose lack of talent was stunning to behold. Helen's first paycheque bounced, and when she went into the bank to enquire as to the state of the Playhouse's finances, she was overheard by a local printer, who then approached her, informing Helen that he was about to place a lien on the Playhouse because he had still not been paid for last year's programs. And there was no budget for the sets and costumes which were to be provided by a group of high school students on government job grants.

"You are not living up to the terms of my contract," Helen said, very businesslike, to the theatre general manager. He looked at her wearily.

"There is a cash flow problem," he said. "It will be taken care of by the first week's box office."

"We don't open for four weeks. What am I supposed to live on? How do we get the production mounted when no one will supply us because they haven't been paid for last year?"

The general manager smiled, again wearily. "You can charge food down at the IGA because the manager there sits on our board. And Home Hardware will let you run a tab, too. The Chair's brother owns it."

The set of the comedy was adapted to take place in the woods instead of a city hostel, to take advantage of the easy-to-assemble shed the Playhouse was given from Home Hardware. After a three-hour conversation with the playwright, Helen also got permission to make the character played by the Chair's granddaughter into a mute. A catatonic autistic mute. Helen gave a talk on homelessness at the local high school and invited the students to attend a preview performance. Word got out, the local newspaper called her a "Crusader From Toronto," and the first week's performances sold out. Her second paycheque didn't bounce.

She even became fond of the shack in the woods. She would arrive back from the Playhouse most evenings in time to admire the sunset, for which the porch, had it been in place, would have provided a sensational view. Helen and the skunks reached a sort of compromise by which none of them would move quickly and startle the others. She would sit on a rock, drinking a tepid beer (the fridge didn't work), watch the western sky ripped to orange and pink shreds and think about what she had accomplished.

She had taught the grant students how to age clothing using bleach and dye and smiled watching the students bent over their work on the costumes, meticulously sewing on sequins, one at a time. Helen's British training again came in handy as she worked the actors' vowels for the Noel Coward revue, teaching them to speak more from the front of their mouths, stretching the staccato in "The Bar on the Piccolo Marina." She even addressed the local Women's Institute on the subject of God and the Theatre, adjusting the perspective slightly to point out that in the theatre, the director was God. And there was the glorious day when she caught one of the high school students reading Pinter.

She felt exhausted, pushed to the limit, yet aware that she was expanding the small world she had stumbled into. She was feeding others, and this fed her. Toronto real estate didn't matter.

***

The canoe slips past Annie's house, and Helen is struck by how small it seems from the river, like a doll's house, with pinpoints of light at the windows. So small a place, yet how large it is in her life. There is no sound from Annie.

"I envy you Malaysia," Helen says.

"Really?"

"Yes, I've always wanted to go there. The rubber plantations, orangutans, that little jewel of an island in the north — Penang, isn't it? I did a project on Malaysia once in elementary school, read everything I could about it. It was part of some sort of Commonwealth geography project, back in the days when great chunks of the map of the world were pink."

"Pink?"

"Yes, don't you remember? The British Commonwealth was always coloured in pink."

"Maybe to mark a more naive world. Nowadays, offshore oil has replaced rubber as the major export, Islamic extremism is on the rise and Penang looks like Las Vegas with all the monstrous hotels on the beach." Duncan pauses, paddles. "In Butterworth, though, on the mainland across from Penang, you can still see traces of the 'good old' colonial days — the wedding cake hotels, the big broad bungalows."

Helen can picture them.

"And the sea hasn't changed much. More polluted, more pirates, but still capable of surprising your socks off with its sudden change of mood."

"Funny how change always seems to be for the worse," Helen comments.

"Change is neutral, neither better nor worse. And it's inevitable. It's the way we handle it that makes it better or worse. I think if you accept it, figure out how it's going to benefit you, it's more likely to affect you for the better."

Helen considers that. "You mean just accept it and do the best you can."

"Something like that."

"Galloping to the grave." Helen can see him smile at her through the shadows, but a strange sadness has settled on her. How brief this moment, even life itself, is.

"Hey! I'm the boatman to the underworld, remember?"

Back at the dock, Helen and Duncan have a quick cognac.

"Thanks for the ride," Helen says. "Amazing how something that simple can get you out of yourself for awhile."

Duncan paces the dock. "Maybe you need to get away more often. Do you ever get a break? Step out for an evening?"

Helen laughs. "No. And where is there to step out to?"

"There's a good place down near the Quebec border, if you like line dancing. And the food's good. Basic, but good. No poutine. Do you think you could get away one evening? Have someone look after your mother?"

"No," Helen says abruptly, then thinks of Mrs. Forbes' offer to sit with Annie.

"In your place I'd be going stir crazy."

"Maybe I should get away. It would be ... great."

Duncan puts his glass down. "Let me know when. And thanks for the brandy."

"Thanks again for the canoe. I'll work on a babysitter. A ladysitter."

As Duncan dusts the seat of his jeans and steps down to the canoe, Helen notes that he has a good firm ass. Down girl, she tells herself again. You've had enough disastrous romances in your time.

True to her word Mrs. Forbes comes over the next afternoon for tea, bearing baked squares and a date loaf encased in plastic. Helen has noticed that Tupperware is as much a part of rural life as fly swatters and wood piles. Whatever the event or crisis — unexpected company, a death in the family, an invasion by aliens from another galaxy — the women tie on their aprons and bake enough squares to feed Somalia, load them into industrial-sized Tupperware containers and deliver them to those in need. The women may think that spaghetti and meatballs is the acme of international cooking, but they all know how to bake sumptuous, high calorie, melt-in-your-mouth dessert goodies.

"Get out the good china and silver!" hisses Annie as she rolls herself into the kitchen where Helen is getting down cups and saucers.

"It's only Mrs. Forbes," Helen protests. "She's known you since Grade 1."

"I'm not having her telling the others at the Women's Institute that I'm not capable of putting on a good table anymore," Annie says, reaching for the silver chest that sits on the sideboard.

"I'll get that!" Helen says, lunging for the chest as it slides off the counter into Annie's lap. She manages to cushion the blow, but much of the cutlery spills onto Annie.

"Now look what you've made me do!" Annie bleats, grabbing at some spoons.

"What I made you do?" Helen's stage-trained voice can be heard on the next concession.

"Everything all right in there?" queries Mrs. Forbes from the doorway, hesitant to enter. She's a trim septuagenerian whose bright floral dress and lively eyes make her look years younger than she is.

"Oh, just a small incident, Mrs. Forbes. Mom was just on her way out to sit with you, weren't you Ma?" Helen bubbles. "I'll bring the tea out as soon as it's ready." She grabs the remaining silver from Annie's lap and gives her mother a push toward the living room. She counts to five then goes into the dining room to fetch Annie's Royal Doulton tea service.

Helen sets the tray, stealing one of the Nanaimo bars as she goes, arranging the cups and saucers, polishing the silver on her sleeve, the way she used to when she worked for the Extra Pair of Hands agency in London, during her drama-school days. As she moves about the kitchen, the events of that time tumble through her mind, not in chronological order, but the way she remembered life during her freefall days in London.

***

Everything was allowed. Rock stars and dress designers, the new aggressive working-class capitalists serving notice on the establishment that their monopoly on what was permitted was over. The unions creating chaos with a series of crippling strikes. One day the trains are not running; the next day electricity is to be rationed because of the coal miners' strike; the following week, the roads are blocked by fuming farmers.

On the social scene, things were equally chaotic. It was the Golden Age of Sex, the brief window of opportunity between the advent of the Pill and the arrival of incurable sexually transmitted diseases. All over the city, Helen and people her age have sex merely because there is no reason not to. Sex takes place even though far too many people share a flat or house. You no longer have to do it in a bedroom with the drapes drawn and no one watching. They don't "make love," they "have sex" and are very proud of the fact that they know the difference. Sex has become a cheap commodity.

Helen is a balloon on the end of a string someone has let go of. Everything is possible, and she intends to have as much of her share as she can. She lives in an old house in Camden Town with two other theatre students, an anarchist arts student, an Irish civil rights worker and a male stripper. The house belongs to a guy named Jeremy, who is in a Volkswagen bus en route to India via Afghanistan to join an ashram. Helen and the other tenants are behind in paying the taxes on the property, the power company is constantly threatening to cut off their electricity and the back of the third floor is uninhabitable because the roof leaks. Helen and two others spend a Sunday tacking up industrial plastic with a staple gun in an effort to control the damp that is also threatening the only working washroom. The house has a widow's walk on the top where Helen goes to work on her lines, the Victorian rooftops of Camden Town her audience.

Throughout her first winter there, it rains almost non-stop. It is dark at 9:30 in the morning and dark again by 3:30. On her lunch break from the theatre school, Helen makes a point of going outside into the drizzle or the rare watery sunlight, just to assure herself that the sun is still operating. The walls of her room develop mould, and she gets a cold at Christmas that lasts until March, despite the gallons of rosehip syrup she drinks. Just when she thinks the winter will never end, she comes out of the Russell Square tube station one morning to find a woman selling small bunches of spring violets from the Scilly Isles. The worst is over.

Despite the material discomforts, Helen is happier than she has ever been. She is twenty years old and free, free to walk the many neighbourhoods of London, to poke in the used book shops on Tottenham Court Road, to flirt in pubs and drink tumblers of ale, to gorge on cheap, delicious Indian food which she had never tasted in Canada. No one wrangles at the dinner table. In fact, she is often alone at the dinner table and she loves it that way. And she is also free to work hard, harder than she will ever work in her life again.

Helen is one of fifteen students at the school, drilled from eight in the morning until six at night, five days a week, with rehearsals most evenings and on Saturdays. The students are run through a shopping list of their trade — voice training, improv work, acting technique, fencing and stage fighting, which sometimes comes in handy for the male students in pub fights.

In the stage and camera makeup classes, Helen learns how to look terrific from forty feet away but grotesque close-up. She retains a life-long abhorrence for heavy makeup, only highlighting her blue-grey eyes when she goes out. The school runs group and individual singing classes, which also help with the breathwork, and dance classes — modern, of course, but also period, in case the students find themselves cast in Henry VIII's court or in a Jane Austen novel.

Helen discovers she has a mania for tap dancing, a passion that almost gets her evicted from the house in Camden Town until she confines her practising to one of the small studios at the school. To this day, she loves the aggressive noisiness of tap, the American vulgarity of it, the individuality of the dance. She is unearthing layers of herself.

The class does two productions a term, beginning with Greek tragedies, moving through history to the present, lingering on Shakespeare and his contemporaries. Helen is judged to be a less-than-electrifying Electra but a spirited Rosalind.

When not working on their own term projects, the students are enlisted in other productions to run sound and lights, sew costumes, build sets and act as dressers, stage managers or general gofers. Helen comes to adore Vera, the school's costume mistress, who operates out of the attic of the school's building. Vera is a post-war Eastern European refugee whose father was a count, and who spends a great deal of her time lovingly caring for the nineteenth and twentieth century costumes that have been donated from old family estates. Helen hides up there with her whenever she can, listening to Vera's accounts of debutante dances in Vienna, and helping her stitch the old silk dresses together.

Although the post-war heyday of new British drama — all working-class rage — is over, Helen immerses herself in the still vibrant theatre scene, sits in the fifty pence seats at the back of balconies and drowns in language. Tom Stoppard and his kaleidoscopic use of English, projected by Diana Rigg in *Night and Day*. Helen watches in despair because she knows she is not beautiful enough to ever captivate an audience the way Rigg does. Then Paul Scofield rivets her in *Amadeus,* and she realizes her profession is capable of providing a stimulating and rewarding life, regardless of how you look.

The theatre school instructors do their best to tear apart their students, to rip to shreds the egos that have been constructed from success in school plays. They are traditionalists who refuse to acknowledge that a revolution in British drama has ever taken place, they wouldn't dream of spelling the word "method" with a capital letter. Stanislavsky is ignored because he is a foreigner. They teach the basics, theatre from the ground up, the classics that helped build an Empire. Most of Helen's instructors have too much contempt for their students to ever sleep with them. They work them with relentless intensity, the way Helen imagines Wellington drilled his troops, and critique their work in pairs, using a "good cop, bad cop" routine.

And it all works. By the end of her first year, Helen has so perfected her English accent that no one can tell she's from Canada. If she gets drunk and lets it slip, people guess she's from Ireland. She moves in a grandly upright manner, as if the point of a stiletto is in the small of her back and her ripe laugh makes her particularly good for Restoration comedy. She can quote long passages of Shakespeare and has read all the plays.

But all is not perfect with Helen. She is aware that her happiness is not really happiness, but relief from pain. She is living in an alternate universe; the other one is still waiting for her back in Canada. She knows she has solved nothing, and she recognizes that she relates closely to no one. There are times when she feels hopelessly alone and unrooted. Usually she gets over it by taking home one of her fellow students or someone she meets in a pub. Sex is a comfort, a release, and given her state of being, the relationships are mercifully temporary.

In a strange way, she misses Canada. Not her family or her few friends, not even Montreal, but the country itself, the sheer size and unmanageability of it. She is a metaphor for her country — wild, developing, not yet knowing her place in the world. On her trips outside of London, she finds the countryside pretty but too organized. Only the moors in England's north resemble the untamed landscape that Canadians carry in their consciousness. Some nights, she walks out on Hampstead Heath north of where she lives and roars till she is hoarse, thinking of the thousands of square miles in Canada where one can do this and never be heard.

Money is also a constant problem. She has her bursary and the small amount Reg and Annie send her each month, but she is constantly broke. Alan, one of the other drama students in the house, an Australian with attitude, comes to her rescue. He introduces Helen to the disappointed spinster who runs An Extra Pair of Hands, an agency that specializes in providing servants for an upper class clientele who, alas, no longer can keep enough servants of their own to deal with a large party. The requirements for the job are basic manners, a black dress and white apron for the women, a tux for the men. It's the perfect part-time job for drama students filled with too much Terence Rattigan, and Alan and Helen make the most of it, working during the month-long breaks between terms, especially in the spring and summer, during "the season." Wages are a pound and a half an hour, all the leftover food you can eat and transportation home by taxi if the party lasts later than ten p.m.

At most of the parties, they are ignored as they pass the Fortnum & Mason caviar and the endless glasses of fizzy wine. But Helen and Alan become the core of a team hired by an American financier trying to raise venture capital in London. The American has an impeccably decorated Regency row house on a private square in Knightsbridge and his household is managed by a fairly inexperienced Mexican houseboy called Rodrigo, who may or may not be the American's lover. It's hard to tell if Rodrigo's nervousness comes from his relationship or the fact that he is way out of his depth in catering to the British Establishment. The second time that Alan and Helen work there, Alan takes Rodrigo aside and assures him that they will take over everything, that he has nothing to worry about, that he will get all the credit for the excellent service. Rodrigo is relieved and Alan delivers, ordering the rest of the Hands staff about and managing a perfect cocktail party. Alan wears a tuxedo he acquired on Portobello Road that looks as if it were made for him, but on his feet are a pair of sneakers he has painted shiny black in the school's props department, and no socks. He glides about the room so elegantly and officiously, no one ever glances at his feet.

The American entertains prospective clients at least once a week. Alan, Helen and two others — a cockney called Maisie, and Connor, the only quiet Irishman Helen has ever met — become regulars, familiar with the wine cellar and pantry. One evening, Helen is alone in the first floor drawing room, awaiting the guests. The room is filled with light from the three tall windows that overlook the square. It is superbly appointed, decorated with leather sofas, antiques and Persian carpets, but it's what's on the walls on either side of the windows that is the main attraction for Helen. Pinned to the wall and on shelves are dozens of Pre-Columbian artifacts — masks, pottery, shards, bits of weaving and small clay fertility figures. Helen has always been fascinated by the Spanish conquest of America — so decisive, so brutal, so New World efficient. She is carefully examining each piece when the American enters the room, asking, "Everything ready in here?"

"Everything," Helen announces. "I think we even have enough ice this time."

"Good," says the American, turning to go.

"I hope you don't mind me saying, but this is an excellent collection of Pre-Columbian art. You don't see a lot of it over here."

"What?" the American asks, looking around the room.

Helen points to the wall. "These artifacts, aren't they Pre-Columbian? Mostly Incan, I think."

The American waves his hand. "Oh, I don't know. The decorator chose them. Said they'd add a nice New World touch. Cost me nearly half a million." Just then the front doorbell rings, and the American goes off to greet his guests. Helen moves closer to the shelves, picks up a small figurine with big ears and breasts and slips it into the front of her bra, adding thief to her repertoire. It still sits on her mantle at home.

The group takes other liberties with the American's ignorance and generosity. At one dinner party, their host announces he is serving Chateau Lafitte that he bought at auction at Christie's. Rather than pour the wine into the Georgian decanters, the staff is ordered to place the bottles directly on the table to impress the guests.

"But it needs decanting," Alan protests. "It's over thirty years old."

"I want them to read the label," the American says, going upstairs to change.

"Boys and girls," Alan says softly. "Get ready for your first taste of two-hundred-pound-a-bottle claret."

As Helen and Maisie serve the dinner, Alan circles the table, pouring the wine while the American draws attention to it. When there is still a third of the bottle left, Alan places it on the sideboard and begins to pour another bottle. The American's eyebrows rise, but he says nothing until Alan finishes pouring the second bottle, again leaving a third of the contents, and whisks both bottles off to the kitchen.

"Excuse me," the American says, reluctant to see his investment go.

"Sediment, Sir," Alan replies, giving the American a look of shock that he doesn't already know this.

Back in the kitchen, while the guests are enjoying their port and cigars in the drawing room, each member of the team enjoys the taste of luxury. Helen notices the wine is very aromatic, smooth, but with no aftertaste, as if her mouth had been cleansed after each sip. Maisie, who is by now sleeping with Alan, obligingly offers her pantyhose to strain the rest of the wine which, sure enough, has a considerable amount of sediment. Helen feels more alive than she has ever been — studying acting by day, living it by night, observing how the Establishment conducts itself, shedding her colonial insecurity.

Not all of her Extra Pair of Hands assignments are as cushy. In her third year at the school, she's assigned a buffet supper for thirty-five where she is the only servant, expected to look after everyone. It is at this post-Ascot party that she meets Guy, her future husband. The flat is crowded with large hats, the air filled with braying laughter. The snotty upper class hostess hisses at Helen that she is not serving the drinks and canapés fast enough.

"You should have ordered a bartender and one more waitress," Helen snaps back. "I'm just going to leave the canapés around the room, so everyone can help themselves."

The hostess protests, but Helen is already headed for the kitchen to scrounge some more tonic water. She's loading up when a perfect British public school accent behind her says, "I say, you seem a little overwhelmed. May I help you?"

"Well, yes. You can tell your hostess that a one to thirty-five ratio of servant to guest is not a successful formula for a party. And if you can persuade some of the guests to drink less tonic, I would appreciate it. "Helen slams more glasses and wine glasses onto her tray and gets two more bottles of wine out of the fridge.

"Here, let me open those," Guy says. "And I can pass them around to those who already have glasses." Helen is taken aback, but grateful for the help. On his way through the door of the kitchen, Guy says, "I'll be back to help with the mixed drinks."

Helen is just finishing the drinks tray when Guy comes back with two empty canapé trays, the angry hostess in his wake.

"How dare you let one of the guests do your job for you!" The hostess actually has colour in her cheeks, despite her overall blondness.

"Steady on," Guy replies. "You can't hold a party of this size and expect one maid to be able to cope. Your family has three servants just to serve breakfast!" The hostess colours further. "Shall I take these in?" Guy asks Helen.

Helen forgets her British accent. "Sure," she says.

At the end of the evening, after the cold poached salmon has been reduced to a skeleton, after pale pink puddles are all that remain of the strawberries and cream, hours after the tonic has run out, while Helen is tossing the dirty plates and cutlery into the Fortnum & Mason hamper, Guy comes back into the kitchen.

"Anything I can help with?" he asks, as if he has known Helen all her life.

"No, no thanks. Just keep the bitch goddess of Winchelsea off my case, will you?" Helen flashes him a genuine smile.

"Glad to. What about those wine glasses though?" Guy goes over to the counter where thirty smudged Victorian wine glasses are lined up. "Surely these aren't going back to Fortnum's are they?"

"After the way your friend has treated me, I'm tempted to take them home with me."

Guy washes the wine glasses then helps Helen stack the empty bottles. "I don't imagine you've had any of the wine yourself," he comments, holding up a bottle. "Not a bad Chardonnay, but a little oaky for my liking."

"I wouldn't know about 'oaky,'" says Helen. "Where I come from, we're more into maples."

Guy stops. "You're from Canada?" Helen nods and smiles. "Smashing country. I spent one summer in Banff."

"Really? Doing what?"

"Riding. Teaching people how to ride horses. On a ranch." He grins back.

Helen tries to imagine Guy dressed as a cowboy and giggles. "On a ranch?"

Guy shrugs. "They were mostly Americans or other Brits or Europeans. They didn't really notice I rode English saddle." They both grin. "I say, you wouldn't like to go for a nightcap after we finish with this mess, would you?"

"I dare say I would."

In a Chelsea wine bar, after she has discreetly removed her apron, Helen learns Guy is a recently graduated geologist, working for a firm in the Midlands, down for the races at Ascot. She also learns that he's an imposter, living above his station, having gone to Winchester Public School and Cambridge on scholarship, where his friends were the sons of captains of industry and heirs to titles. Guy's father has a small tailor's shop, but it is his mother, the daughter of a solicitor, who has the social ambitions. Guy cheerfully tells Helen he owes far too much money.

"If this were a play, you could say I'm a bit of a bounder," he adds, going to fetch more wine, even though he's already a bottle or two ahead of Helen.

His candour and the fact that he too is an actor of sorts, playing a role he hasn't yet mastered, appeals to Helen, and the evening ends with Guy spending the night in Camden Town. It doesn't hurt that he is also tall and good-looking in a bland, blond Anglo-Saxon way.

Over the next several months, she ignores the fact that Guy votes Tory, that most of the people living in her house don't like him, that he knows everything about rugby and nothing about theatre. Otherwise, she'd see that they have nothing in common. But Guy takes her to parties in Kensington where people snort cocaine and use exclamations such as "Capital!" and "First rate." They spend a weekend in Cambridge, where Guy shows her the colleges, then punts her down the River Cam, which he does fluidly, Helen lying back in the punt, living a Henry James novel. Helen even forgives Guy when his credit card bounces as he's paying the bill in the hotel. Guy has an eagerness to get ahead that is energizing.

Exploring their many differences keeps them interested in each other, even though their arguments can be fierce. Toward the end of one post-rugby dinner party, as all the county-type guests are denouncing union supporters as leeches, Helen reverts to her Canadian accent and says, "The only leeches in this country are the land and factory owners who have screwed the working class for centuries. The only way out of your class system was to emigrate. They should have slaughtered you instead."

There is a very awkward silence until one of Guy's teammates says, "If you don't like it here, why don't you go back where you came from?"

Helen takes a sip of wine and answers, "I am back where I came from, buddy. And I'm not going to take this shit the way my ancestors did." At which point she gets up and leaves.

In the silence of the car on the way home, Helen is remorseful, recognizing she has gone too far, acknowledging that she doesn't feel that passionate about anything, let alone politics. Hers is just a generalized anger. "You must hate me," she says matter-of-factly to Guy.

Guy waits a moment then says, "No, I don't. I rather like you."

"Really? You wouldn't want to change me?"

Guy thinks another moment. "I might want to modify you somewhat. But I'd never want to change you." And he squeezes her knee. "You have spirit."

At that moment, Helen falls in love, because Guy is the first person to see her faults as virtues. Spirit. Such a great word. So much better than show-off, or any of the other words her family has used to describe her. Even better, he's a man who knows exactly what he wants out of life, and he's well on his way to getting it. He's the anchor to her balloon.

\*\*\*

Annie and Mrs. Forbes are talking old times when Helen brings in the tea

"Now you and Maggie MacRae were tight," Mrs. Forbes says, delicately extending her little finger as she picks up the tea cup. "I remember you two going off to Montreal together."

"Ah Maggie, poor thing." Annie tries to pick up her cup, but it rattles like a tambourine. Helen slips alongside her to guide it to her lips. "Died so young. Barely fifty. Breast cancer. Never had much of a life, really. Never married again after that flier ... what was his name? Lord, and I was matron of honour at their wedding ... Patrick, that was his name ... nice lad, a redhead, but killed over Germany during the fire-bombings. Maggie never got over it."

"Are you talking about Aunt Maggie?" Helen asks, mopping up some crumbs off Annie's chin.

"Who else?"

"But I remember her quite well. She used to come for dinner. I thought she had quite a glamorous life. I used to try on her hats."

Annie lets out one of her snorts. "Well, it might have looked alright on the surface. After all, she was personal secretary to one of the most important mining men in the country. Actually, she was more than personal secretary, if you know what I mean."

"She always was fast," Mrs. Forbes concedes.

"But he was always taking her places," Helen interjects. "Remember? She went to the Bahamas every winter and to Switzerland with him. She had this beautiful diamond watch he bought her in Switzerland."

"Hmm," says Annie. "Money he should have been spending on his wife."

Mrs. Forbes sucks her teeth in agreement.

Helen presses on. "Well, we don't know what arrangement he had with his wife, do we? She might have known about Maggie all along."

"And do you remember that she used to come and spend Christmas with us? She and your father going through whisky like it could cure the common cold?" Annie snorts again. "What kind of a relationship is it that leaves you alone at Christmas?"

Helen thinks of the Christmases she has spent with strangers, usually when she was in a show. The spontaneity of those times, the immediate closeness of people making the best of things, the great fun she had. No expectations to be disappointed. And she thinks of her father and Maggie, downing whisky, Reg with his arm on Maggie's shoulder, singing naughty songs in the living room while someone played the piano. But she says nothing.

"Yes, it's at times like Christmas when you most appreciate you have a family," Mrs. Forbes says, leaning in for another square.

"And when you are old," Annie reinforces. "That's when you need your children most. Why I'm lucky to have you, Helen."

Yes, but am I lucky to have you? Helen thinks. A realization sweeps in. She will never do this to someone. Her childless state is suddenly a bonus. No one will ever feel obligated to give up their own life for her. It is a strangely liberating thought, masking the reality that she may be truly alone. But she won't allow Maggie, Maggie of the smart suits, the risqué jokes, the lavish Christmas presents and the exotic souvenirs from Morocco, Paris and Hong Kong, to be relegated to the status of "poor thing."

"She didn't need children when she was old because she never got to be old," Helen says. "More tea?"

"But she died alone," Annie says softly.

"We all die alone," Helen retorts, a little too quickly. "In that no one comes with us," she adds more softly. She notices the tears welling in Annie's eyes and instantly regrets her words.

"Well, we each take a different path in life, I guess," chirps Mrs. Forbes. "I suppose that's what makes it interesting. It would be pretty dull if we were all the same." And she beams at Helen. The UN could use Mrs. Forbes, thinks Helen. Ditto Actors' Equity.

The older women chat on about the fates of other locals. When Mrs. Forbes leaves, Helen sees her to the door.

"Now you let me know if there's anything I can do," Mrs. Forbes says, patting Helen's wrist. "Maybe sit with your mother while you take some time off." Another pat.

"Well, now that you mention it, I have been invited out to dinner, if I can get away."

"Wonderful! It'd do you a world of good. When are you going?"

"Whenever I can arrange it. How does tomorrow night sound? Or any night, really."

"Wednesday night would be best. I have my missionary group tomorrow night."

"Wednesday's fine. Now, I'll see that she has dinner and is all ready for bed. It's really just someone to be with her."

Helen receives more pats. "Don't you worry about a thing. We can manage. You go out and enjoy yourself." Mrs. Forbes seems pleased that she's chocked up another good deed and waves gaily as she drives away.

After she puts Annie to bed, Helen puts away the supper and tea dishes, carefully replacing the good china in the cabinet. The TV is still on in the living room with an in-depth report on an African country, now celebrating twenty-five years of civil war, with up to half a million of its citizens killed or displaced. The program goes to a commercial break promoting a new breakthrough in kitchen technology that has resulted in deep-fried potato products shaped like small animals. Helen switches it off.

Beside the china cabinet sits the bag containing her new silk caftan, still wrapped in tissue paper. Wondering what the protocol is for a moonlight rendezvous by the river, she smiles to herself. What's the dress code?

The moon, an irregular apricot hiding among the trees, is just rising as Helen sets out for the river, caftan trailing, cigarettes, brandy bottle and two snifters in hand. She feels a little foolish, but light-hearted, as if she is improvising her own romantic comedy. Duncan is pacing along the path, flicking ash into the river when she comes into view. He gives a low whistle.

"If I'd known it was a fancy occasion, I'd have changed my socks," he says.

"You said I should wear it. My mother wants me to look glamorous in my leisure moments. I'm afraid you are the only leisure I have at the moment. I'm just grateful she didn't buy one made of gold lamé. She has a very Hollywood view of the acting profession."

"Well, Glengarry County could use a little more Hollywood, don't you think?" Duncan dusts off the boards on the dock with his shirtsleeve, making a place for Helen to sit. "The view from a tractor is very limited."

"I'm wearing this because we have something to celebrate. A friend of my mother's has offered to sit with her while I go out one evening. How does Wednesday night sound?"

"Perfect! I happen to be free, as I am for the rest of the week. The rest of my life, actually, but let's not get into that." Duncan takes the proffered glass of brandy. "It'll be my turn to treat you for a change, okay?"

"You bet," Helen replies, and they clink glasses. "To Wednesday night." She sweeps around, swirling the caftan around her and sits suddenly, so that it fans about her, the silk softly brushing her legs. Theatrical training can come in handy off the stage as well, she smiles to herself.

"This robe reminds me of my Aunt Maggie. She wasn't my real aunt, just a friend of my mother's from around here. My mother and Mrs. Forbes were talking about her this afternoon." Helen takes the cigarette Duncan holds out to her. "She was a woman who never got over an early trauma — the wartime loss of her new husband. She spent the rest of her life on her own. She had a successful career, a long-time lover, a good salary ... she travelled a lot, was very stylish and great fun. She was my godmother and my favourite adult when I was growing up. Yet all they could do was pity her, because she was on her own."

Duncan takes a sip of brandy and says quietly, "And you thought they could have been talking about you."

Helen is puzzled. "Me? No, I ..." and she stops herself. "Well, I suppose they could have been," she adds flatly. "Except she had a more exciting life."

There is a brief silence in which Helen curses herself. Why does she go on about her mother? She used to have other things to talk about.

Where does all this self-pity come from? What is it about this man that stirs up old emotions?

"Tell me more about Maggie," Duncan says.

"I don't know much more. I was a child when she died. About eleven or so. Cancer. When you're a child, you only ever see glimpses of who adults really are. Snapshots. They spend far too much time trying to make sure you never know too much." Helen fingers the caftan, the silk sliding down her hand, remembering her aunt. "Maggie always said she wanted a good time, not necessarily a long time. Guess she got her wish." Helen gives a short bark of a laugh. "My mother was furious that Maggie's dowdy sister-in-law got her diamond watch."

"But you remember her. Fondly. I think that says something about her. Quite a lot."

"Oh yes! One time when she came back from Spain, she brought me an embroidered shawl and some castanets. Said I would make a great Gypsy."

"And she was right. Dressed in that thingamajig, you do look like a great Gypsy."

Helen blushes. "That's your profession, isn't it? Travelling the world?"

"And how much time did you spend at home in the last year or so? 'Hi, diddly-dee, an actor's life for me ...' Isn't that how it goes?" Duncan hoists his glass. "To Gypsies everywhere. May we always run into each other."

Kind, Helen thinks. Loneliness isn't absence of people, it's absence of kind. Kind, kin, kindred. She offers her glass. "To Gypsies everywhere. And a good time Wednesday night. Speaking of which, where is this roadhouse and what time?"

"It's called Zoot's, and it's in Point Fortune. As they say in the country, you can't miss it. How's 7:30 sound?"

"Perfect!"

Duncan hoists his glass. "To Maggie and good times."

My God! He's attractive, he's perfect! Maybe too perfect, Helen thinks. After all, you've been fooled before.

Even so, she tilts her head the way Maggie would when she was flirting with Reg. My godmother, Helen thinks. My role model.

## chapter 14

I CAN TELL BY THE AMOUNT OF NOISE she's making that Helen is being careless with my good china. Never put Royal Doulton in the dishwasher. How often do I have to tell her? That girl! I have to get stronger. I can't have her ruining my things. I feel like going right out there and telling her right now, but ... Oh damn! My leg! Won't move the way I tell it to. Why is it any little thing makes me cry? I used to have nerves of steel. Now every bit of me is as weak as wool. Feels like I could break so easily.

I'm not broken yet. And at least Helen hasn't broken any of the dishes yet. They mean a lot to me. They remind me of Reg's one good quality. That's what we were supposed to look for in a man in my day: a good provider. Ah! If only they didn't come with all the rest of that male paraphenalia. A man who gave you his paycheque was more important than a man who gave you affection, or so popular wisdom went. Don't know who made up that rule, but whoever it was, they didn't know women very well. Didn't know me, anyway.

When I think of all the things Reg provided: a lot of bull talk, a lot of lies, a lifetime's worth of irritation. Even in the money department, the flow was sometimes erratic, what with his weakness for the horses and the stock market. He never could turn down a poker game. Get rich quick, he believed. It's old-fashioned to earn it. While I was raised to be just the opposite. It's hard work that gets you results. Anything worthwhile has to be paid for with effort, whether it's love or a crystal ashtray.

Well, I certainly paid for my love of you, Ewan, didn't I? That is you in the corner, isn't it? Fancy you just slipping in here with the cool night breeze, when you were gone so long. How long was it? It must have been fifteen years after I'd married Reg before I saw you again. Fitting that I was heading home, my father dead and my mother sick with what we first thought was kidney stones, but which turned out to be much worse. Me, the daughter who was always useless going back to the farm for a few days to help out Alma in nursing her. A real sticky summer day it was, and I first thought I saw you across the great bay of Windsor Station. But the haze under the glass ceiling was so thick, with blinding streaks of sun cutting through, I wasn't sure until I got on the train and there you were, at the other end of the car, facing me. Older, much older than you look right now. Still with that great shock of hair, starting to go grey, your face tanned and lined from all those years in the fields, but your eyes still the same, pale and open as a summer sky. Tired, even a bit stooped, but with a worker's shoulders, and when you grinned and said "Hello Annie," it was as if fifteen years had been yesterday. Remember what you said? "Guess you never thought you'd see me at the end of an aisle, Annie." You always could make me laugh.

It all seems so clear. The windows of the train open, but with the air so close I could see the sweat form then slide down your neck as I came to sit opposite you.

"You going home?" you asked, and so I filled you in on how my mother was ill.

"Just to help out," I said. "Not that I was ever much help when I lived there."

"That's true. You always were more of an ornament, Annie. Still are." And he winked.

I think I blushed, surprised that I still could at thirty-seven. Did I look ornamental? I was wearing a smart blue dress, with a hat to match. People still dressed up to travel in those days.

"What brings you to Montreal?"

"Tests," you said, casual as anything. "I had to go up to the Royal Vic for some tests. It's my stomach. Maybe an ulcer."

"Farmers aren't supposed to get ulcers, Ewan. Businessmen get ulcers."

You shrugged. "That's right. It must be the easy life I lead," and you grinned again.

The heat. I remember the heat and the humidity, dirt and steam blasting through the open windows, clogging the air further. Almost too hot to speak, but then the train picked up speed, and we began a cautious investigation into what had happened to us in the past fifteen years. I prattled on about how we'd moved from Lachine to the West

Island, that we now drove a Buick and had a stereo — all the comfortable aspects of my life, including a suite of Scandinavian furniture.

"A teakwood dining room set," you repeated after me, shaking your head in wonder. I couldn't tell. Were you genuinely impressed or merely mocking me?

On and on. The many train stops, me going on about the summer camp Barbara had attended, Sean's new bicycle, the elaborate inventory of my life, making sure I avoided the emotional mud where more important matters might be hidden. Ah! And wasn't it easy to talk? As if I'd slipped into the seat beside you in the truck, stopping for ice cream on the road back from Alexandria. Eventually, the conversation got back to us.

"How's Flora?"

"Pretty good. Between the farm and the girls, she's pretty busy. My mother died last year, you know."

"Yes, I think I heard that from Alma. I was sorry to hear it."

"Now Annie, there was a time when you'd have been mighty happy to hear that." You eyed me for my reaction but I wasn't about to give you one.

"Not happy, Ewan. Although it might have made things easier between us. She was always against me."

It was then you leaned forward and gripped my wrist. You had a fierce look in your eye. "Never against you, Annie. She was for us. For me and my family. She knew I was the only hope she had of keeping the farm, of proving that her whole life wasn't a losing battle, a total waste. And she was afraid you'd persuade me to leave it, like I wanted to."

"I never tried to persuade you to leave."

You sighed and let go of me. "True. I didn't need any persuasion. But maybe you should have. Doesn't matter now, does it?" You looked out the window.

Well! The conversation had certainly taken an uncomfortable turn. I remember I was confused, as if I were learning something now I should have known years ago. So I joined you in looking out the window for awhile, looking at the landscape of escape.

"How's what's-his-name ... Reg? I hear he's a fine fellow."

"Yes, he *is* a fine fellow. Doing very well in sales." I spoke almost automatically. I couldn't let you have a glimpse of my marriage.

Mustering all my sophistication, I dismissed Reg with a toss of my hand and fetched a cigarette out of my purse.

"You've got … what … two kids, I heard?" You leaned forward to give me a light.

"Yes. A girl and a boy." I hoped you hadn't noticed how my cigarette was shaking slightly.

Travelling through the afternoon haze, the city and the suburbs had slipped away, replaced by small holdings, small towns, small hardscrabble farms.

"He a good father?"

"Oh, perfect. The kids adore him. He's great fun." And to keep going, to show the fun we all were having, I launched into an account of a trip we had taken to Old Orchard Beach, the number of lobster I'd eaten and Lord knows what else, when suddenly the train lurched. The brakes and whistle screaming, me falling across onto you, your moist smell, the car in total confusion. Luggage falling from the overhead racks and people pitched into the aisles as the train came to a halt in a series of convulsions. A child fell face forward beside us, screaming, you and the child's mother collided as you bent to pick up the little one. Everyone looking around for an explanation, people with their heads stuck out of the windows, the conductor and trainmen swinging down from the cars and running alongside the tracks.

It was only a matter of minutes I suppose, but it seemed longer. We'd all started chatting to each other and helping to sort each other out. The conductor came back and announced that the train had hit some cows on the track and that the engine was off the rails. "We're not too far from Côteau Landing," he said. "We've telegraphed ahead for help. It won't be too long."

The train emptied, with people sitting on the grass on the shaded side of the train. You and I, and everyone else who was curious, walked up to the engine. So much blood. One of the cows so mangled it was hard to tell what creature it might have been. The farmer stood beside one which was still alive, her belly heaving, his rifle in his hand, crying softly, muttering curses in French. We stood back in silence, in awe of so much destruction, embarrassed at being witnesses. Then you did a very kind thing, Ewan, remember? You stepped forward, put your hand firmly on the farmer's shoulder, took his rifle, walked up to the cow and shot her in the head. She shuddered, then was still. When you gave the farmer back his rifle, he muttered, *"Merci."* You nodded, your eyes on the cow for a few moments.

An hour or two later, wasn't it? I know we were all hot, tired and thirsty. A couple of noisy old school buses came down a nearby road to take us all into Côteau. We were told to leave our luggage, but still people took stuff with them, bags and wilting flowers. We were packed in for the short ride, with only the old people and women with children getting the seats, the smell of dust, overripe fruit and stale sweat almost overpowering. The circles of sweat spreading under the arms of my new dress, me leaning against you, Ewan, your arm around me to steady us, as we jostled over the rutted dirt road.

The bus stopped on the main street, right by the railway station where we could see the engine being prepared to go and rescue our train. Women flocked to the washroom in the station, but you spied the railway hotel across the street and said, "Come on, Annie. We deserve a beer."

Now back in Glengarry or even in Montreal, I wouldn't have set foot in a hotel beverage room to save my life. No respectable woman would have, and in small towns, your reputation means more than your life. But I wasn't in Glengarry, or Montreal, was I? I was caught somewhere between my old life and my current one, a million miles away from either, in a situation not of my making. I didn't even think about how Gordon might be at the station, worried. In the heat and boredom of waiting, the situation had become ... what do they call it? Surreal. Like in *The Twilight Zone*, with mist forming at the edge of the picture, the details uncertain. The only familiar object was you, Ewan, your hand under my elbow as if it had always been there, leading me through the Ladies and Escorts entrance.

Cool and dark in the bar, with three fans blowing from different directions, rattling the flypaper. The beer deliciously cold, and I remember rubbing my neck with the frosted bottle, the room filling up with other passengers who followed us in, the owner's wife bustling in to help cope with the sudden demand. You and I in a booth at the side, with the noise and activity swelling around us. You taking your first sip of beer, wincing and pressing your stomach. For some reason I started babbling on again, worrying about the luggage I had left, a matched set of blond leather, a gift from Reg, Christmas past.

"It might be stolen. It's almost brand new, and this type of accident attracts looters."

You suddenly rose and pulled me to my feet. "I've heard enough about all the stuff you own, Annie. I'm not interested in Swedish furniture and blond luggage. I'm going to rent us a room." I was stunned but let you lead me through the bar into the lobby.

How many times over the years have I tried to explain it to myself? And I can't, except to say that it was the most logical thing in the world to do. A delicious lick in my lower stomach, my legs not working very well, but I followed you to the desk, up to the room, leaning against the door frame for support when you said, "Now, Annie. Where were we?"

Well, we can't pretend it was all stars and fireworks, magic after all those years, can we? You were rough, rougher than you'd ever been, perhaps because we didn't have much time. Ah, but it was also unbearably sweet and satisfying, as natural as breathing. I remember I cried, a great rush of feeling I didn't know I had flooding over me, you wiping away my tears, knowing better than to speak. The strange thing was that at the same time, you seemed to be someone I had never known at all, and someone I'd held all my life. The familiar slope of your back and thighs. A scar on your left shoulder that hadn't been there when I first knew you. You smiling apologetically, acknowledging the distance between us. Always a smile with you, Ewan, whispering, "We finally made it into a bed together, Annie. We've waited a long time for this."

Only about two hours until the whistle blew at the station, announcing that the train was there, with a new engine. The shadows in the room were long by then — suppertime, time for chores. We dressed quickly in the fading light, but just before we left, you touched my hair, fingering the curls, and said something strange.

"Did you get what you wanted, Annie?"

Of course, I thought you were referring to what had just taken place between us, so I kissed your hand and whispered back, "Yes."

Now I'm not so sure what you meant. How often have I repeated that question to myself over the years? How often did the answer change? It still hangs here in this room. And now, you can't tell me what you meant.

Not much talk for the rest of the journey. At Maxville, we got off at opposite ends of the car, you going to your truck to drive back to the farm, me hearing from Gordon that my mother was worse. The ordinary world, carrying on, tugging us apart.

\*\*\*

The rattling of the dishes has stopped. She must have gone out for her cigarettes and brandy. She drinks and smokes too much for her own good, that girl. Says it helps ruin her vocal chords, makes her voice project better on stage. Sounds like some sorry excuse, if you ask me. Oh, what's the use? She'll never change. I never did. And she's nothing if not my daughter. Stubborn, willful. Not very lucky in her choice of men. I'm tired. Tired of remembering, tired of wishing things had turned out differently.

## chapter 15

ANNIE AND HELEN ARE LYING ON THEIR BACKS on the living-room floor, swinging their knees from side to side, while Eric, the Swiss physiotherapist, dances in front of them saying, "Und right, zen left, zat's it. All ze vay over," leaning down to guide Annie's knees in the right direction when she gets stuck. On the television in the background, a talk show host is interviewing a couple who keep 650 cats in their suburban home, a Guinness World Record. The woman looks severely depressed, despite the fact that people from all over the world send them money and tins of cat food.

Ostensibly, Helen is learning how to guide her mother through the exercises, but in fact, she enjoys the activity on her own account. She fits in some stomach crunches and stretches while Annie labours to lift her bad leg. The living-room floor is littered with soup-can weights, bands of elastic and towels for stretching. A portable set of parallel bars stands along one wall. Annie doesn't seem to have made much progress in two months, but neither the physio nor Helen will acknowledge this. Helen knows exercise is good therapy, for broken spirits as well as broken bodies.

In the fading days of her marriage, Helen attended aerobics classes, dance classes, yoga classes and learned tai chi. Unconsciously, she seemed to believe that if she kept moving, the obvious wouldn't catch up with her.

\*\*\*

She has been married for three years, and she and Guy live in a Victorian house in Toronto's Cabbagetown, part of the chic professional masses who have bought up slum houses in the area and gutted them, preserving every scrap of *de rigueur* gingerbread trim. The newcomers regret that they can't renovate the working poor who don't want to move. The renovations — wall removals, exposed brick, pot lighting, built-in wine racks and sanded pine floors — have left them hugely in debt, especially since they're relying on Guy's salary.

Helen works in a series of temporary typing and reception jobs trying to keep her acting career afloat. During the 1970s, Toronto theatre burgeoned if not actually blossomed. New theatres and new playwrights shot up like dandelions, and the trend was toward collective shows, where everyone was part of the creative process. By the end of the decade, there were close to forty theatres operating in Toronto, making it the third largest theatre centre in the English-speaking world, after London and New York. Not quite the scale of London or New York, mind you, but by the mid-1980s, mega-musicals are beginning to change that.

Helen goes to auditions and even lands some parts — a Depression farm wife, characters in a couple of Pinter plays, one of the minor "Belles Soeurs" in a revival of Michel Tremblay's play. But the problem is, she doesn't fit in. Again. Her British elocution is a liability, not an asset; in fact her whole British training works against her. The Toronto theatre scene is quite closely knit, the actors, playwrights and directors knowing each other from theatre in such major centres as Regina, Kelowna and Fredericton, from the National Theatre School and summer stock. Helen doesn't share their history nor does she hang out with them enough to become known.

On the surface, Helen and Guy's life looks good. They entertain and go out a lot, usually with people Guy has met through his work. He has become a mining authority in a brokerage firm on Bay Street, using his geology background to advise the company on its new explorations and investments. He travels a lot, and when he's home, they mix with the bankers and investment people he meets on the job, many of whom have tidied-up Victorian cottages a few streets away.

By now, Helen and Guy realize that they have nothing in common, but hide it by discussing wallpaper or the type of deck they should put out back. Although they had briefly lived together in England, they had married to shorten the immigration process when Guy wanted to work in Canada. Now they drink a lot and discuss what's in the daily paper, trying to steer clear of politics and an argument. This is the ruthless eighties, and Guy is a big fan of Margaret Thatcher.

The other thing they argue about is money, or the lack of it. Guy's attitude toward Helen's chosen profession is ambivalent. On the one hand, he likes the cachet of introducing his wife as an actress, and encourages this image by buying her actressy gifts for birthdays and other occasions — dangly Burmese earrings, a gold cigarette case, a lace bodysuit. But Guy likes money more than he likes this outré image. He wants it all — trips back to Europe, a second house in the Muskokas, a European car. He carries in his head the image of the grand houses he visited with his friends from Winchester. The wages of an actor playing to eighty people in a converted garage theatre in Toronto don't support a life like that. Nor do the hourly temp rates for typists.

"Look, if you insist on being an actress, work! There are television parts," says an exasperated Guy, pacing the new cedar deck. "Commercials pay good money. I know because one of my clients directs commercials, and he makes wads of money. Des Mooney does most of General Foods stuff. I could arrange for him to meet you. And movies! They're making movies all over the place! Right now they have old City Hall standing in for some castle in Prague."

"I don't want to do commercials. I'm an actor, not the backdrop for a cereal. Besides, I hear they're a waste of time. Cattle calls. You're at the audition for hours, and you get thirty seconds in front of the director. Not even long enough to flash your tits." Helen has drunk too much wine, and her speaking voice has become very West End London.

"At least try, for God's sake! Or teach acting! Now why couldn't you give acting lessons, to kids or something?" Guy pours himself another brandy.

"Because I don't want to." As a reason, it sounds hollow even to Helen. "Speaking of kids, maybe we should start thinking about it."

Guy looks over the backyard, surveying it as if it were a stretch of the Hampshire Downs. "I want kids when we can afford them. Afford to give them what they need. And when we're settled."

"I never want to *settle*," Helen mutters.

But she does try. She acquires an agent, a fat, chain-smoking ex-model, who is very impressed with Helen's accent and bearing and sends her off to every cattle call going. And Helen enjoys a modicum of success. She plays an awkwardly dancing raisin in a chocolate bar commercial and a snotty English lady in a series of three tea commercials. She plays a pioneer housewife in a TV series about the good old days of Loyalist settlements, and she is a lawyer's secretary in a made-for-TV movie. While she does make some money, going for all the auditions cuts into the time she's available for temp work. The net financial gain is minimal, but the effect on Helen's self-esteem is devastating.

Guy's business travels leave Helen with enough time on her own to consider her failure as a wife and actor. She doesn't dare consider whether she wants this dance to continue. Frightened by the amount of time she spends drinking or crying, she acquires a therapist, a woman who poses interesting questions. "How is it your husband is directing your career? Do you direct his?" and "Your parents don't get along, you and your husband don't get along. Is that a reasonable sample from which to conclude that no married couple gets along?"

Helen is still pondering these questions when she gets a call from her agent. A theatre company in Nova Scotia for whom she auditioned wants to offer her a full summer's employment, parts in three plays — the lead in one and good character parts in the other two. Plus the chance to direct a workshop. Five solid months of work, at minimum Equity rate, but with cheap room and board available. By the ocean. With a director whose work she admires. One lead and two solid character parts.

She finds it hard to concentrate as she buzzes around the kitchen preparing dinner. Gail, a costume designer she's worked with, and her partner are coming for dinner, along with a lawyer and his wife who live a few blocks away. As Helen lifts the lamb cubes from the marinade and threads the shish kebabs, her mind is somewhere in Nova Scotia. She can't wait to tell Gail and her therapist the good news. It does not even cross her mind to tell Guy.

Helen hands Gail a glass of kir and news of the offer, while Guy and the lawyer discuss how the Reagan administration is affecting oil prices. The lawyer's wife overhears Helen and murmurs, "Nova Scotia is very beautiful in the summer. Guy could join you for a holiday."

"What holiday?" Guy wants to know. "I thought you wanted a cruise next fall."

"I did. I do," Helen replies. "And maybe we can afford it if I work for five months at The Wharf Playhouse. Which I've been offered. Three plays. The lead in one and the chance to direct a workshop."

"Congratulations!" says the lawyer.

"Five months!" says Guy.

"It's a very good company," adds Gail. "They don't do the usual summer schlock. Bill Patterson has a good reputation. Could get you a bit better known."

"We'll have to discuss this," Guy says darkly. "Another martini?"

Helen hides her tears as she fusses with the salad in the kitchen. Amy, the lawyer's wife, comes out to help and notices. "You could always leave him five months' worth of casseroles," she says, and Helen has to smile.

"I've never been too great on casseroles."

"No one is great on casseroles because there are no great casseroles. He'll get used to the idea."

Helen has always considered Amy to be the perfect fifties-style housewife — stay-at-home, well-groomed, a matched set of two children, given to decorating and cooking courses. "You think it would be right for me to go? Even if Guy disagrees?"

Amy shrugs. "Either you're an actress or you're not. Even Liz Taylor travels to find work. Of course, she gets to go to Rome to do Cleopatra, not to Lunenburg. But it's what you do, isn't it?" Helen is suddenly very fond of the woman and feels a sense of loss over never having had a close confidante. Therapists don't count. Amy smiles, clinks her glass against Helen's and says, "Go for it."

There are arguments, but she does go, and Guy takes a week off to join her down there when she does her star turn. There are more fights. By the time she comes back, neither of them is in the mood for further combat. Guy is having an affair with a client's secretary. Helen has had an affair with an actor who's six years younger than she is, and she is booked to tour Western Canada in the play she starred in in Nova Scotia.

\*\*\*

Annie is making constipated grunting sounds as she tries to lift her left leg. Her forehead is damp and her mouth twisted from the effort. Her good hand is clenched in a fist and her weak arm is shaking as her leg rises two, maybe three inches.

"*Gut!* Very *gut!*" the physio praises. "Now *vunce* more!"

Helen is sitting beside Annie but can't look anymore. It's like watching a fly on flypaper. "You're doing great, Ma!" she says rising. "I'll go make us some tea." She pauses at the door, watching her mother vibrate with effort, her lame leg wobbly as an infant's. Determination, thinks Helen. Will. She has so much, I have so little.

Later in the day, Helen's benevolent attitude has vanished. Can anything else go wrong? she wonders. She's agreed to meet Duncan at the roadhouse at 7:30, and it's already after 6:30. Annie isn't ready for bed, and Helen's still in her grey sweats with spaghetti sauce dribbled down one arm, thanks to Annie's attempt to roll her spaghetti on a fork at supper.

"It's not cooked enough," Annie declares, as Helen cleans up the trajectory of pasta and sauce. "If the noodles were cooked properly, they'd stick together and this wouldn't have happened."

You're right there, thinks Helen, recalling the gluey spaghetti dinners of her girlhood.

Next comes the salad, with Annie trying to pick out the bits of green pepper so they won't make her burp.

"You're doing this on purpose, aren't you?" Helen says, exasperated. "Because I'm going out for the first time in two months, you're doing everything you can to see that I don't make it, right?"

Annie pokes the salad a little more. "You don't even know who this boy is," she sniffs, relegating him to the same status as the green pepper.

"Well, for starters, he's probably near fifty, so he's well out of the 'boy' category. And it's not like it's a real date. I'm meeting him in a restaurant — that is, if I can ever get out of here."

"I think we're imposing on Mary Forbes' goodwill, and I don't think we ought to."

Helen is rattling the supper dishes through a stream of water at the sink. "She volunteered, Ma. She's your friend."

"And what if something happens? What is she supposed to do?"

"Same as I'd do. Call 911. Now are you finished torturing that salad?"

Next Helen gets Annie ready for bed, dressing her in her nightgown and bathrobe ready to go to sleep, her hill of tablets set out beside the bed with a glass of water.

"I won't be able to fall asleep while Mary's here," Annie pouts, her arms jamming in her nightgown at a scarecrow angle.

"Then don't. Stay up. I won't be late."

"And Mary shouldn't stay up too late, either. She has to drive home."

Mrs. Forbes arrives just after seven, her cribbage board tucked under one arm, and Helen has the chance to duck into the bathroom, brush her hair and teeth, and add a dab of mascara, tugging off her sweats as she heads for her bedroom. She has had no time to think about what to wear, but she finds a clean pair of slacks and a shirt. A quick spray of perfume, a flurry of last minute instructions from Helen to Mary, and Annie to Helen, and she's gone.

# chapter 16

WHERE AM I? WHAT ... what is this? Oh lordy, a dream. It was a dream! What we used to call a wet dream, I guess, although who would credit it, an old woman in a wheelchair, scarcely able to move, yet this rhythm happening inside me. And a nightmare at the same time. I can't even tell you who it was because he didn't have a face, just the ability to drive me wild, to take me to a place I want to go, again and again.

Who's that in the kitchen? Reg? Helen? Why it's Mary Forbes! That's right. I must have nodded off. Now I remember. Helen's out gallivanting with some man who just wandered up from the river. Never did have enough sense, that girl. While I've always had too much, too much to ever be truly — what do they call it? — transported.

That's all sex really is, isn't it? It's not about Ewan or Reg, Tom, Dick or Harry. It's not about a man. It's a means of transportation, a road to take you somewhere else, somewhere where neither your body nor your brain matter. Somewhere outside the muddle that is you.

Not that I've felt that way very often. With Reg, occasionally, when we'd been out painting the town, me with just enough drink in me to let my guard down, and he with enough drink in him to take advantage of it. Brief shining moments we never talked about afterwards. More often with you Ewan, especially that time when more than the train engine was derailed. That time when we forgot who we were supposed to be or who we wanted to be and just became ourselves.

Ourselves. Myself. Alone with myself. To this day I can remember how it felt when I realized I would never see you again. The pain. I can't actually feel the pain, of course, because no one can ever precisely remember pain. If they could, no second child would ever be born. But the emptiness. The great emptiness, as if I'd been abandoned on a road in the desert, with nothing but sand for miles. No relief. For years, without realizing it, I had consoled myself with you. The idea of you. That you were out there, that you had loved me and would always love me, as if time hadn't happened. Suddenly, I wasn't going to be able to fool myself anymore. It's important that, you know. To be able to fool yourself. It allows you to skate over some awfully thin ice.

Ewan. The whole time back at the farm, nursing my mother, I was aware of you, only a concession road away. You going out to chores, reading the paper with your morning coffee, throwing sticks for your dog. I never imagined you with your wife, with Flora, or your girls, just you on your own, as if you existed just for me. I was in a dreamlike state, doing the laundry, changing my mother's dressings, reading to her, helping Alma in the kitchen, reading to my nieces and nephew to keep them quiet so they wouldn't disturb my mother's fitful sleep. Only speaking to Alma and Gordon when spoken to, Gordon remarking how I seemed to have "simmered down." How can you simmer down if something inside you has *always* been simmering? I even forgot to call the children on Sunday as I'd promised. Never thought of Reg at all. My secret — our secret — was a peaceful zone in which I moved.

It was about three weeks later when I got back to the city that my panic set in. An emotional witch's brew; the recognition that my mother was dying, that I was married to a man I didn't love, couldn't love, that I had children who tied me to him. But most of it was you, the awful ache of knowing that you were living your life apart from me, that you survived without me, when I felt I could not survive without you. I now had proof that we belonged together, and that knowledge made the house claustrophobic, Reg's banter unbearable, my children's questions irritating. And it wasn't just feelings, it was tangible. My skin itched, I broke out in hives, my stomach swirled, a constant headache pressed against the back of my eyes.

The emptiness. A dark corridor leading nowhere, with no doors. And only one hope, that I would see you again, that the accumulation of fifteen years — your wife, my husband, our children — would be wiped away as if they hadn't happened. A mad hope that a great mistake in my fate would be discovered and corrected, the slate erased, no harm done to anyone. Insane of course, but then I *was* a little insane, I think. I tried writing down what I felt and that became a letter to you, filled with impossible hope. How much you meant to me, how you and I belonged together, how God or His mad brother sometimes moves in mysterious ways, such as a train accident. I told you I wanted to see you, to talk this over with you, that I would go back up to the farm again on the pretext of caring for my mother and that we could meet somewhere to talk, maybe down by the river like the old days, where no one would see us, no one would know.

How often did I write that letter? Ten times? Almost every day. Tearing up each version, carefully choosing my words, then not sending it, worrying that Flora might be the kind of wife who opened her husband's mail. Should I send it by registered mail, so you'd have to go in to the post office to sign for it? Or send it via Gordon, making up some convoluted excuse for doing so? My panic focused on getting the letter to you, but as long as I didn't mail it, it kept the hope of you, the hope of us, alive. Nothing irrevocable could happen.

The letter was still sitting in the drawer where I kept my monthly stuff and my diaphragm, when Alma called to say my mother was worse, that the doctor had ordered morphine to make her more comfortable. My breath quickening, great gulps of air, my emotions in shreds, the sadness that her gentle, steady force soon would no longer be there for me. But there was more. Alma said quietly, "Now I know you don't need any more bad news, Annie, but Gordon and I thought you should know. Ewan's dead."

A moment when everything stopped. I couldn't speak, couldn't even breathe with this stone in my chest. "No!" was all I could manage.

"He took his own life, Annie. He'd been up to the hospital in Montreal for tests, and they found cancer. Stomach cancer. Said there wasn't too much they could do for him. The pain was pretty bad, I hear, and I guess he wanted it to end his way, not with some disease. He was found in the barn, with his shotgun between his knees. Flora! That poor woman! As if she hasn't had enough tragedy in her life." A long sigh from Alma, little gasping breaths from me.

"I'm sorry to have to tell you, Annie. I know he meant a lot to you at one time. It's a shame, isn't it? A man in his prime, those girls of his not yet grown. The funeral is Tuesday."

To this day, I don't know how the conversation ended. I remember Barbara, only ten, taking the phone out of my hand and going to fetch Reg. Reg guiding me into the bedroom to lie down, then calling Alma back. Everything put down to grief over my mother, and if Alma knew differently, she never let on, God love her.

Less than a month later, my mother was gone, too. The funeral, a bleak fall day, the sky spitting into the open grave. And there in the crowd Flora, still with her sad lopsided smile, dressed in dark navy, with her grey hair making her seem older than she was. I went over, took her in my arms and hugged her till I could hear her gasp. I couldn't help myself. What was I doing? Trying to find a trace of the smell of you on her skin? Folding myself into the last arms that held you? Both of us crying, neither of us saying anything, then Reg lightly pulling me away. "It's her condition," he said, patting my belly, flashing Flora one of his big, boyish grins. Flora nodding and wiping her eyes.

It's a terrible place to live, a place without hope where the oxygen has been taken out of the air, but you still have to stumble around in the hazy ether. Years ago, when Helen had a breakdown in her first year of university, I recognized her symptoms. They absolutely terrified me. She was mute, the way her eyes darted the only indication of her inner flight. And I was useless in helping her, not knowing how I ever made it out of that trough myself. All I could see was that I had passed on my helplessness to her, and that enraged me. Worse of all, I kept my distance from her, blamed her weakness on Reg's instability. It's one of the things I'm most ashamed of.

But I knew the territory she occupied. The awful moment when you wake up, and the day sinks ahead of you. Did I look after the children during that time? I don't remember. I remember moments like Reg in the kitchen, making french fries for the kids, the room full of smoke. And him with a cigarette dangling from his mouth, cursing as he tried to tie ribbons for Barbara's braids, her late for school. Barbara finding me in the park one time and leading me home. And I remember crying uncontrollably when the flour canister slipped from my hands and flour covered the kitchen floor.

But I didn't stay in that zone forever. You can't stay there. Life pulls you on, puts things in your path that force you to move on. Breakfast happens, a child gets the measles, a cake is baked and the laundry flaps on the line. It was still the late fifties; we were encouraged to pretend bad things didn't happen. As long as the lawn was mowed, there was an ornamental shrub on either side of the porch, matching furniture in the living room and a tasty but nutritious casserole in the freezer in case company dropped by, you were alright. There were no demons hidden in the basement, just knotty pine wall panelling, Lazee-Boy chairs and a naugahyde bar.

I guess I knew the worst was over when I could finally talk to someone about how I was feeling. Maggie. Dear Maggie. Just back from a long stay in the Bahamas, sitting at my kitchen table one afternoon, smoking a cigarette, shaking her head and patting my hand. "I wish you'd told me sooner, Annie. I might have been able to do something for you."

"What could you do? What can anyone do? He's dead. I'm not." Another snuffle or two there.

She patted my arm again. "I mean the baby. There are doctors who can fix that, if it's early enough."

I remember looking at her, shocked, because I hadn't thought of the baby as any kind of problem. It was my trophy, my souvenir of the great love of my life. It was at that moment that I realized that the baby was the force pushing me back into life. Helen. Growing fiercely inside me, insisting on life, energetically taking over the body that I no longer had a use for. The first time I felt her kick, I realized with dread that I would survive. As my stomach swelled, so did the recognition that I was climbing out of that trough. I was giving her life, and she was giving me back mine. I could think, *I will never see Ewan again,* without sobbing.

I tried to explain this to Maggie, who smiled and said, "That's good. I take it Reg doesn't suspect a thing."

I dismissed Reg with a sigh. "You know how sensitive Reg is. He'd only notice if the baby was born coloured." We even managed a giggle with that thought. "You ever want to have kids, Maggie?"

A flick of her cigarette. "Yes and no. The reason I know about those doctors is that I once had an abortion. The baby was an accident, of course. But it was out of the question, what with James' position and his wife and all. And I realized I had nothing really to give a child."

"Surely James would have looked after you?"

"Oh yes, of course. But I'm not talking about money. I mean I didn't want to share my life, never wanted that responsibility. Maybe it's from seeing all those dead bodies at my father's place back home, but I've always tended to detach myself in certain situations. Emotionally, I mean. And you can't do that with children. They demand your all."

"But you're so good with kids. My kids, anyway."

"Ah well, that's easy, isn't it? It's a night out, not a commitment."

She sighed and lit another cigarette. "I think far too many people have children blindly, when they don't even like children. At least I like them."

"And I don't. Not really. Don't have the patience."

"That's because you can't see things from their point of view, Annie. And that's always important, no matter who you're dealing with."

"Oh, you should have had that child! You'd have been a natural mother, Maggie. Why didn't you tell me about the abortion? Was it awful?"

"The decision was awful. But the procedure was easier than a trip to the dentist. And I couldn't tell you. You were up to your knees in dirty diapers at the time. You'd have thought I was a monster."

"Never, Maggie. We're friends, even though we're very different."

Maggie flicked her cigarette again and examined her nails. "Not as different as you think. We're now both old hands at adultery, after all. Imagine! A passionate encounter in Côteau Landing!" She hooted then caught herself. "Sorry, Annie. I know you loved him. And he was a fine man."

It must have been more than a year later, after Helen was born, after my moods and rages were put down to the death of my mother, the shock of another pregnancy and the post-partum blues, that the shift really happened. Reg had to go to Chicago on a sales trip and suggested I come along.

"It'll do you good," he said. "Get you away from the nursery rhymes, put a little colour in your cheeks." Him leaning across the table and pressing money into my hand. "Buy yourself some new clothes. Get your hair done. You used to sparkle at cocktail parties."

So I packed my bags — that blond luggage I had been so worried about — and I went. Even managed to have a good time, joking with Reg's customers, drinking too many Whisky Sours, shopping up a storm. But I was not the same person I had been. There was a hardness there, a new greediness that came out of the great wound inside me. I had left a large part of myself behind, and I couldn't retrieve it, so I had no choice but to move forward. I remember I was very impatient with that new little girl who moved far too quickly across the floor of the kitchen. But I had no choice but to care for her and love her.

Love! I can't believe how much importance we attach to it, especially since it rarely goes to plan. Yet women in particular always think all the forms of love are important. And when we're young, love means sex. "I love you" means "I want you." But it's only after you've been through a lot with a man that you can honestly say, "I love you." Love's an assessment, not just a hope.

Have I loved? Been loved? I think I love my children, although I'm not sure what that means, and I'm deeply suspicious of what they mean when they say, "Love you, Mom." Love between parents and children doesn't really count, does it? It's almost always automatic and it never ... what's that word I'm looking for? — transforms. That's it. It never really transforms you. It might clarify your thinking, give you a focus, whereas the love I'm talking about replaces your thinking, renders you unable to think at all. Love. So many ways you can mean it. In the end, as he lay there dying, the bluster all gone out of him, I could say that in a way, I even loved Reg. Not always, not even most of the time, but in a deep part of me that neither of us ever explored. That tight cord between us that kept us tense and alert to each other. A cord that grew thicker, more comfortable, the longer we were together.

\*\*\*

My dream just now started with me, just a young woman, riding our old workhorse Blanche along the Dominion in the evening. There was a man with cows on the other side of the river. It was hot, a cinnamon atmosphere, and the cows naturally gravitated to the water. So did the man, taking his clothes off and wading in. He couldn't see me behind some trees. Him striding in and out of the water as if he were Adam before the fall. Beautiful, innocent and doomed. Suddenly, he spotted me and waved me down to join him. I felt as if I had never wanted any-thing more. I leapt off Blanche, running down, tearing off my clothes, giving myself to the cold water, the current pulling me toward him. I shut my eyes and gave way to the tug, till I felt my skin brush up against another's. Opening my eyes, I was terrified, because I was surrounded by cows, all shoving me and mooing at me, pushing me away from the shore. I cried out, but my mouth wouldn't open, and the man was gone. Yet something was moving in me down there.

Pull yourself together, Annie. Mary Forbes is here to play cribbage and you need all your wits about you. Filling your head with a lot of girlish nonsense you should have left behind ages ago. You can bet a good deal that Mary Forbes doesn't waste her time dreaming such foolishness. I imagine it's the green peppers that have done this to me. I told Helen to leave them out of the salad. Here comes Mary with the tea. That'll settle me down.

# chapter 17

HELEN ARRIVES FIFTEEN MINUTES LATE to meet Duncan, the roadhouse shining like the new Jerusalem in the light of the setting sun. When Helen enters, smoke from cigarettes and fragrant fondue pots stings her eyes. Edith Piaf warbles from the sound system that she has no regrets. Already Helen feels as if she has entered another space, the way she feels when she steps on stage, as if her real life is being left in the wings.

The place is almost full and decorated with bizarre ceramics, plastic plants, hurricane lamps and other Gypsy touches that would make the room appear full even if no one was there. It's definitely friendly. Duncan waves from a booth and comes over to greet her. His touch on Helen's arm as he guides her back to the booth further eases her into an alternate state.

"I'm sorry I'm so late. My mother ..." and she makes several hand gestures instead of finishing the statement.

Duncan smiles. "I figured that was it. No problem. I'm just a glass of wine ahead of you." He pours Beaujolais into Helen's glass, then hesitates. "Maybe you'd prefer something else?"

"No! No! The wine looks yummy." Helen greedily takes a long draught. "Maybe I should get a glass of water, though, so I don't finish the bottle before the menu arrives."

The waitress comes over, a chubby Québécoise whose skirt is too short and too tight. Actually, everything about the woman is too-too. Hair, smile, machine gun delivery of the specials. They decide on a beef fondue, with Helen ordering escargots as a starter. She rolls the little nuggets in her mouth, savouring the garlicky richness of them.

"These are so good. It feels like years since I ate anything not approved by a dietitian." She sponges up the rest of the sauce with her bread, then checks herself. "God! Do you think I'll ever again be able to talk without a reference to my mother?"

"It's a tough gig you're on," nods Duncan. "Any idea how long it might go on?"

"No. They were supposed to have a place for her at St. Andrew's by now, but nothing's come up. And I'm supposed to be teaching a course at the National Theatre School in October. So I don't really know." Helen suddenly panics. "How long are you going to be here?"

"Don't know. I've got to use my airline ticket by the end of the year."

Helen feels an inner joy. Something to look forward to at the end of the day, for at least the next little while.

"Look," says Duncan. "Botulism. An outbreak of E. coli. That's what that seniors home — St. Andrew's or whatever they call it — needs. I could sneak into the kitchen, do a little commando work, and there'd suddenly be plenty of vacancies. We'd have your mother in there in no time."

Helen giggles, then sobers at the realization of how vulnerable people like her mother are. "Those poor old dears. I wouldn't want to rush them."

"Some of them wouldn't even notice." Duncan pours more wine. "What's the course on?"

"'Language and techniques of the Restoration.' Now aren't you sorry you asked?"

"That isn't 'restoration' as in furniture restoration, is it?"

"No, as in 'Restoration of the monarchy.' Seventeenth century. Don't roll your eyes, it pays the rent. In this country, hockey players succeed, artists subsist."

"I know. And it isn't the government that subsidizes the arts. It's the artists."

Helen looks at him curiously. "I know that. But you're not supposed to."

"Had a girlfriend once who produced documentaries." Duncan grins. "A while ago."

The fondue arrives with a sizzle and a selection of sauces, all of which Helen pokes her finger into, all of which are delicious. They exchange stories about best and worst meals ever, Duncan winning the latter category hands down with his story of snake stew served up by headhunters in Borneo. The sound system plays more Piaf, Jacques Brel,

French café music. Halfway through their fondue, tables are cleared at the back of the restaurant, and people start to drift in, settling around the bar. Three middle-aged men with long hair, who look as if they ought to know better, bring in a keyboard, guitar and fiddle and start plugging them in.

"I warned you it was a roadhouse," Duncan says, pointing out that their waitress is flirting outrageously with the fiddler.

By the time they have finished their meal and the bottle of Beaujolais, the band is ready, enthusiastically pumping out a lively mixture of traditional kitchen jigs and French country and western hurtin' songs. Helen thinks they are all wonderful, the perfect complement to the dinner, wine and Duncan. She beams at him across the table, knowing she will remember the smallest details of this evening years from now. That symphony of sensations when you are falling in love. Couples get up to dance, including two middle-aged women who might be sisters, dancing with each other in a stiff detached way. Helen looks at Duncan.

"I'm a terrible dancer," he announces.

"Well, some of those lyrics sound pretty terrible. I think he just sang 'Stand By Your Man' in French."

"He did, but it became something like 'Stand By Your Femme.' You like to dance, don't you? I can tell."

"I don't like to dance. I *love* to dance. And sing. And nobody does either at parties anymore, beyond a certain age. It's a shame."

"I can't sing either," Duncan grins. "And it goes without saying, I can't act."

Helen smiles, pulls him to his feet and nods toward the other couples pumping their way around the floor. "That isn't dancing. That's the Ottawa Valley two-step, and anyone who can count one, two can do it."

They find a break in the circling couples and charge in, rocking from side to side with the best of them. After one circuit, Helen faces Duncan. "You lied. You've been doing this all your life."

Duncan pulls her closer to him, "*We've* all been doing this all our lives," dramatically twirling Helen around. A young couple, bent on coming through, make their way by them out to the centre of the dance floor. The man winks at them on the way past. Helen leans back against

Duncan's arm. She is aware of every point at which her body touches his — shoulder, chest, arms, hands, hips — yet she feels free, wonderfully untied. The wine and music course through her.

After an abortive attempt at line dancing, Helen picking it up quickly, Duncan twice kicking himself in the shins, they sit down and order coffee. The music is too loud for conversation so they communicate mostly through touch and facial expressions. The band is definitely non-union because the only break they take is to sip the large glasses of beer the crowd sends their way, along with their requests. Mostly the band leader, the fiddler, talks into the mike in French, but this time he leans forward and says, "Dis tune is for 'Elen." The band starts sawing away at "Can I Have This Dance?"

Helen looks at Duncan in surprise, but he just grins and hauls her onto the floor. With each movement, Helen's desire for him grows. She feels every pressure of his hand, notices the rivulet of sweat that rolls down in front of his ear, resists the urge to lick it off. She's sure he feels the same way, the way his lips brush her hair, the thickness in his jeans when he holds her close. "Will you be my partner every night?" the singer croons, and Helen silently answers, *Yes!* Suddenly her eye is caught by the starburst metal clock on the wall over the bar, and her lust retreats.

"Oh my God! It's nearly eleven! I'm supposed to be back by now."

"What, this early? Okay, then let's go. I'll get the bill."

Out in the parking lot, the air is cooler, with a breeze off the Ottawa River. Duncan opens the car door for Helen, but they end up kissing and groping like teenagers against the door frame.

"I really must go," Helen says with difficulty.

"I'll follow you home." Duncan's voice has deepened.

"Yes! Then we can have a brandy after Mrs. Forbes leaves." Helen jumps in the car, revs the motor and takes off when she sees Duncan's headlights in her mirror.

The lights in Annie's house are blazing when Helen arrives at the driveway. Duncan pulls alongside. "I'll park up near the bridge and meet you down at the river when you're free."

"Okay. I'll be as quick as I can."

"Take your time. It's still early for those of us who aren't yet geriatric." Duncan pulls away, and Helen turns into the driveway.

"Well, it's about time," is Annie's greeting as Helen comes in. The two women are still playing cribbage, the teapot and cups on the dining table between them, but Annie's head is nodding.

"Don't you let her make you feel guilty," Mrs. Forbes tells Helen. "She had a little nap in her chair earlier, and she didn't want to quit because she was winning."

"Winning, but I'm that tired," says Annie pushing herself away from the table, declaring the game at an end. "Now, Mary, you'll want to get home."

"Did you have a good time, dear?" asks Mrs. Forbes, packing up her cribbage board.

"Lovely, thank you," Helen replies, then pointedly looks at her mother. "It's so nice of you to ask."

"We had a grand time, too, Helen," Mrs. Forbes adds, patting Helen's arm. "We'll do this more often. Give you a chance to get away."

Goodbyes are said, Annie and Helen watch Mrs. Forbes back slowly out of the driveway. Before the car lights have swerved onto the road, Annie is pushing herself down the hall to her bedroom. "You said you'd be back by ten."

"Eleven," Helen reminds her.

There is more fussing in the bedroom as Annie wrestles her dressing gown off, complains about the garlic on Helen's breath and chokes on one of her pills.

"Just swallow it. If you weren't trying to scold me at the same time you're drinking, this wouldn't happen."

"Don't know why you're in such a hurry now when you sure took your time coming home," Annie mutters. "Now what have you done with my slippers?"

"I'm in a hurry because I have a very nice man waiting for me down at the dock," Helen says evenly.

"What?" Annie's wide awake again.

"We're going to have a brandy after I've tucked you in."

"You're going to go out again and leave me?"

"I'm not leaving! I'll be down by the river. I can hear you if you call."

"That's no place to be entertaining. Bring him up here. I'd like to meet him."

Helen is so astonished she can't speak for a few moments. "You want to meet him? Tonight? You just said you were tired."

"Never too tired to meet an attractive young man."

"Uh, he's not that young."

"He is compared to me," Annie states. "Now give me back my dressing gown. You go invite him in."

"Ma, I'm not sure ..."

"Don't worry. I'll go to sleep, and you can carry on."

This turn of events is so surprising that Helen does as she's told. She smiles as she heads toward the glowing cigarette tip. "She wants to meet you," Helen says, grinning broadly. "Won't go to bed until she does."

Duncan puts his arm around Helen. "Then we'd better not keep her waiting."

Helen pours out two brandies in the kitchen, and they take them down the hall to Annie's room. Annie's sitting upright in her wheelchair, a royal personage about to receive one of her subjects.

"Ma, this is Duncan," Helen says with a sense of déjà vu she can't quite place. "Duncan, my mother Annie."

Duncan comes over to shake Annie's hand. "A pleasure to meet you, Ma'am."

Annie eyes him carefully, holding onto his hand. "Duncan. And where are you from?"

"Duncan's been living in Malaysia," Helen interjects.

"But I was raised around here," Duncan smiles.

Annie scrutinizes him more closely, pulls him closer. "Now who are your people? I bet I know them from the old days."

"Urquart's my last name."

"Urquart, yes," Annie murmurs, then just stares blankly at him for a few moments. "Lots of Urquarts around here. And MacLeods, MacSweyns, MacDonalds ..."

Helen recognizes the sign of Annie's fatigue. "We mustn't keep you up, Ma. You're tired."

Annie switches on again briefly. "Yes, well, it's nice to meet you, Mr. Urquart. Your people, they farm?"

"My brother farms on the Sixth Concession."

"Ah! Yes, the Sixth," Annie's mouth continues to move after she's finished speaking.

"You're tired, Ma." Helen moves forward. "You've got to get to bed."

"Stroke." Annie announces to Duncan. "A bloody nuisance. And me being so careful of what I ate. If anyone should have had a stroke it was Marjory Follows. She still smokes."

"I don't think fairness really enters into it, Ma," Helen counters.

"When you have a setback, I guess it's only natural to want to blame someone," Duncan smiles.

"Exactly!" Annie nods in satisfaction, but her speech is slurring. "Thank you for taking my daughter to dinner. I only wish I could. She's been a marvel to me."

Once again Helen has the sensation that Annie is talking about someone other than her, someone Helen doesn't know very well. She looks at her mother, who nods at her.

"Time for bed, Ma," Helen says softly.

Annie rallies again for a moment. "It was awfully nice meeting you, Mr. Urquart."

"Duncan," Duncan says, and bends to softly kiss her on the cheek. Helen feels extraneous to this scene.

After Duncan disappears, Annie's head falls. Helen tries to guide her to the bed.

"Not yet!" Annie struggles with Helen who's trying to remove her dressing gown, each arm feeling weighted. "I want to tell you something ..." Her voice trails off.

"Later, Ma! In the morning." Helen thumps the pillows.

"In the morning," Annie whispers, leaning back. "Yes, in the morning. Now you should call it a night, too."

"Ma, I'm forty years old. Now go to sleep." Helen pats Annie and kisses her good night.

Helen joins Duncan in the darkened living room. "My mother," she states simply.

"I know," Duncan says, wrapping his arms around her. "I know."

## chapter 18

WHY HAVE I NEVER TOLD HER? I always meant to. I've been meaning to for years. Especially since Reg died. Poor Reg. I never knew he knew, until he was dying, those last few weeks when my nerves were like corn silk, frayed, flying, frightened that he was dying, impatient for him to get it over with. Impatient, as I always was with him. Haranguing him about eating so little, and with him insisting on a martini before dinner.

"This is so hard on your liver," I said, him shakily pouring the gin into the cocktail shaker. A silver one I got on sale at Birks. Only plated, mind you.

Despite the liver cancer, we had never actually talked about him dying, so it was a shock when he turned and said, "What possible difference can it make now?"

Me fussing with the dinner plates on the table, not wanting to get into that territory. "It can make looking after you easier," I said. "Typical of you, to try to make my life as difficult as possible." As if his death was about me. But then, in a way, it was.

He dipped just a touch of vermouth into the shaker. "Not always," he said quietly. "I've been a little more tolerant of your weaknesses than you have been of mine." He sighed and looked out the window. "Though I admit I've indulged mine a bit more than you've done yours."

"What weaknesses?" Like I didn't have any.

"Could you get the olives from the fridge?"

"No! What weaknesses?"

He started to shuffle off to the kitchen. "Well, you've always been too fond of spending money, Annie." He stopped, thought for just a moment, then said, "And then there's always been the question of where Helen came from." He swung open the door to the kitchen and went through.

It felt like he'd punched me, dealt me a physical blow, which he'd never done in all the years we'd been warring. A slap out of nowhere. A gasp for air, my head becoming lighter, as if someone had taken the top off it and the contents were spilling out. Then, my heart hammering, I followed him into the kitchen.

"What do you mean by that last crack?"

"I mean, I'm not so stupid about female matters as you might think. I can count. And you seem to forget the state you were in when you found out you were pregnant again. It wasn't just that it was a surprise, now, was it?"

I couldn't look at him. I just knew I had to deny it. "Don't be absurd! It was a mistake! I must have forgotten my diaphragm! What do you mean, you can count? Babies are born late or early all the time! As for my ... breakdown, you seem to forget that my mother had died!" All the excuses I had prepared for myself thirty-odd years ago came back. Despite the years of going over them in my head, they still didn't sound convincing.

Reg took the jar of olives out of the fridge and said, "I don't really care, Annie. It doesn't matter now, does it? I told you when I first met you I wouldn't want a woman no one else wanted. And it's never mattered. Helen's a fine girl, in her own way. A little flighty for her own good perhaps, but she's got a good heart."

Finally, control over my panic. "This is absurd. You're just looking for an excuse for your own peccadillos."

Reg started to shuffle back into the dining room. "Have it your own way, Annie. You've always wanted to." Then he stopped. "I'd just like to make it clear that I didn't try to make your life difficult. You mostly did that yourself, Annie. And that one time, I tried to help. I did try to help, really." The door swung back, and he was gone.

We never spoke of it again, and I never again objected to his martinis. Oh, I meant to bring it up with him. To confess and tell him I wasn't some slut who'd had a casual affair, that it had been Ewan. But I think that might have hurt him more than if it had been a stranger. And the time never seemed right. Besides, nothing was going to make up for all those lost years, was it? We'd never been good at talking to each other, at saying what we really meant. So we just declared a truce. Settled a score, recognized we'd both made mistakes. And then he died.

But I always meant to tell Helen. Poor girl. The last child. The awkward child, keeping to herself, living through those stories in her head. Like she was paying me back for the mistake I'd made. But she has a right to know ... Tomorrow I must tell her.

Almost told her when her marriage broke down. "Good for you," I wanted to say. "Recognize your mistakes and get on with it. There are no children, so no harm done." But I couldn't say that. Not then. She was already fragile, already on some medication. She didn't need any more disturbing news, did she? And at a time like that, she needed me to be strong, not show weakness, didn't she?

But I was thinking about how I once left Reg. Just after the first time I caught him red-handed, so to speak, after he came back from a trip to Winnipeg with scratch marks on his back. Funny, but I thought of you, Ewan. How you were not a man to meet a floozie in a bar, ply her with liquor and take her back to your hotel room. Remember how sacred and mysterious sex was for us, reserved for special moments in the dark? Not a drunken struggle with strangers. Each time he was caught, like the time when the woman answered his phone in the hotel room, he'd say it didn't mean anything, that it was just like scratching an itch. Well, sure cured me of any itchiness I'd ever had. Couldn't bear him to come near me for weeks at a time afterward, imagining I could still smell cheap perfume on him. In Glengarry, sex had been something to be sniggered at, never talked about and never elevated to a lofty position. But it was Reg who made me think sex was dirty. Sex with him became dirty.

The time I actually left — Sean was still a baby — Reg had also sunk our savings into a bauxite exploration investment scheme which had gone bust. That did it. Left a note. Packed up Barbara and Sean and took the train back to Glengarry, to my parents. I remember my father sitting at the kitchen table, smoking his pipe, unable to look at me as I asked if I could come back for awhile, just until I could find work and a little place for me and the children. I knew I was asking a lot. They'd built an extension onto the house for Gordon and his family, but it still meant the house was crowded. Before we got on to the subject, Gordon, Alma and the kids found that they had something very important they had to do in the drive shed. My mother made tea, patted my hand, rocked Barbara on her knee and nodded as I blurted out some of the details of our marriage, censoring Reg's excesses for the sake of decency.

My mother. My sweet, sweet mother. "What you need is a good night's sleep." More pats. "We'll talk about this in the morning."

Lying awake upstairs, I could hear them murmuring in the kitchen, Gordon pouring himself a whisky, not a good sign.

After breakfast, before he went back out to do chores, my father spoke for the first time. "We think you ought to go back to Montreal," he said, again finding it hard to look at me. "A woman's place is with her husband. You've always been high-strung, Annie, a little too hasty for my liking. Now you're a mother, you need to calm down, sort things out with Reg. He's a good provider, after all."

Me upstairs crying, Alma coming in, putting her arms around me, rocking me.

"I'd have you here in a minute. It's not that we don't want you and don't love you. You know that, don't you?"

Me blubbering, blowing my nose.

"You know you'd never be happy back here. Not after living all those years in Montreal."

And I knew she was right. I'd come back home out of desperation.

"I'll bet you don't even own a pair of rubber boots anymore," Alma said softly. Had to smile at that. "Now Gordon's willing to get some of the lads from down the road to go down and straighten Reg out, if you like."

A bitter laugh. "That would sure surprise him."

"Nothing serious," Alma said. "Just so's he wouldn't dream of fooling around for a while."

So that was it. I went back, had to go back, and none of my family ever spoke of it again. And I think my exit had made Reg reconsider things a little. Shortly after, we bought our first house, a little bungalow in Lachine that looked like a Monopoly house. And he began to take me with him to some of his sales conferences and conventions — not all mind you, but enough to let me know he wasn't straying. And I have to admit, I loved that aspect of my life — the parties, dressing up and flirting with men old enough to be my father. Didn't make me feel any warmer toward Reg, but it did help me forget the disappointment I felt — as if there were some big, beautiful garden next door that I wasn't allowed to enter. I can still remember the sound of the front door closing behind me, that time I came back from the farm, my options at an end. The terrible "clunk" of the door.

Ah, what does any of it matter now? Reg. Poor Reg. We made a life together. The important word here is "made," because it was something manufactured, something put together and made to work. A life bought block by block — houses, new cars, Scandinavian furniture, flagstones on the patio. Children filling the space between us. Parties and trips and an occasional slice of swift sex were the mortar that held the flimsy structure together. But we created something, and if it wasn't quite what I thought it would be, well, I had enough sense of accomplishment, of moving forward, to feel satisfied, if not happy. Of course, you can't keep up a front like that all the time. There were explosions. But Reg and I, we made a marriage, found a formula that allowed us to carry on. Couples today don't even try to do that. We made something of ourselves.

But Helen's not made of the same stuff as me. Still, she's come through it well enough. She's independent, free to do what she wants. Manages to live a full life without a man, unless you count that fellow who rents from her. There's her little house, work she enjoys, some friends. Never enough money of course, but then, money always meant too much to me and too little to her. I mean, it wouldn't be what I'd want, but she's in control of her own life.

Like I was in 1944. Married, but free. Strange, that, isn't it? In those days, marriage gave you a status that you could never have as a single woman, even if you were earning your way. Reg was overseas, flying Lancasters, bombing the Germans, and I had the little flat. On the third floor of a triplex it was, in the east end, just off Lafontaine Park. Flats were hard to come by in those days, because people had flooded into Montreal for jobs, like Maggie and me. But the triplex was owned by an uncle of one of the French Canadian girls I worked with, and I managed to get it. Small, it was — a little parlour at the front, a bedroom. A sort of living-dining room that led into the kitchen, all strung out along a long hall.

By that time, Maggie was married too, and we both felt that as respectable mature women, we shouldn't be boarding in someone else's home. So she moved in with me, taking over the parlour as her bedroom. Oh, the fun we had! It was a long way from where we worked in the north end of the city, but we didn't mind, setting out in the dark of a winter's morning, stomping our feet to keep warm while we waited for the streetcar.

I was in charge of a team of five other girls at the factory, earning good wages — more in a week than my father saw in a month. Spending almost every cent I had, furnishing the flat, making it mine. Going to auction sales in Westmount with Maggie, picking up furniture, including that drop-leaf dining table over by the window in the living room. I remember bidding on a set of highball glasses and Maggie telling the man I was bidding against that the glasses had belonged to a woman who died of TB, that the germs would still be on the glass.

Let's see. The living-room furniture — an overstuffed wine-coloured velour sofa and two chairs, new, from Eaton's, along with the big carved mahogany radio and phonograph machine. Every week, each of us buying a record and most evenings, dancing together to Glenn Miller or Benny Goodman. To this day, I still tend to lead when I dance. When I still could dance.

Oh! And our war brides club! A bunch of us at the factory all in the same boat, husbands overseas, wives on their own. Every Wednesday, treating ourselves to a night out, going to Au Lutin Qui Bouffe one time, daringly trying frog's legs and taking turns having our photo snapped feeding the baby pig they kept on the premises. Or we'd just go to a club like the Chez Parée and drink Singapore Slings. Showing how risqué we were by going on to the Music Box at the Mount Royal Hotel and flirting with the dozens of soldiers and airmen who hung out there. In fact, that's where Maggie had met her husband. For us married women, it was safe — if a fellow got too close, you'd flash your wedding ring and point out that your husband was actually fighting the Germans, instead of hanging around waiting to. What a great feeling it was to know you were still attractive to men and you could call the shots.

Once a week, our Red Cross evenings, where a bunch of us would get together at our place to roll bandages or knit socks for the troops, sipping sherry or tea, exchanging gossip. To this day, I don't knit very well, can never maintain the right tension, probably because I laughed so much when I was knitting then. The socks I produced looked as if they were designed for Frankenstein's feet, Maggie always commenting that she hoped they were going to be sent to the Russians. And the book club once a month. Nothing too heavy, although I remember a big argument over how moral Ernest Hemingway was. Mostly books like *Gone With The Wind*, all of us siding with Scarlett.

A wonderful time. Seems terrible to describe a war that way. But at night lying in bed, part of the walnut bedroom suite that my wages had bought, covered with a candlewick bedspread, I'd slip into sleep, feeling whole. I worked hard, kept myself smart, made a home to my own liking, dined out in all the right places and answered to no one. A complete transformation. Never missing you, Ewan, nor regretting my choice a bit. Writing twice a week to Reg, he seemed farther away than England. I was in my own new country.

The only other time I felt even remotely like that was when I moved back here ten years ago. The first house I'd ever bought on my own, and I remember the sense of confidence I had signing the deed. On moving day, waiting for the furniture to arrive, I sat down by the river and thought how it had always run through my life. How far I had travelled away from it, yet somehow been tugged back. Not as the farmer's daughter who left, but as someone in my own right, gathering my life around me.

Oh! I feel as though the river is flowing through my brain right now. A strange sensation. A pressure. A rush of memory, a current of regret, even though it could not have been any other way. It washes away any other possibility. That pressure, ah, it's you, Ewan. You've come for me, I know. Pulling me into the river again, the sound of water filling my ears, making all other thoughts float away. Ah, Ewan!

# chapter 19

HELEN MOVES TOWARD DUNCAN in the darkened living room. He puts out his cigarette and runs his hands along the seductive silk of the caftan she's put on. Helen feels shy, strangely so, especially when her eyes fall onto the large sofa in front of the window, the scene of her first sexual attempt twenty-five years ago. She shivers slightly, remembering the shame, annoyed that her mother is still a factor in her sexuality.

Duncan misinterprets the shiver as one of desire and pulls her toward him. His lips on her neck and collarbone help stir her own lust, but still she feels an uneasiness that she can't quite shake, and she pulls back.

"I'm not sure she's asleep yet," she says stupidly.

Duncan hands her the brandy snifter. "And what does it matter if she's awake? Cigarette?"

Helen takes one. "I can't tell you how foolish I feel about my mother."

"Foolish? Now that's one word you should never use to describe yourself. Let other people do that."

"When I'm around her, I become someone else. Someone I don't like a lot. I act for a living, but when I'm dealing with her, I feel that I'm doing the worst acting job of my life. I can't be honest with her. It seems we never let our guard down. Although we did the other day, in Cornwall."

"Maybe it's because she's acting, too."

Helen thinks of the scene in the bedroom. "Maybe. It's hard to say. I don't feel I really know her."

"Maybe she doesn't want to be known."

"Doesn't everyone?"

"Does *anyone* really know you?"

Bernie flits across Helen's mind, accompanied by a stab of guilt. "Yes," she says, blowing out a stream of smoke and thinking of the instant rapport they had when they met. "Sometimes you only just meet someone and you click so well, you feel you've known each other all your life. You know what I mean?"

"Like you and me?"

This is just irresistible. Helen inhales so sharply, her throat burns with smoke and brandy. She reaches for Duncan at the same moment he reaches for her, and any lingering guilt or unease is pushed onto the floor by the heat spreading through her. She feels removed, not just by sex, but by a connection with Duncan. The feel of him, his taste, the sound of his breath are all an extension of her own. They are moving by instinct and everything else is forgotten until the clock on the mantle clangs, and Helen hears a heavy thud from down the hall.

"What was that?" An alarm switch has been flicked inside her.

"What was what?" Duncan is prepared to let the house collapse around them. There is a crash down the hall, the music of glass breaking, and both of them stumble off the couch, pulling on clothing, and racing down the hall.

Annie is on the floor, rigid, her mouth working like a fish.

"Oh, God! Ma! Ma! What happened?"

Annie's body spasms several times in reply. Duncan moves Helen aside, checks for Annie's pulse, watches her eyes roll back. One foot kicks rhythmically, as if at a door.

"I'll call 911," and he's up and out of the room.

Helen grabs at Annie's hand which is grasping at nothing, murmurs over and over "It's alright, Ma. We've sent for the ambulance. You're going to be all right." But Helen doesn't believe herself, pulls a blanket off the bed to wrap Annie in, tries to cradle her. "It's okay. It's okay." Annie is flopping like a mackerel in the bottom of a boat. Helen places a pillow under her mother's head and pushes the broken lamp into a corner with her foot.

Duncan is back in the room. "They're on their way. I'll go up to the road to guide them in. Okay?" Helen nods. "Are you okay? You want me to stay?"

"No ... no, meet them at the road."

The emergency room in Cornwall is all swift efficiency for Annie's case. The other people waiting for treatment look as if they live there. A young man with a carved-up face, slouched on a bench; a large woman, child asleep in her lap, fixated on the corner television set; an older woman, knitting in a chair beside an old man stretched out on a gurney; a family conferring in the corner.

Annie is hooked up to an IV, a heart monitor and a couple of other monitors, the ambulance oxygen tank removed so she can be plugged into the hospital's main oxygen supply. Helen is fearful, but the clerk is merely bored.

"Health card, please."

Helen hasn't brought it. She barely had time to pull on her sweats before the ambulance arrived. She explains to the clerk that her mother has been in this hospital before.

"I need the card. Otherwise, there can be fraud," the clerk says, chewing her gum audibly.

Who would want to be in my mother's position? Helen wonders.

"Is there someone else who could get the card?"

"At two o'clock in the morning?" Helen's stage voice soars across the waiting room.

"Bring it in tomorrow then. Mother's maiden name?"

It's the routine that keeps everyone sane, Helen realizes. She wants to scream: It's in your bloody records! But instead she fills out the forms, her hand trembling.

The staff won't let her near Annie, and their equipment makes it impossible anyway. So she drinks putrid coffee, tries to figure out what time it is in Los Angeles, decides she'll call Sean there when she knows more. As she waits, she flips through magazines that are six months old. A recipe for Mock Beef Wellington involves a pound of hamburger meat, covered in canned liver paste and rolled in Pillsbury crescent rolls. Helen's stomach rolls over.

A very young doctor comes out. "It's another stroke," she says. "On the left side of her brain this time, so it's affected her speech. We've given her a drug that's proven to be very successful in minimizing the effects of a stroke. But we won't know for hours what the damage is. Needless to say, the next twelve hours are critical."

Helen nods stupidly.

"We've taken her up to intensive care, if you want to go up. Or you can go home, try to get some sleep."

"I'll stay with her."

Entering Annie's room, one could be forgiven for thinking a space vehicle has arrived to transport Annie to the next world. The monitors are all blinking and beeping, the oxygen is wheezing, an intravenous is in one arm and a nurse is extracting blood out of the other. Electrodes are attached to her head and chest. Annie alone is still, her mouth in an expression of surprise. There is a television on above Annie's head, tuned to one of the nature channels. Helen watches as a shark tears apart a young seal.

Feeling totally useless, Helen asks the nurse, "Can I change the channel?" There isn't much on, but there doesn't seem to be a switch to turn it off. The Shopping Channel. Black and white sitcoms from the fifties with forced laugh tracks, a program on which a hostess looking like a 42nd Street hooker interviews quasi-celebrities about their pets. The hostess' dog is green. Helen turns back to the shark.

Having taken her limit of blood, the nurse leaves, and Helen pulls a chair up beside the bed, takes Annie's cold hand in hers. The tears come easily now that no one — not even Annie — can see. She whispers reassuring things to her, "You'll be all right. Just rest. I'm right here. I'm going to call Barbara and Sean. Are you comfortable? Can you hear me?"

Helen thinks she feels a slight pressure in her hand, but then recognizes that she can imagine anything. She works in theatre, a world of illusion. The nurse comes back in wheeling a lounge chair with a folded blanket on it.

"Here," she says. "Why don't you try to get some rest yourself? Your mother's been given a sedative. We'll keep an eye on her from the station," and she nods to the set of monitors set up in the middle of the ward. Mission control.

But Helen can't rest, not while the main heart monitor is dipping down to 30 then up again to 130 or 140. How can so much erratic activity be taking place in a body so still? She can't tell how much time passes, but soon the sky outside the window has pale peach streaks in it. Another nurse comes in.

"I'd like to talk to you a moment. Outside."

Helen is immediately on guard, but follows. "Is she worse?"

"No, no. About the same. But there is something we must discuss."

"Yes."

"I know it's difficult to talk about this, when you've just had this shock. But as medical staff, we have to do it. If there is another ... crisis ... another stroke or heart attack ... Do you want us to resuscitate?"

Helen stares at her. "You mean just let her die?"

The nurse has rehearsed her lines well. "We, of course, would do all we can to make her as comfortable as possible. Provide the necessities. But no extraordinary measures. Had your mother completed a Living Will?"

I'm not even certain she filled out a dead one, thinks Helen, her mind backing away from reality. "You mean do I want her put on life support, is that it?"

"She's already on a life support system," the nurse says softly. "To help her recover. I mean, do you want us to try to restart her heart if it stops?"

Helen feels her own heart has stopped. "I don't know. I mean, how bad is the stroke? Will she recover? Is it possible she will be able to speak? And tell you what she wants?"

"She cannot speak. It's been quite a damaging stroke, we know that much. We don't yet have the EEG. But her heart is very weak. We have to know what to do in case there is an immediate crisis."

"I don't know," Helen stammers.

"Take some time to think about it. I see by your mother's chart that you have siblings. Maybe you want to discuss it with them. Or with your husband."

"I don't have a husband." Helen receives her first pitying look from the nurse. She wonders where the models for all those compassionate nurses and doctors on TV come from. "What would it involve? Resuscitating her, I mean."

"It isn't pretty. We have to get a tube down her throat, then her chest is pounded to try to restart her heart. Electric paddles are used. I have to tell you, on a small woman like your mother, we sometimes break ribs." The nurse nods grimly.

"I don't think I could watch you do that."

"Don't worry. We don't let you. You're sent out of the room."

Helen thinks of how awful it would be to die like that, gagging on a tube in your last conscious moment, while someone breaks your ribs. All for your own good. At the international court in the Hague, they put people on trial for doing that. And this isn't just anyone. It's her mother.

Through tears she murmurs, "I'll think it over. Let you know."

The nurse pats her arm in acknowledgment to let Helen know she knows how hard it is, but she can't possibly care really, not if she is to go on doing this job.

Weighted by exhaustion, Helen goes back into the room where Annie lies, her mouth still open in protest. Dry, her mouth must be dry, thinks Helen and moistens her lips with water from the tap. She holds up a glass of water with a little bent straw to Annie's mouth, but Annie doesn't take any.

Hugging the blanket, Helen settles back in the lounge chair, her tears flowing freely now. This is the first time Helen has consciously contemplated the fact that her mother might die, right here and now, in front of her. Through her sorrow comes the irony that Annie's life is now in her hands. After forty years of feeling it was the other way around, she now sits there, in control while Annie lies helpless, waiting judgement. Why is there no satisfaction in this? she wonders. Because our differences have never been about power. They've been about the choices we made. And she is my mother. She thinks of the way Annie finally ruled the roost when Reg was dying, triumphing in the end, outlasting him.

\*\*\*

Helen remembers her father's death. She had two weeks off between finishing a new play in Edmonton and starting rehearsals for a Neil Simon comedy in Halifax, so she went to Montreal to help her mother nurse Reg.

"He won't eat," are Annie's first words to Helen as she came through the door.

"He has liver cancer, Mom. It's probably hard for him to eat."

Reg is seated in the living room, wearing a paisley robe, a cravat knotted at his neck. His skin has a yellow glow, and he has lost a lot of weight. What he hasn't lost is his bonhomie.

"Theda Bara," he says, a little too jovially, recalling his childhood nickname for her. "Finding time in her busy acting schedule for her old man."

"Hello, Dad." Helen embraces him, appalled at how frail he seems.

He has always been a booming presence in her life. "Sorry I couldn't make it sooner, but in my position, I can't turn down work. How are you feeling?"

"I've been better. But I'm better for seeing you. How was Edmonton?"

"Cold. But the play went over well."

"Well, we must have a drink to celebrate. Annie? Cocktails."

"You're not supposed to drink. It's bad for the liver. And you're not drinking when you're not eating." Annie with the upper hand, relishing it.

"I had an egg sandwich for lunch," Reg protests.

"Half an egg sandwich."

Here we go again, thinks Helen. He's dying and they can't call a truce. This battle has lasted longer than the Thirty Years War.

"Ma, maybe because it's a special occasion," Helen tries. "I know I could use a drink after that flight." Annie capitulates.

Helen sits on the ottoman at Reg's feet, and Annie perches on the sofa across the room while they sip their martinis.

"So when are you going to get a real job?" Reg wants to know, and Helen instantly regrets backing him up on the drink issue. It's an old line of his. She will no longer snap at the bait.

"Do you have much pain?"

"No worse than sampling some of your mother's cooking." Annie leaves the room in a huff, off to cook dinner for an ungrateful husband. As soon as she's gone, Reg stage-whispers, "You got any cigarettes?"

"Dad, they're not good for you." She is used to smoking out on the front steps in her parents' house.

"Nothing's good for me anymore," Reg says, matter-of-factly. "What difference can one smoke possibly make?" He grins tightly.

Helen realizes that he knows he's dying, and that he has accepted it. It shocks her. Reg has never been too fond of grim reality. Although she has mentally registered that Reg will not recover, up until this moment she hadn't absorbed it emotionally. She fumbles in her purse for her cigarettes, to hide the tears filling her eyes.

"Open the window so your mother won't know," Reg stage-whispers again.

Throughout dinner and the rest of the evening, Helen observes how the balance between her parents has tilted in favour of her mother. Annie refuses to serve Reg his dinner until he has taken his pills. When he leaves the brussels sprouts and part of a pork chop, Annie says, "If you ate more, you'd have more strength."

Reg, who has had to lean on Helen to get to the table, says, "I have as much strength as I need right now."

"Easy for you to say, but I'm the one who has to help lift you and get you into the bath."

"Well, I suppose I could give up bathing," at which Annie snorts.

Helen has never understood why her parents didn't divorce, especially after divorce became commonplace and she, the last of the children, had left home. She'd harboured the idea that her parents got along better after the kids were gone, that they had drifted into a more mellow old age together. In the two weeks she is there, she sees what a fantasy that is. Annie, at sixty-eight is still vibrant, quick in her movements, looking ten years younger than she is. That she now has to look after her ailing husband when she should be enjoying her retirement is just one more example of life's unfairness, which she has always chafed against.

Once Reg is put to bed, Helen and Annie drink their coffee in the living room.

"Did the doctor say how long he might have?" Helen asks as gently as possible.

"Two months, maybe more if it hasn't metastasized. He'd last longer if he obeyed the doctor's orders." Annie's lip begins to quake. "But he'll never do what he's supposed to do."

"Do you ever think that he might not want to last longer?"

"Life is a gift. You're supposed to make the most of it. He even refused chemotherapy."

"But that would only have slowed the disease, right?"

"It's just like him to take the difficult way. He's always been trouble." Annie fusses with a handkerchief in her pocket.

"He won't trouble you too much longer, Ma. And I'll come back to help out when I'm finished in Halifax."

Annie pats Helen's hand. "You're a good girl, Helen, when you choose to be."

Helen doesn't feel as if she has chosen anything. She merely feels weighted, immobilized by the recurring game her parents have trapped her in.

During her stay, as she watches Reg steadily decline, having to stop to rest twice instead of once as he climbs the stairs, Helen tries to find a new closeness with him. After she arranges him in his chair in the morning, she pulls up the ottoman, asks him about his past, his and Annie's past, her own past. She is looking for clues to explain the impasse, but Reg reveals none.

"What was it like in the war, Dad?"

"Piece of cake, really. A lot of fun. Spent more time in the English pubs than I ever did in the air."

"But it must have been frightening on some level. You could have been killed. Lots were."

"Oh, you don't think about that. Not if you're smart. Let's see what's on TV." Reg looks over Helen's shoulder. But Helen doesn't quit easily.

"Did you marry Mom because you were about to be shipped overseas?"

"No. I married your mother because she was the smartest, prettiest little thing around. And the only way I was going to get any closer to her was if I married her, if you know what I mean. You know your mother."

Helen nods. She knows how her mother views a woman's so-called most precious commodity. "But you wanted to marry her?"

"Ah! I was ready. People get married when they're ready to." He sighs. "I think it must be time for those girls on the *20 Minute Workout.*"

As Helen leaves the room, Reg is glued to the set, watching three sets of firm buttocks pumping while a female voice with a southern accent urges them to do "Three more, two more, one more and again."

\*\*\*

By the time Helen is back from Halifax, Reg is bedridden, almost mute, what few words he says slurred by massive doses of morphine. Annie has the visiting homemaker stay with Reg while she takes Helen shopping for something appropriate to wear to the funeral. Annie already has plans for her widowhood. There are travel pamphlets and real estate agent cards in the den, and Annie has sent three bags full of Reg's clothes to the Salvation Army. Annie has always masked her feelings with activity, and Helen tries to gauge her mother's true state of mind.

As they have a martini in the living room, Helen says, "It shouldn't be too much longer now, Ma."

"No, any day, the doctor says. Although his heart's still strong. Poor man." She sips her drink. "Poor Reg, he deserved a better ending than this." Annie sounds detached.

"How are you doing, Ma? You holding up? I know this has been hard on you."

"He wants to die at home. I'm seeing to it that he gets his wish."

Helen thinks of the many times Annie would have gone out of her way to do the opposite of what Reg wished for. She realizes some sort of acceptance, if not reconciliation, has taken place in the six weeks she's been gone.

Reg quietly dies eight days later, without protest, without a trace of his former self surfacing. Annie wears a new navy blue suit to the funeral, dabbing her eyes, but holding up very well.

\*\*\*

Helen finally dozes in the hospital lounge chair and the next thing she is aware of is a new team of nurses bustling in, turning Annie onto one side. "Prevents bedsores," one of the nurses explains as they change the IV, change Annie's diaper, record the readings on the various monitors.

"Breakfast is here. Would you like some?" one of the nurses asks.

"Yes, thank you. But what about her, my mother? How will she eat?"

The nurse gently says, "She's being fed intravenously. Have you decided on the DNR?"

"The DNR?"

"Do not resuscitate," the nurse nods.

"Right. Yes, well, give me a moment."

Helen finds a pay phone in the hall and calls Barbara, praying she hasn't left for Germany yet.

After several rings she hears, "Hello?"

"Barbara, it's Helen."

"My God, Helen, it's only seven thirty. You're up early. You got me out of the shower."

"It's Mom, Barbara. She's had another stroke. A bad one. She can't speak."

"Oh, no."

"I'm in the intensive care ward in Cornwall. She might not make it."

"Oh, why does everything have to happen at once? I have a meeting with a new client at nine. And I'm due to fly out to Germany tomorrow."

Helen feels her face redden in anger. "Well, I'm sorry it's not convenient for you, Barbara. If Mom had only known, I'm sure she would have chosen another time to die!" An orderly walking by in the hall turns around at the sound of Helen's voice.

"You think she's going to die?" Barbara's voice has assumed a little-girl quality.

"They've asked me to decide whether or not she is to be resuscitated if her heart gives out. And I don't know what to say, Barbara." Helen's voice is now loud with anguish.

"Is she conscious? Can you talk to her?"

"She can't speak. As far as I can see, she can't even move. Barbara, what do I tell them?"

"Gee, I don't know. I guess you'd better do what you think is right, Helen. I mean, you're the only one there to assess the situation."

"I'm the only one who's been here all along. Sorry to have disturbed your shower."

"Helen, listen! Don't be so goddamn snotty. Give me time to think. Look! Where can I reach you? I'll call you back after my meeting. See what the situation is. Can you get some sort of prognosis out of the doctor by then?"

"I have no idea." Helen is exhausted. She gives Barbara the number of the nursing station and hangs up. Alone. I'm so alone, she thinks, then pulls herself together. You've been alone all your life, she tells herself.

Her next call wakes up Sean's latest girlfriend in Los Angeles, who doesn't even know that Sean has a sister, let alone two. The girlfriend tells Helen that Sean is either in Pittsburgh or Philadelphia, she isn't sure which, but she expects he'll call sometime today, and he should be flying back tomorrow, when they are going down to Baja California for a few days. The woman sounds dumb, but Helen reminds herself that she was asleep. She resists asking her how old she is.

"This is a family emergency. My mother may be dying. Is there a hotel in either Pittsburgh or Philadelphia where I could reach Sean?"

The woman giggles. "You know Sean. Mr. Mystery. Plays it close to the chest. I really like that in him, though. It's liberating, you know?"

"It's mind-boggling." Helen gives her the nursing station number and begs her to call the airline, Sean's children, anyone who may know where he is.

"Okay," the woman says. "You stay cool, now, you hear? You're in some rough water there, I can tell by your voice. I'm with you, Elaine. Stay cool."

Helen hangs up, chuckling, giddy with fatigue. But I'm cool, she tells herself, heading back to Annie's room. I'm cool.

Annie has her eyes open, and they flicker when Helen comes in. The effort causes all the monitors to go wild, so that a nurse comes in and looks at the monitors worriedly. The nurse leaves, and Helen moves to the side of the bed, with Annie's eyes following her. Holding Annie's hand, she says quietly, "It's me, Helen, Ma. Can you hear me?"

No response. Annie's eyes focus on a place beyond Helen's shoulder.

"Ma? If you can hear me, let me know. Squeeze my hand."

Still no response, although Annie's lips quiver.

"You'd be better off with the other hand," says another nurse, coming in to look at the monitors. She checks Annie's pulse.

Helen takes Annie's other hand, which twitches when she puts pressure on it. Annie's breathing is laboured, as if she is attempting a great task. Which in a way she is, Helen realizes, her eyes brimming again.

"Squeeze my hand if you can hear me."

The hand jitters, but not so that Helen can definitively say that Annie has connected with her. Annie's eyes seem dazed, and they continue to wander. A weak cry comes from her throat, and Helen begins to lean forward to listen, just as the nurse pulls her back, presses the button on the wall and says, "I think you better wait outside for a moment."

*chapter 20*

So much confusion. No idea where I am. Green walls and someone's here, someone I recognize, holding my hand in an old familiar way. So much swirling in my head. Light and dark.

Nothing seems to work. Like one of those dreams where you try to run, but you can't, like your shoes are stuck in quicksand. Trying to speak, but nothing comes out. Mouth moving, but no sound. Can't hear anything over the running-water sound, the rushing of water, torrents of water through my head, all going where?

Who's holding my hand? Reg? Ewan! Should have known it would be you. You look different, as if your head is lit from within. Your hand. Not at all calloused, the way it used to be. But that old connection is still there, isn't it? Why won't you speak? It's alright, I don't seem to be able to either, and we've never needed words to convey our feelings anyway, have we? A lot I need to tell you. You never knew about Helen, never knew you had another daughter. Never knew how much you meant to me. Never knew ... Ah, there's time. Right now, this moment has its own rhythm. I can feel it becoming stronger, through your hand. I am whole, calm, even happy, because what is missing in me is made up for by you, my other half, the other glove, the piece of china that makes the place setting complete.

So much time spent fussing about things. Place settings. Cars. The right dress. You remind me of what really matters, Ewan. Rain must fall so crops can grow. Cows have to be milked, twice a day. Children come into the world, and because of that, part of who you are is lost, because you must look after them. Another part emerges. You go on, absorbing loss. Then someone holds your hand and you realize that it's really all you need.

So much water, flooding all around. And you trying to lead me into the flood. So tempting, to just float in the liquid pleasure of it, feel it lift me up and carry me, the way I've always wanted to be carried, lightly so I can still move, still do what I want, but know that there's this great force holding me, supporting me. That the touch of someone else's hand — the right person's hand — can convey all that.

Ready now. I can feel your tug, the flow of the water gaining strength, roaring now, buoying us over the rocks, through the rapids, the water boiling white, ready to deliver me, ready. Yes, now.

## chapter 21

AFTER THE NURSE CAME TO TELL HER, Helen stayed with Annie for the hour and a half it took for a doctor to come and pronounce her dead. Annie's mouth was still open, eyes still dazed. A hospital social worker came along with a nun to guide Helen into a room where she made the phone calls — to Barbara's answering service, to Sean's bimbo, now fully awake and informing Helen that her mother had joined the "cosmic ether." The funeral director arrived, and Mrs. Forbes was called. After being reassured that Annie's second stroke had nothing to do with their game of cribbage, Mrs. Forbes undertook to call all of Annie's local friends. There were calls to old friends in Montreal, to the local minister, the details repeated over and over, a mantra to mark Annie's passing. The final call did her in. Bernie was not there, and when the answering machine came on, all Helen could say is, "She's dead, Bernie. She's dead. And I never did tell her ... never really talked to her ... Oh, God, I'm sorry. Call me. Please."

The social worker took the phone from her hand, suggested she rest and asked if she had any friends in the area. Helen thought of Duncan but had no idea where to contact him. He seemed very far away, belonging to another part of her existence.

It is past noon when Helen finally makes it back to Annie's house. She stands in the living room, the same thoughts circling in her head that swooped in as soon as they told her: I should have been there with her. No one should die alone. Alone. She wonders why that word carries such weight. She has never felt more isolated in her entire life than she does right now. Annie feared being alone more than anything else on earth, Helen remembers. Or is it me that fears that? But I have always been alone.

Helen goes to the mantle and strokes the mahogany surface of the clock, hoping its steady metre will steady her. There is so much to do. So much she has already done.

Helen sleeps for an hour or more before the phone wakens her.

"Helen, I'm so sorry," Barbara says. "I'm so sorry you had to be there on your own."

Helen is groggy. "At least it was quick, Barbara. Not like Dad." There is a pause, while they both remember the months of Reg shrinking.

"I'm catching the six o'clock train. Trevor and the children will come tomorrow in the car. Can you meet the train?"

"I thought Trevor had to go to Germany."

"He'll fly out of Montreal after the funeral. We'll all be there."

Now, thinks Helen. They'll all come now. When she's dead. When I can go.

"Helen?" Barbara continues. "Have you finalized the funeral arrangements? Can you meet the train?"

Helen wants to giggle over the redundancy of "finalizing" a funeral. It certainly isn't tentative. "The funeral director's taken her body, I'm ... we're to go by tomorrow to select a coffin, bring her clothes. We've talked about the funeral for sometime Monday, but I was waiting to hear from you and Sean to see what you want."

"Good, I thought that at least in the arrangements, I could be useful. As a professional, I mean."

Yes, thinks Helen. Now what wood would go well with death? Will the flowers have to be colour coordinated? We wouldn't want Annie's dress to clash with the coffin silk, would we?

"Have you heard from Sean?"

"No. Apparently he's in Pittsburgh or Philadelphia, according to his latest girlfriend. I've asked her to try to reach him, but I don't think she's too motivated."

"Is the girlfriend Charity somebody?"

"Verity, she said her name was."

"Must be the same one. She's an aromatherapist."

"She sounds as if she's still in high school."

"Can you meet the train, Helen? Otherwise I'm sure I could get a taxi or whatever. I know you've been through a lot."

Yes, I have, thinks Helen. "Of course I'll meet the train. Gets in about ten, doesn't it? I'll check. It'll be good to have you here."

"I guess we only have each other now," Barbara says, her voice breaking.

Helen has barely had time to plug in the kettle when there is a knock on the door. Three women with ice-cream-coloured bouffant hairstyles are there, with stacks of Tupperware between them.

"I'm Irma MacLaughlin," says one, placing a covered tray of sandwiches on the kitchen table. "I went to school with your mother, poor woman. These are egg salad, ham salad, liver paste and chicken salad. I'm real sorry about Annie."

There are cookies, a lasagna, a carrot cake, an arrangement of vegetables and dip and the ubiquitous Swedish meat balls. Helen is amazed that these women have organized and delivered the food so quickly. Do international relief organizations know about rural matrons as a resource? She thanks the women, invites them for tea, tries to memorize which name belongs to which woman — Doris, Edith, Irma. They decline the tea.

"You must have so much to do. We feel for you in your loss. She was a grand woman, your mother," says Edith, and they're gone as abruptly as they arrived.

A call from Sylvia, Sean's second wife, the only one Helen could ever relate to, is next.

"Sean's latest little girl called me to tell me about your poor mother," Sylvia says, her soft southern accent having a soothing effect. "Was it sudden, honey?"

Helen recounts the past months since Annie's first stroke.

"Y'know, that brother of yours never even mentioned anything to the kids or me. My Gawd, he must be getting worse."

"He tried to pretend nothing had happened, Sylvia. You know what he's like. Few of us improve as we get older." It feels good to be able to trash Sean with someone who understands him.

"Nevertheless," Sylvia draws out the word so that it has at least five syllables, "I'm trying to teach the kids to be a little more responsible than he is."

"They shouldn't have far to go. How are my little niece and nephew, although I guess they are not too little anymore?"

"Jason is six foot two and still growing even though he's now in college. His pants keep gettin' too short, which is terrible at eighteen, don't you think?"

Americans have always struck Helen as being too tall. "If he's still growing at thirty, cut back on the vitamins." As she says this, she chokes. It's the idea of growth that stops her.

"Sue Ann and I are comin' up," Sylvia announces. "We got us a flight out of Atlanta tomorrow. Thank Gawd for Sean's pass. The only good thing he ever did for me. You heard from him yet?"

"No. I'm going to call the girlfriend back tonight. Listen, it's very sweet of you, Sylvia, but it's a long way to come for the funeral of your ex-mother-in-law. You sure you want to come?"

"Hell," says Sylvia, "I always liked your momma and in fact your whole family. So do the kids. It was your brother I couldn't stand. Now don't worry about puttin' us up or anythin', honey. We've got us a hotel and we'll look after ourselves. We'll be there. After all, we're family."

Helen takes a moment to consider the evolution of that word in recent times. "It'll be good to see you, Sylvia. And Sue Ann." She hangs up the phone. My family, she sighs, moving toward the kettle. She thinks of Sean, Barbara and herself. Maybe we were all abducted by aliens at birth and programmed to dysfunction. No, she remembers. The dysfunction came from Reg and Annie, and it doesn't matter any more. Make the tea. Meet the train. One step at a time.

*chapter 22*


IT IS AFTER TEN IN THE MORNING when Helen wakes up. She has slept for a long time, but the lift into consciousness is quickly torpedoed by the events of the past thirty-six hours. When Barbara arrived the previous night, she had with her a list of things to be done between then and the funeral, with little boxes to be checked beside each item. She had a timetable, a task list for both herself and Helen, a suggested menu for the post-funeral reception, a list of people to be called and a list of items she wanted from Annie's house. Barbara handed Helen her task list as they were driving home. Helen, keeping one hand on the wheel, took the list and without looking at it, ate it. Even chewed up, the paper was hard to swallow, but it was well worth the look on Barbara's face.

"I'm only trying to help," Barbara had said. "You don't have to be so childish."

Once back at Annie's, Helen took her brandy down to the river, realizing Duncan would be long gone for the evening, but hopeful that he had heard about Annie's death from others. In a small community, a death is big news, the equivalent of the discovery of the Dead Sea Scrolls. She sat on the dock and, for the first time, felt the absence of Annie, felt the absence of knowing Annie had always been there for her, even though it hadn't been in the ways Helen needed. I'm an orphan, Helen thought, looking up into a black sky that had never seemed so immense before. She felt a heaviness descend upon her, the full weight of self-reliance, made even worse by the uneasiness she felt about Duncan's absence. Where is he?

Now Helen closes her eyes and rolls over, but the sound of the telephone, and Barbara's bright voice answering it, pulls her back. Wrapping herself in her flannel housecoat, she finds Barbara at the kitchen table, dressed and in full makeup, the phone and her lists in front of her, the coffee machine gently hissing behind her.

"Ah, good morning. I was about to go in and wake you. I turned the ringer down so it wouldn't disturb you earlier. I figured you needed the sleep."

"I guess. Thank you." Helen's eyes are heavy. She has never been a morning person; just acknowledging another's presence required the entire extent of her verbal skills at that time of the day. Luckily, Bernie is the same way, so that on days when they are both in the kitchen at the same time, they communicate in one-word sentences — "Coffee?" "Juice?" "Sports?" "Cigarette?" "Working?" — followed by a nod or a shrug.

"Now I've set up an appointment with the undertaker for 11:15, to select the coffin and whatever type of service we want and so on. Do you think that outfit would be right for her?" Barbara points to a dress and jacket which Helen has never seen before, draped over a chair.

"That one of Mom's?"

"No, it's something I picked up on my way to the station yesterday. Mom always liked strong colours but I don't think they would be appropriate in the circumstances."

Helen thinks about the bulging cupboard in Annie's room and the acres of clothes downstairs. Annie as she wanted to be seen. It doesn't matter now. "Whatever you think."

"The cost of the outfit can come from the estate, as part of the funeral expenses. Anyway, then we can go to the bank before our appointment with Mr. Currie at 1:30."

"Mr. Currie?"

"The lawyer, Helen. About her will. Honestly, you'd think that since you have power of attorney, you'd be more aware of these things."

"I didn't want power of attorney, remember? You were the one who said it was logical, since I was here." Helen shuffles over to the coffee pot, trying to get up to speed. "Have you heard from Sean?"

"Yes! He called at about nine o'clock. He'll be here this afternoon, driving down from Dorval. He isn't bringing the teeny-bop with him."

"Good."

Helen would pay anything to have ten minutes of silent inactivity, to sit out on the deck in the sun and wait for the caffeine to kick in. She is shuffling in that direction when Barbara says, "She did make a will, didn't she? After Dad died?"

"Yes."

"Have you read it? Is it in order?"

"It's in the safety deposit box in the bank. I've never looked at it."

Barbara snorts at this. "Really, Helen! You and your artistic temperament! I do wish you'd be more practical, especially where other people are involved."

And I do wish you'd shut up, just for a few moments, thinks Helen, continuing in the direction of the back door.

"Don't you think you should have a shower and get ready? We have to leave in less than an hour. Let me whip up some breakfast for you. Eggs, or are you a cereal person?"

"I'm a never-eat-before-you're-awake person. And I'm going to sit in the garden until I finish this cup of coffee. After which I will prepare myself for the day's events," Helen says in her best Stratford accent. "No more chat for ten minutes." And she's out the door.

By 1:30, Helen is starving, not having eaten anything, ready to eat another of Barbara's lists as they sit in Mr. Currie's office. Barbara offers her a half package of mints and she puts all that are left in her mouth. The session at the funeral home took longer than expected, with Barbara questioning whether the mahogany coffin should be that much more expensive than the oak, while dismissing the plain pine number Helen had her eye on. The discussion of a silk lining versus a rayon one took even longer, as did the merits of an "Eternity Package" which required placement in a lead-lined container. The arrangements would have gone on longer had Helen not said, "Listen, Barbara. Any money you're going to spend on the funeral will mean less for us from the estate. You realize that, don't you?" The oak casket with a pale peach rayon lining to match Annie's new outfit, and without a lead lining, was quickly selected.

Mr. Currie comes in, offering condolences, remembering Annie as a fine woman, a slim file folder under his arm.

"Ah! You are familiar with the will?" he says.

"No," Helen replies. "It's in the safety deposit box. We didn't have time to get to the bank. Are you the executor?"

Mr. Currie seems surprised by Helen's lack of knowledge. "Yes, I am co-executor. Along with yourself."

"Me?" Helen looks at Barbara, who tries to hide her disapproval of the arrangement. "But I don't know anything about ... wills. I find it tricky to pay my phone bill on time."

Mr. Currie smiles. "I'll attend to all the legal arrangements and tell you all you need to know."

"I live in Toronto, you know."

"So I've heard. You both do, don't you?" He smiles at Barbara.

"The Beaches," Barbara smiles back. "And the details of the will?"

"Well, your mother made provisions for her funeral arrangements, you probably know that, and asked to be buried in the local St. Andrew's churchyard. She bought a plot there just last year."

The two sisters look at each other, and Barbara speaks. "But she has a plot next to our father, in Mount Royal Cemetery in Montreal. Are you sure?"

"Please check your own copy of the will."

"Why would she do that?" Barbara wants to know.

Helen smiles ruefully. "She was happy here, until the stroke happened, of course. She was never very happy with Dad."

"Helen!" Barbara doesn't think this is appropriate information for Mr. Currie's ears.

"Okay, she was afraid her grave would be ransacked by Quebec nationalists?" Helen finds she's becoming quite good at handling Barbara.

"What other surprises do you have for us, Mr. Currie?" Barbara asks brightly.

"Well now, her total estate, aside from her house, which is paid for, and its contents, comes to about $134,000." Helen whistles, and receives another critical look from Barbara. "Dad must have finally learned to invest against the advice of his cronies," Helen says anyway.

"Deducting the funeral expenses, probate costs and my fee," Mr. Currie continues, "That leaves about $110,000 to be divided equally between you two and your brother."

Helen quickly calculates what improvements $36,000 could make on her house. "I can get the roof done," she says to no one. "Put the rest into a retirement thingy."

"Then there's the money from the sale of the house," Barbara says. Helen is still considering the windfall she never anticipated.

"Well," says Mr. Currie. "Now each of you — the two of you and your brother — are to have whatever of your mother's personal effects and furniture you want. If a dispute arises, with both of you wanting the same object, a coin is to be tossed." Helen smiles at the whimsy of this, before Mr. Currie continues. "The house is to go to you, Helen, to dispose of as you wish."

"What?" Barbara can't believe her ears.

"Again, I would refer you to your own copy of the will. Your mother specified, 'In that my son Sean and daughter Barbara both own a considerable amount of property and have careers which pay handsomely, and in that my daughter Barbara is married to a man of means, I wish my youngest daughter Helen to inherit my house, to provide her with some financial security which her career in the arts does not afford her.'"

Helen and Barbara are both stunned, but from opposite emotions. "I have children to educate," is Barbara's first response. Helen is totally unprepared, especially considering the type of financial conversations she'd had with her parents over the years.

\*\*\*

Helen is driving up to Montreal to let Reg and Annie know that her marriage is over, that she's moved out to a small apartment. It's hard enough even to think about it, to explain it to herself, let alone to her parents. She's cruising on Elavil antidepressants, shouldn't even be driving, going too fast through a brilliant autumn day. But she feels the separation won't be a reality until she faces Reg and Annie.

"I'm sorry to hear that, Helen," is Reg's reaction, mixing martinis for all in the living room. He shakes his head, "Aren't you ever going to really settle down?"

"Listen to who's talking," Annie chimes in, bringing in some seafood canapés she's made. "You've never grown up. Why do you think your kids should be any different?"

"Now Annie, I've held a job. Provided for you and the kids. Well, I might add. All I'm saying, is that Helen should take some responsibility for herself." They are talking about Helen as if she weren't right there in the room.

"I *am* responsible. It just hasn't worked. Guy and I are just very different people, with very different values." Helen feels all her inner resolve disappearing. She is the errant child again. Why, oh why didn't she just write to them?

Annie sits beside Helen, pats her arm. "Are you asking him for support?"

"No! I wouldn't get it anyway. I'm capable of working. He's already balking at giving me my share of the house."

"Well, he pays the mortgage," says Reg, swirling the contents of his cocktail glass.

Helen rallies. "My name is on the mortgage. And the deed to the house. I've never made as much money as Guy, but I contributed everything I earned." She realizes her voice is quavering slightly. Mixing Elavil with alcohol is a very bad idea.

"How do you propose to support yourself?" Reg wants to know. Helen feels as if she has no support at all, not emotional, physical or financial.

Annie leans forward confidentially. "Are you getting counselling? You know, for your nerves?"

"I'm fine, Mom, really."

"I want to know if you've really tried to make this work," Reg says, pacing the floor. "Have you seen a marriage counsellor?"

"Yes. It didn't seem to help much. It just highlighted our differences." Helen recalls sitting in Stella Weizman's office, Stella smiling and asking them each to remember one small thing they really liked about the other, one endearing characteristic. "Oh Christ!" was Guy's reply.

"How long have you been trying to work this out?" Reg seems to be a tiger for process.

Helen feels whipped, but she presses on. "Why are you so eager that we work this out? You never seemed to be too fond of Guy. At one point you called him a jumped-up little prick."

Reg nods. "He could be a jumped-up prick. But I thought he was good for you."

This is news. "Good for me? In what sense?"

"He kept you in line." Reg's words are a noose tightening around Helen's neck. She excuses herself and runs upstairs, hearing Annie say, "Couldn't you save the Inquisition? Can't you see that she's upset?"

Kept me in line, Helen thinks. Like I was some delinquent, a crazed dog, a circus animal in need of a benign keeper. She shakes her head slowly. Over the years she has come to see Guy as a benign keeper, too.

She couldn't wait to leave the zoo.

After several minutes, Annie comes upstairs, ostensibly to announce that dinner will be ready in about ten minutes. She sits beside Helen, pats her hand.

"I once left your father, you know. Before you were born, when Sean was still a baby. Took him and Barbara back to the farm, told my parents that my marriage was over, that it had been a mistake."

"I didn't know that. What happened?"

Annie gives out a small puff of air. "Nothing happened. Your grandparents were of the 'You made your bed, you lie in it' school. My father put us on the next train back to Montreal. Your father hardly even had time to read the note I'd left." She pauses. "We didn't have too many choices back then. We made the best of it. And of course, there were you kids to consider. But you ..."

"What about me, Mom?" Helen wants to keep Annie open, to keep her talking.

"You know what's best, I suppose." She pats Helen again. "Don't pay any attention to your father. You know I never have." She gives a little sigh. "You do what's best for you. I'm going to get dinner on the table."

Helen hears the sounds of plates, pots and pans being positioned. Also Annie saying, "Don't you think you've had enough, Reg?" They made the best of it, she thinks, then stifles a giggle. The best. My God, what would the worst have been like?

\*\*\*

"Well, of course, she's allowed to leave the house to whoever she likes," says Barbara, her voice brittle, "But I know our father wanted the state divided equally. And after all, it was he who earned the money."

"Mom earned every penny of her share, Barbara. We both know that," Helen says quietly, her tears starting. Barbara sits up straighter, recognizing she has revealed more than she wanted to in front of the lawyer. Helen continues, "I think that house meant more to her than real estate. We can talk about the arrangements later."

Mr. Currie straightens his papers, then rises. "It'll take me a few days to sort things out and there'll be some papers to sign. I'll get the copies of the death certificates we need from the funeral home and call when you need to come in. I am very sorry for your loss," he adds leading them to the door.

"We'd better get to the safety deposit box before the bank closes," Barbara says on the way out.

"We'd better get to the chip stand before I faint," Helen counters, suddenly more eager to assert herself.

*chapter 23*

THE MORNING AFTER THE FUNERAL, Helen sits at the kitchen table, drinking coffee, surrounded by the remnants of the wake. She feels the coffee hit her stomach, join the other gallons she has drunk in the past three days, turning her stomach into slow-burning stew. She lights a cigarette even though she knows it will make the stew worse. Only the dishwasher chugging in the corner disrupts the morning silence. Scenes from the past few days wash into Helen's head like waves.

The arrival of Sylvia and Sue Ann, a tall stalk of a girl with sunflower hair, bearing armloads of flowers.

"How you doin', honey-child?" is Sylvia's greeting and her soft southern voice pours like caramel over the other mourners at the funeral home. She charms the locals, making them smile by referring to them as Precious, Dear Heart and Angel Heart. The only one who isn't charmed is Sean, when she corners him after the funeral to demand two months of child support he still owes from last year.

The funeral itself. There was a good crowd, an amazing number of people who remembered Annie from sixty years ago — neighbours who used to farm down the road, old friends who went to school with her and folks who had known Gordon and Alma. The minister reads the scriptural passages Helen and Barbara have selected, beginning with "The Lord is good at animal husbandry" and going on with other tortured phrases before Helen realizes this is supposed to be the 23rd Psalm. In reading Ecclesiastes, the minister drones "A time to plant and a time to pluck up what is planted." Helen has some insight as to why the church may be losing members. The plain text Bible? Well then, how about "a time to harvest what has been planted" or "reap what has been planted"? Who says "pluck up what is planted"? She thinks of all those people who have "improved" Shakespeare, insisting that he was a cool dude, composing songs out of his verses, the songs he presumably didn't have time to write. Her indignation keeps her sorrow at bay during the service.

But no amount of mangled words or sprays of flowers can hide the raw reality of the empty rectangle of earth in the cemetery, ready to swallow a life. The earth walls are so unrelentingly solid, as is the casket, that they smother the flurry of memories sifting through Helen's mind. She feels a hollowness far greater than the grave. It's Sean who saves her.

"Why isn't she being buried beside Dad?"

"I don't know. It's in her will. She bought this plot just last year."

"That means there's a spare plot beside Dad. You might want to consider joining him, Helen." Sean gives her a nudge.

"Looks like you'll have to be cremated, Sean, so that each ex-wife can get a piece of you."

"None of them liked it much when I did give them a piece of me," Sean retorts and Helen has to giggle, is still muffling giggles, disguising them as sobs, when the minister says his "Ashes to ashes, dust to dust" speech, mercifully keeping to the original text. The thud of earth clods being tossed on the casket brings her back to her great sense of loss.

Back at the house after the funeral, the kitchen is filled to capacity with Tupperware containing mountains of squares, dyed green and pink sandwiches, casseroles and homemade pickles with names like Slippery Jacks, Harvest Medley and Special Crunch. Helen is aware she is in one of the last places on earth where people cut the crusts off white bread sandwiches. Annie's friends have brought a coffee urn from the church as well as their own silver teapots and are making coffee and tea. Sean forces a small tumbler of sherry on each of them.

An anxious presence for Helen is Megan, Barbara's anorexic daughter, whose body is all sharp angles, her jaw looking as if it might break through her skin. She is hauntingly pale, listless, and she moves like a giraffe. Helen watches her pick up a pickle, nibble at it then put it down. She moves on to the desserts, pressing her fingers into the crumbs around a cake, brushing them on her lips.

But when Helen puts an arm around her shoulders and says, "How're you doing Sweetie?" Megan brightens, in fact over-brightens.

"I'm fine, really. Fine!" she says, then realizes her role. "Of course, I'll miss Grandma."

"So will I, Sweetie. So will I. You know, she always said she wanted to live to dance at your wedding. Looks like I'll have to take her place." Megan smiles wanly.

Later, thinks Helen. I must try to have a word with her later.

At one point the kitchen door opens, and haloed against the light, like a Sunday School picture of Jesus, is Bernie. The locals stare as if they have never seen a Black man before.

"Sorry I missed the funeral," he says, pressing Helen's head against his shoulder. "Worked until three this morning and needed some sleep before I drove down." Helen is so glad to see him, she starts crying all over again, introducing him to everyone between snuffles. Even after the introductions, some of the village women continue to stare.

"It's alright, I'm used to it," Bernie says tersely when Helen takes him aside to apologize for their behaviour. "Good thing I didn't wear my leopard-skin thong." But he is awkward, sullen and tries returning the stares, long years of race and class differences being played out. He finds solace in the sandwiches, muttering to Helen, "Who ever thought of putting cheese, pickles, tuna and mayonnaise in the same sandwich?" He has lived all his life in Canada, travelled across the whole country and met scores of well-meaning people who smile too broadly and ask him if he is from The Islands. "Yes!" he replies. "The best one — Cape Breton." Helen recognizes that most of the time she has spent with Bernie it has been just the two of them, and sometimes Jed. He is always so easy with Helen that she has forgotten how closed he can be with strangers.

Only after the friends have left and the members of the family have taken off their shoes and ties does Helen allow Bernie to pour her a drink and take her outside, down to the river. Barbara is busy tidying, replacing the extra chairs. She has already taken Sean aside to discuss the lopsided will. Sean just shrugged. "Hey! Maybe the old lady was right. Helen needs the money more than we do. And she's the one who looked after her."

Bernie and Helen settle down by the collapsing dock.

"I'm sorry I wasn't here for you when your Momma died," Bernie says, shaking out a cigarette for Helen.

"It was sudden, Bernie. She could have gone on for years, the doctor said after her first stroke. No one really expected it to happen when it did so there's no way *you* could have planned for it. Besides, I know the show biz tradition. The only funeral an actor can miss a show for is his own."

"I'm not an actor. But I do like a paycheque. And I can't stand to see a director cry."

"How is it going?"

"Terrible. The set, when I left it, was, in the words of the designer, 'A post-apocalyptic medieval fortress jungle gym.' The actors have to leap a hurdle to exit stage right." Bernie shakes his head. "Maybe it's a comedy after all."

They smile, and each silently remembers the disastrous productions they have been involved in. Bernie breaks the spell with, "So, how're you doing?"

In a small voice Helen answers, "I should have been there with her. They sent me out of the room. She was alone with strangers. And if there was one thing she hated, it was being alone. I should have been there."

Bernie holds her, rocks her. "She knew you were there, my dear. So tell me what happened."

Helen repeats the now familiar series of events, leaving out Duncan, even though she is sitting in the spot where she first met him. Although Duncan has hovered uneasily in the back of her mind for the past few days, his absence unnerving her further, he is not someone she can talk to Bernie about.

"Sure is a pretty place your Momma picked." Bernie smiles at the bushes, tosses a stone into the river.

Helen swallows, straightens herself. "She's left it to me, Bernie. Just me. The house, the property. That was quite a surprise."

"I guess. How are your brother and sister taking that?"

"Brother doesn't care. Sister does. Big time."

The sun is sinking behind the trees, bringing out swoops of birds preparing to settle down for the night. "So you're now owner of a city and a country property," Bernie says, looking around. "If you're not careful, you'll become middle class."

Helen smiles at her new status. "She left me some money, too. I'm not sure I can take the security."

"You can handle it. You gonna keep this place?"

Helen hasn't considered that yet. "I don't know Bernie. These past few months, I haven't dared look into the future. This area has its attractions," is all she says, hunched over her drink, protective of it, hoping it will erase the fatigue.

"I have to go right back to Toronto," Bernie says softly. "They're still playing with that frigging set."

Helen turns and hugs his legs. "You shouldn't have come all this way just for me. I'd have understood."

Bernie's a bit abashed. "I had to come. See if you're alright."

"I'm alright. Or I'm going to be." Helen tries to hide her disappointment. "You'd better get going."

Bernie stands and kisses the top of her head. "You look after yourself, Schweik. Remember I'm at the end of the telephone. And come home soon."

After seeing Bernie off, Helen comes back down to gaze at the silken surface of the river. Immediately she thinks of Duncan, the thought causing a backflip in her groin. She is hurt that he didn't come to the funeral. Surely he had heard about the death through his relatives. Everyone else in the village was there; the announcement was in the local paper.

As she relaxes, she rationalizes Duncan's absence. He didn't want to presume. After all, the relationship is new, not yet fully consummated. He hates crowds. After all, he's been living in a remote village in Malaysia. He respects her grief and is waiting until she is alone. After all, the place has been crawling with people. None of these excuses quite fit, but then she further rationalizes that she does not actually know him well. She just *feels* as if she knows him well.

\*\*\*

Sean leaves in a rented red convertible, looking older, more jowly, but with his hair dyed and a tan that looks as if it came from central casting. During his two days here, he titillates Annie's friends, telling them risqué airline jokes, recommending they go to California rather than Florida this winter. When Helen asks about his latest live-in girlfriend, he shrugs and says, "She's nobody important. Great ass, though."

As he is packing to leave, Helen stands in the doorway of his room, "Don't you want any of Mom's personal things? You're entitled to them."

"Nah! It's just old lady stuff. Maybe Sylvia or the kids might like something. Just send me the cheque when the will is probated."

Helen sucks in her breath. "Don't you care anything at all about her? Or about the past?"

Sean looks at her straight for the first time. "No, no I don't. I was never so glad as the day I left her house."

Helen is shocked and speaks through the thickness in her throat. "You were always her favourite! She did so much for you! She even borrowed from Uncle Gordon to post your bail."

Sean balances a folded shirt in his hands, weighing his words. "Yeah, I guess she did a lot for all of us. But it was always to her plan, never to ours. She and Dad had their own agenda. We didn't really figure much in it, except as pawns."

Helen knows this is true, but her raw sense of loss pushes her on. "Don't you feel *anything* for her?"

Again Sean carefully considers his words. "No, not really. The trouble is, you always felt too much, Helen. You never learned to tune them out. I did. Barbara did in her own way." He places the shirt in his suitcase and zips it up, ending the conversation. Helen sniffles in the bathroom for several minutes, knowing he is right, but unable to accept it.

\*\*\*

At the kitchen table, Helen takes a long drag on her cigarette and feels a stir in the acid bath that is her stomach. There is now only Barbara left. Helen is exhausted, but when she awoke at six, she was unable to get back to sleep. Thoughts kept rolling through her head: What did Annie think of in her final moments? What did she think of any of them? Did she know she was dying? Helen realizes that what evades her is her mother's psychology. Helen could predict how Annie would react in any given situation, especially if it involved Reg, but she never knew where her reaction came from. In stage terms, she doesn't know Annie's spine. How is it that Annie in life could only show her disapproval of me and saved her support and affection for after her death? Hadn't I made it clear what I needed? Helen's eyes, lids already swollen to twice their normal size, fill with tears.

A door bangs, the toilet flushes and Helen stirs herself to make some coffee for Barbara. This is the first time I've been ahead of Barbara in anything, she thinks wryly as she fills the coffeemaker. "Good morning," she says, as Barbara comes into the kitchen.

"Mom didn't allow smoking in the house," Barbara says as she sits down.

"In her house," Helen replies. "This is now my house." She instantly regrets the comment and fusses with the coffee to hide her indiscretion. Barbara looks around the kitchen, biting at her bottom lip as she does when she's annoyed.

"Sorry. Yes. Your house."

"Listen," Helen says, finally giving voice to what she has been wanting to say for three days. "I realize the will is unfair. You can have some of the money from the house, if you want it. If you need it. The thing is, I'm not quite sure I want to sell it right now. You can certainly have the other money she left me."

"You might move down here?" Barbara is waking up.

"I don't know. I haven't had time to think, let alone plan."

"Are you mad, Helen? You've always lived in the city. You're an actress! You'd go out of your mind here!" Barbara has found her normal pace. "You've always been so impractical!" she exhales.

Helen feels a surge of energy, too. "Nice to see you've taken up the job of criticizing me now that Ma's gone," she says, grabbing for another cigarette. The sisters face each other across the kitchen, both looking like prize fighters with their bulky housecoats, puffy eyes and matted hair.

"I didn't mean it that way, Helen. It's just ... I am your older sister."

"The last time I needed an older sister, I was nineteen and committed to a loony bin, Barbara. And you weren't there. You're a little late." Helen is startled by her own harshness. Where has this been living?

The reference to the past hangs in the air, mingling with the aroma of coffee. The atmosphere is similar to that of Reg and Annie's kitchen, with the children waiting to exhale. Helen verbalizes it. "We sound like Reg and Annie. If there is one family tradition we should break, it's that one. You and Sean are all I have left as family. I don't want to fight." She takes a deep breath. "When I went off the rails, you were a young mother living in Toronto. There was nothing you could have done. I'm sorry."

Barbara measures milk and sweetener into her coffee the way she does everything — carefully. "I'm sorry, too. And I'm also sorry you had all the responsibility for Mom these past couple of months. The truth is, Megan's eating disorder is worse. You saw what she looks like. We're considering sending her to a residential clinic. We've made her stop gymnastics, in fact all physical stuff, because she's just too frail to continue. To make matters worse, Trevor is having an affair with one of his colleagues. That's why I wanted to go to Germany with him. She'll be there."

Barbara takes a long draught of coffee. "I was afraid to leave and come down here to help. Afraid there would be nothing there when I got back."

It's Helen's turn to feel a deep remorse. "I'm sorry. I didn't realize. You should have told me. But then, we've never talked much, have we?"

"No," Barbara nods, and the sisters drink their coffee in silence for a few minutes, thinking of the thousands of conversations they might have had. "The thing is, I could never think of Mom as really frail. I guess I was in denial, but she was always so strong, so feisty, like she could overcome anything, even Dad." They both chuckle.

"I think she felt that way till the end. Never much self doubt there." And there is so much doubt in me, Helen adds to herself. "I can see where you might need some of the money from the house. For the clinic. Is there any question of you and Trevor divorcing?"

Barbara quickly tidies up that perception. "Oh, no! Nothing like that! He's had the odd dalliance before. Claims it's his way of dealing with stress," she barks bitterly. "Doesn't do much for my stress level, though. God! His girlfriend is twenty-seven years younger than he is. You can't even begin to compete with such youth."

"Or stupidity," Helen adds. "Wow! I never realized Trevor could be such a prick!" She has always thought of Trevor as plodding and boring, a man who would spend New Year's Eve filling out his income tax forms. She can't even imagine him in his underwear, let alone seducing a series of young chicks. It's as if he's Jekyll and Hyde. "It's very worrying about Megan," Helen says. "Maybe running amok as a teenager is hereditary; maybe she takes after me."

Barbara nods. "She's very creative. And admires you a lot. She's always telling friends her aunt is an actress, and she tapes you when you're on TV, like that part on *Storefront Lawyer*."

"Really? I was on for something like forty seconds, that's all it took to establish me as a battered wife." The mysteries of the family are deepening. Next, someone is going to tell Helen that Sean is a sensitive and caring individual.

"When you had your ... breakdown," Barbara says, "we never did get the full picture of what happened. I mean what caused it. Mom and Dad always glossed over everything, and I never did really find out even how you got over it. And then you just went off to England."

"A really bad love affair was the official cause. But it's never that simple, is it? I suppose I had felt inadequate, lonely and isolated all my life, and that I substituted fantasy, acting, whatever you want to call it, to fill the space inside. When I turned my fantasies onto another person, John, he let me down big time. I just fell apart. Lost all direction."

"You felt isolated?" Barbara's turn to be surprised. "But you were the centre of attention, the family favourite! The baby. The one Dad jollied, the one Mom always worried about!"

"Loneliness isn't absence of people or attention, Barbara. It's about absence of kind. Absence of people like me. Sure the folks worried. And criticized. Because I wasn't like you — feminine, soft-spoken, conciliatory, obedient, etcetera, etcetera. The ideal daughter. It took me years to realize I didn't want to be like you. As for 'favourites,' Sean wins hands down."

"You're right, there. Mom was so determined he shouldn't turn out like Dad. Well, he's a lot worse than Dad, don't you think? At least in the number of women he's gone through?"

"Dad went through a lot of women?"

"Lord, yes!" Barbara pushes up her sleeves to deliver the details. For the rest of the morning, while they make toast and boil eggs, clean up the kitchen and begin emptying the drawers in Annie's room, the sisters exchange memories, each one different, each a piece of puzzle that fits together across a great divide. Barbara reveals how Annie had a breakdown just before Helen was born. How Reg's philandering seemed to subside after that. The brief happiness in the family when they bought a new house. Helen asks Barbara if she remembers when Annie left Reg.

Barbara pauses with a stack of sweaters in her arms. "Hm, no. But I do remember we went up to the farm for a day or so without Dad."

The pattern is spun out, identified. Not the origins, but the pattern of Annie and Reg's life. At lunch, Helen again brings up the subject of Annie's will.

"I know you feel cheated somewhat." Helen fetches leftover sandwiches from the refrigerator. "Even if I decide to keep the house, I can probably get a mortgage on it. Pay you something."

Barbara smiles. "You've always been too soft for your own good, Helen."

"But it's unfair. The will is unfair."

"Mom was always unfair, Helen. She played us against each other. They both did. It was their way of getting back at each other."

"That's a terribly cruel analysis."

Barbara pauses. "I'm not saying they were conscious of doing that. Just that they did it. Sean and I realized it and dove for cover as best we could. You were always trying to please them. And they couldn't be pleased. Especially not Mom. The only things that pleased her were a good sale and a good fight."

Helen knows this to be not quite accurate, but cannot pin down what it lacks. "I will give you part of the house."

Barbara has a real inner struggle going on. On the one hand, the living room contains several cardboard boxes filled with her selection of Annie's things, all of them the best the house has to offer — the Royal Doulton china and figurines, an almost Persian carpet from the entrance hall, all the silver, Annie's gold necklaces, her pearls, her wedding rings and other jewellery. She has already amply demonstrated her greed. She could spend a third of the price of the house in one morning, without trying. But she does care for her sister and, like Annie, worries about her. She recognizes that if she robs her sister of what is legally hers, she will have overstepped the boundaries.

"Sean's right. You're the one who looked after Mom. And Dad too, for that matter. And you need the money the most. It's what Mom wanted, and we all did what she wanted, didn't we?" Barbara grimaces and gestures toward the boxes. "I've put aside the odds and ends I'd like. I hope that's okay." She's biting her lower lip again.

Helen nods. "There's only one thing you've packed that I would have liked. The mantle clock."

Barbara leaps to the boxes. "Then you shall have it! I never thought you wanted any of this stuff. You've never been what is called materialistic." She has carefully marked every box, so the clock is quickly found. "It's not even that attractive. I only took it because it's an antique and a dealer would pay a good price for it."

"It was Grandma and Grandpa's. It reminds me of them, even though I never knew them." Again, Helen's eyes fill with tears, a reminder of how close to the surface her emotions are.

Barbara hands her the clock. "They were good people. It's right that you should have it." Then she expands, "Anything else I've taken that you would like?"

## chapter 24

TWO DAYS LATER, HELEN SITS on the bottom stair to the basement and looks over the army of boxes that are stacked there. She promised herself after Barbara left this morning that she would keep busy until sundown, then go down to the river to wait. Surely, now that she is alone, Duncan will show up. Surely there'll be an explanation. Upstairs, the things Annie used day-to-day have too much recent memory attached to them. After she tripped on the ball of bright orange playdough this morning, Helen cried for five minutes.

In the basement, the atmosphere is more neutral. The boxes only contain Annie's past and are therefore safer to view. The quiet, the perfect calm of the room is the antithesis of Annie. The boxes don't rage, sigh, or accuse you with their energy. As Helen rises, she groans with the effort. How can I feel so empty and so heavy at the same time? Aloud she says, "Mom, are you here?" then feels slapped by the silence. One thought rescues her: She will never criticize me again.

The first few boxes are easy to handle. A set of melamine dishes, the pastel colours stained beige, one plate missing. A box filled with leather purses of different colours. Christmas cards going back many years. Loads of handcrafted items from the charity fairs Annie attended — crocheted poodles that hold a roll of toilet paper, macramé plant hangers, Christmas reindeer made out of wooden spoons and little needlepoint sachets for potpourri. She gazes in amazement at a tissue box holder quilted to resemble a sofa, with the tissue going up between the seat cushions. Who comes up with these ideas? Who bothers to do this work? Why aren't they quilting blankets for children in Afghanistan? These items are easily labelled "Garage Sale" and put to one side. Annie was never a fan of holding garage sales, estimating that if the goods had a value to someone else, she should keep them.

Helen opens a box filled with letters tied in ribbon and card boxes of photographs, with a ledger or diary on top. Curious, she flips open the cover to find biweekly entries:

*October 18th 1947*

| | |
|---|---|
| *Salary rec'd* | $80.00 |
| *Household expenses* | $40.00 |
| *Milk* | 2.00 |
| *Light & gas* | 2.00 |
| *Doctor* | 1.50 |
| *Fuel* | 1.50 |
| *Water rate* | .75 |
| *Telephone* | 1.75 |
| *Christmas club* | 2.00 |
| *Insurance* | 3.00 |
| *Rent* | 12.00 |
| *Savings* | 13.50 |

There are over 100 entries, representing four years worth of careful budgeting. Helen notices "Teeth — $10," and that it wipes out a large portion of the savings. Beside "Household expenses," guilty luxuries are detailed along with the socks and shampoo — a magazine at 10 cents, lipstick at 29 cents and a tantalizing entry that says "$1.65 for night with girls."

Helen has always seen her mother as extravagant, her purchases the source of many a fierce argument with Reg. Here is Annie the responsible housewife, making the most of her husband's hard-earned salary, before Reg's sales commissions put them in a different category. Helen pauses to consider this new person — Annie, the post-war bride. How she filled her spare time is indicated by a "To do" list that appears beside some of the entries. For a week in April 1948 it reads:

*Drapes for living room*
*Remove wax in hallway*
*Wax hallway*
*Clean windows*
*Finish socks*

There is an energy, an optimism, in these entries that Helen has never seen in her mother. An entry late in 1948 reads "Cloth for diapers!!! — $1.89" indicating that Barbara is about to be born, seemingly with some enthusiasm on the part of Annie.

Helen opens a card box that has a baby book, shower cards and birth announcements in it. The cards are yellowing, with babies that look like angels, little dogs and storks on them, late forties kitsch. Most of the cards are signed by women Helen has never heard of, although a lavish one with lace on it is signed, "From your old partner in crime, Love, Maggie." The baby book has dutifully been filled in, all the landmark weights and heights recorded. As Helen flips through it, a strand of Barbara's fine, blonde baby hair slips to the floor.

I knew you too late, Ma, Helen thinks, which again starts her tears. She dabs at them, then puts the box aside to be forwarded on to Barbara.

She turns to the first bundle of letters, tied with red satin ribbon that crackles with age when Helen undoes it. The letters are from Dulcie, Annie's mother, a reminder of the days before cheap long distance phone calls, when people took the time to write, to keep in touch. Dulcie apparently wrote on Sundays, as there are references to just being back from church. Helen smiles as she reads the local news — Hector Logan's wayward pig run over by a pickup truck, Harriet MacKenzie's cow giving birth to a fourth set of twins, a new entranceway at the bank. The small dramas and forward steps that add up to the life of a community.

Helen hungrily absorbs every letter from the grandmother she never knew, piecing together a contented and simple woman who daringly grew artichokes in her garden one summer but didn't like the taste of them, who made all the period costumes for a Dominion Day pageant in 1956, who made raspberry and rhubarb jam with mixed success, who had corns and a plantar's wart that just stubbornly couldn't be removed, and who also had a pet hen named Mamie.

Dulcie shows her concern for her daughter, too, offering to come up to Montreal to babysit the children while Reg and Annie attend one more sales conference, sending along a guaranteed cure for colic and asking Annie to parcel up her mending and send it down to the farm, so she can do it for her. It takes Helen several hours to read all the letters and, when she finishes, she feels that in losing her mother, she has gained access to her grandmother. The past has pockets you can slip into and find comfort in. Where you can rest. She carefully reties the bundles and puts them in a box of items she will keep.

After lunch, she tackles the next bundles which are letters from Reg overseas. "Hello Old Girl" is Reg's typical greeting, and the letters are filled with antics in English pubs and games of pickup football on airfields while waiting for the next bombing mission. Reg gleefully reports that Dresden looked like a birthday cake filled with candles as his plane turned and headed for home. There are a few dark reports such as "Ted Downie didn't make it back," but for the most part Reg seems to be on an extended vacation. He describes how many pubs there are in Leicester Square, says St. Paul's looks in need of a good wash and gripes about the food but raves about the camaraderie now that the tide has turned and Gerry is on the run. Helen smiles, remembering how much Reg liked winning. He'd gamble on anything, just for the possible rush of a win.

At the same time, she feels a sense of loss, because although there is affection in the letters — he calls Annie his "little squeeze" — there is no intimacy, no sense under the chipper words of them being connected. Reg comments on Annie's furniture buying as "preparing the nest for a future line of Bannermans," but that is the only clue to the life they expected from one another. There is passion — Reg says he'd give his eye teeth to be able to see Annie's new black silk slip, so he could toss it across the room. But no inner workings. No indication that Reg might be in danger, that they might not see each other for years, that there is connection beyond the words on the paper. And none of Annie's letters to Reg have survived. Men aren't sentimental that way. So Helen's view of the marriage is closed, left as a memorable tableau of heated fights and glamorous evenings out, with none of the scaffolding visible.

It's a different age, Helen rationalizes. No pop psychology then. After all, her parents were not poets. They hardly knew each other, given the length of time between when they met and when they married. But Helen still wants a glimpse of something visceral, to know the underpinning that drew them together and kept them married for over forty years. She sighs and bundles the letters back up. As she returns them to the box, she sees at the bottom of the box another letter she hadn't noticed before, the envelope not sealed. As she turns it over, she hears the phone ring upstairs. Damn! Why didn't I bring it down with me, she thinks as she scrambles up the stairs to catch it before the fourth ring, hoping it might be Duncan.

"Miss Bannerman?" Helen instantly recognizes the bright voice, the voice that would announce the end of the world and still conclude with "Have a nice day!" The lady on Prozac from Health Services.

"Hello, Mrs. MacPherson. How are you?"

"Just fine, thank you! And isn't it just a glorious day!"

"To be truthful, I hadn't noticed."

"Oh! You're that busy, hunh? I'm sorry to hear that. I imagine Mother is quite a handful."

Helen can't help herself. "No! No, she's not a handful, although I imagine she soon will be, what with the worms and all."

There is a slight pause. "I beg your pardon?" The voice has flattened somewhat.

"Were you calling to say there was a vacancy at St. Andrew's, Mrs. MacPherson?"

"Why yes! A lovely private room, which I think you indicated your mother could afford, facing south, so you get all that sun and a view of the golf course, too!" The voice simply bubbles with the details. "And it was freshly wallpapered by the previous tenant!"

"Well, I don't think I'll be needing it for a few years yet, Mrs. MacPherson, and Mother certainly won't. You see, she died last week."

"Oh!" Mrs. MacPherson is at a loss for words. "Oh, I'm just so sorry to hear that! My deepest sympathy, Helen."

"Thank you. It was quick. She didn't want to go into care, and in a way, it's a blessing that she didn't have to."

"Oh yes! But ... How are you doing, Helen?"

Helen has to smile at the good intentions of this worthy woman at the other end of the phone, whom she hasn't met.

"I'm okay," she says nodding. "I'm sad, but I'm okay."

"It's always hard to lose your mother," Mrs. MacPherson croons over the phone.

Helen thinks about that a moment. "Yes. Especially if you feel you never knew her."

"Oh, but you two were so close!" Mrs. MacPherson gushes. "The way you looked after her! And she was so proud of you! Almost the first thing she said when I visited her in hospital was that you were an actress!"

So was my mother, thinks Helen, suddenly feeling tired. "Yes, well, I want to thank you for all you've done on our behalf, Mrs. MacPherson. I know you tried."

"That's what I'm here for! To help!"

I'd kill for a copy of her prescription, Helen thinks as she hangs up the phone. She walks through to the living room, now bare of ornaments, just its dignified furniture basking in the late afternoon light. The only sound comes from the mantle clock, wound by Helen this morning. She opens a window, acknowledging that yes, it is a nice day. As if on cue, she hears the soft cooing of a mourning dove at the bird feeder in the garden.

God! I'm tired! she thinks as she stretches out on the sofa, not even kicking off her shoes. She is asleep before another thought hits her, dreaming she is going from room to room in an old farmhouse, the rooms dim, the light through the clouded windows stark. Cobwebs obscure her view into the next room, where shadowy figures move about.

At nine o'clock that night, Helen is on the dock, her cigarettes, brandy and two glasses beside her, her mood sinking fast. She's already had one brandy and it only seems to have made the blood in her veins heavier. She pours another, lights a cigarette. An owl hoots and there is a small anguished squeak from the bushes. We are in a season of death, she thinks. The crickets thrum in agreement.

None of her rationalizations for Duncan's absence make a bit of sense anymore. If he had to go away, goddamn it, he could have dropped her a note, left a message on the phone. She wracks her brain. Did she inadvertently say something? Do something? Could he have left a message that Barbara picked up and forgot to tell her about? Even if she meant nothing to him, it would only be polite to tell her he was going, and he always seemed polite. Christ! He was there when her mother had the stroke!

She takes a deep drag on her cigarette, followed by a swallow of brandy, feeling the deadly mixture curl in the back of her throat. Even though she has slept for three hours before dinner, she feels tired. No, not tired: used up. As if the events of the past few days, her dead mother and her all-too-alive siblings have consumed her, leaving only the outer skin of who she was before all this happened.

The phone rings back at the house and again she curses herself for not having thought to bring it with her. She is out of breath when she answers, a throaty "Hello."

"I think that's the kind of greeting you get when you call phone sex numbers," says Bernie. "How are you?"

"Low. Blue. A little bit drunk."

"A little bit drunk alone?"

Helen considers telling Bernie the whole story of Duncan, but instead just says, "Yes."

"That's not good. Things seem to be piling up on you?"

"Good use of words. I've been going through my mother's stuff. Letters from my grandmother and Dad. Letters from dead people."

"You know, Helen, maybe you need a break. Why don't you just leave that stuff, come home for a few days? I could come down with you later in the month and help you sort it out. You know it'll keep."

It'll keep all right, thinks Helen. I've kept most of this baggage with me for forty years. "I don't know, Bernie. Maybe you're right."

"Cato caught a pigeon for you, hoping to tempt you back. Shall I tell him it worked? I'll make your favourite clam chowder. Or maybe you should go away somewhere for a few days vacation. Now that you're an heiress."

Helen smiles. "I guess she really did give me what I needed, Bernie. A little security."

"What you really need, woman, is to accept yourself and value yourself as you really are. And there ain't nobody in the whole wide world can give you that except yourself."

Helen shakes her head. "I accept myself," she protests. Then she thinks of her vigil down by the river and recognizes how she has switched Duncan's bad behaviour into the possibility that she has behaved badly. "I don't know, Bernie. Maybe coming back for a few days would be a good idea. Let me think about it."

"Think as long as you like. We're here."

Helen goes down to the dock and pours herself yet another brandy, and this time it works. Her self-pity gives way to anger. She thinks of the high octane battles that took place between Reg and Annie and the memory of the energy of those conflicts seeps into her. Okay, maybe they never got what they wanted. But they never stopped trying. Annie would never sit around waiting for a man, feeling sorry for herself. Resolved, Helen decides to look for Duncan's relatives on the Sixth Concession. They should be easy enough to find. Let's at least get an explanation. Nobody just abandons me without telling me why. She drains the brandy and heads up to the house, a little unsteady on her feet, the lights from the house drawing her in.

# chapter 25

AT THE END OF A LONG DRIVEWAY, overhung with maples, is a typical Eastern Ontario farmhouse, red brick with white gingerbread trim, a tin roof glowing dully in the sun. It's in a T shape, with an addition on the back where the summer kitchen and woodshed would have been. Some work has been done to modernize it — new windows — but the veranda that runs in an L along two sides of the house lists a little and in back are the barn, a sway-backed drive shed, the milk shed and what was once a chicken coop. The condition of the smaller buildings does not inspire confidence, although the milk shed is covered in shiny new siding. The barn is in pretty good shape too, and there's a bright green John Deere tractor in the yard.

Helen has parked her car at the road and is walking up the driveway to the house, the heat quite intense even though it's only ten in the morning. She's sweating, possibly the result of the fuzzy hangover she has from last night's brandy. The hangover has also dulled her anger somewhat, although she's determined to push on. Three-quarters of the way up the drive, she sees a man emerge from the barn and walk toward the house. She recognizes him instantly, and he slows his pace when he notices her.

When she gets closer she cries in her best stage voice, "Good morning, Duncan."

He stops, shields his eyes, squinting at her. She walks more quickly now, more determinedly. Closer up, he looks different, his face broader, his hair greyer. He looks older than she remembers and a little shorter. She repeats, a little less sure of herself now, "Duncan?"

The man looks at his boots, then at her. "No, Duncan's my brother. My twin brother."

Helen is taken aback. Duncan never mentioned a twin, but now that she looks at this man, he is obviously not Duncan. More hesitant in manner. Not the same fan folds around the eyes.

The man steps forward, extends his hand. "I'm Alistair. How d'you do?" He looks at Helen with great curiosity.

"Helen, Helen Bannerman," she says recovering, shaking his hand. "I'm sorry. Duncan mentioned he had a brother, but not that you were twins."

"Well, you get sick of people comparing you. You know Duncan?"

Helen gestures down the road. "Oh, yes. He came by the house where I was staying. By the river. I'd been looking after my mother, but she died last week."

"Right. Yes, Mrs. Bannerman. I read about that in *The Glengarry News*. I'm sorry for your loss. You must be the actress daughter."

Helen smiles at how the rural bush telegraph works.

"Would you like to come up to the house for coffee?" Alistair gestures.

"Thank you, but really I was just wondering what happened to Duncan. I hadn't seen him."

Alistair stops. "He left. Didn't he tell you?"

Helen feels her stomach drop. "Oh. Was there some emergency?"

Alistair looks Helen up and down. "No. He always does things on the spur of the moment."

Helen swallows. "I thought maybe he had to go back to Asia."

"Nope, I don't think he's gone there, but I don't know where he's gone. Although he does claim to have a wife back in Malaysia."

"A wife? He didn't mention that either."

Alistair looks at the ground. "Yup, and two young kids. I think the wife's Malaysian, although I can't be sure. We've never met her."

"He lied to me, " Helen says, feeling very foolish. Her face reddens.

"He's lied to quite a few people in his time," Alistair says. "He lies to everyone. He likes to charm people, and the truth doesn't always do it. I'm sorry."

Helen's mind is rioting. A mixture of foolishness and anger. It's like when you're on stage and your mind goes blank, and not only can you not remember the next line, but all the lines that come after that, and you are not sure where exactly you are in the script. An actor's worst nightmare. Duncan has handed her the wrong script.

"Have you known Duncan long?" Alistair asks.

"A few weeks. But I felt I knew him."

"Yeah, folks do."

Helen can't help it and starts to cry. "Maybe you should come into the house," Alistair moves toward her, recognizing that his brother has left another mess that has to be cleaned up. He feels resignation rather than anger. "I'm sorry, especially since this comes on top of your mother's dying."

Helen backs away, rage and sorrow competing to destroy her composure. "No! Leave me alone! And damn your son of a bitch of a brother!" And she is gone down the driveway, running.

Alistair shakes his head and says, "Poor woman," followed by, "Christ, Duncan!"

Hours later, Helen is sitting cross-legged on the sofa in the living room, hugging a pillow, crumpled balls of soaked Kleenex fanned out around her on the floor, a cold cup of tea on the coffee table, her eyelids unrecognizable. She rocks herself, the cast list of men who have betrayed her running on a continuous loop in her head. How could I have been so wrong about him? she thinks. I'm an actor. Knowing character, deciphering the depths of character, is my trade. At which I am obviously not very good. Which explains why I've never succeeded. My family is right, I am just a child who's never grown up. A failure, in relationships as in life.

Years of psychotherapy are wiped away and her Domino Theory of Emotional Response comes into play, in which one setback leans into another fragile area and her entire sense of self-worth collapses. Momma, she cries out in her head, and again dissolves into tears.

She has bitten every nail on each of her fingers, paced the living-room floor and stared out the window. She has reached the nadir, wondering if there are any razor blades in the house. She calls Bernie, desperate to talk to someone, but gets the answering machine. She leaves a semi-coherent message, then returns to the sofa, empty of tears but not of despair.

"Very Wagnerian," a voice in her head says. "Or if you insist, Puccini." Dr. Glickstein, using her sense of irony to help her. Other lessons she learned about herself from the good doctor seep back in. You knew Duncan for less than two weeks, she reminds herself. If he lies all the time, as his brother says, he might be psychopathic, which means he's very convincing and even capable of conning mental health professionals. You were vulnerable, are vulnerable. Cut yourself some slack.

Although she is still filled with self-loathing, she decides she must make an effort to move her mind into new territory by doing something physical, something that will stop all her energy going to her brain. She makes another cup of tea, drinks it this time, practises some deep breathing and heads downstairs to work on the mess.

In the basement, the bundles of letters are where she left them, with the half-empty box waiting to be dealt with and the unsealed letter on top. For the first time she notices the name on the front. Ewan Urquart. Annie's old flame. Annie's dancing partner. A stab of ice runs through her. Urquart. Duncan's last name. But it can't be! Don't think about it, she tells herself. There is nowhere to go but forward.

Helen feels a bit queasy as she opens the letter, because she knows instinctively that here she will find the emotion that was missing in Reg's letters to Annie. The paper is a good quality vellum, Annie's hand sure.

*My dear Ewan,*

*I have written this letter at least ten times and much more often than that in my head. I don't know if I'll have the courage to post this one either, afraid as I am of Flora or someone else reading it before you. But I know I must tell you things, so they will stop echoing in my mind.*

*I have convinced myself, and I hope to convince you, that it was fate that put me on that same train, in the same car, as you. It was fate that let those cows out of the field and put them on the track so that the engine was derailed. And it was fate that led us to the hotel in Côteau Landing.*

*The biggest mistake I have ever made was in letting you go that time you came up to Montreal and said you wanted me back. Or perhaps my biggest mistake was in marrying Reg, just because he was so different from you. Whatever the case, I have rued my error a long time. Not at first, because the war was on and my life was changing so quickly. But certainly once my daughter was born and I could see what the pattern of my days would be. As you know, I have always hated any sort of routine, thinking it dull. But to share a routine with a man you don't love, who has no understanding of you or wish to understand you, is a prison sentence that no amount of diversion can make you forget. And I don't think I realized that fully until you and I locked in that hotel room and our understanding of each other flowed without words being necessary.*

Helen puts down the letter, finding it hard to breathe and feeling she is violating Annie. A daughter should not know about her mother's adultery. It is written down somewhere in the Survival Manual for Families. She wipes her eyes. Poor Annie. Poor Reg. But Helen's resentment of Annie's hypocrisy regarding sex surfaces, creating a conflicting mix of reactions. Then Helen realizes the significance of Annie's having kept the letter. She had kept it, put it with these others, moved it from Montreal to this house. She must have known someone would come across it, would probably read it. Even after her stroke, when she couldn't make it down these stairs, she could have asked Helen to bring up the boxes and destroyed it herself. Helen snuffles, finds a Kleenex and turns to the next page of the letter. What harm can there be in reading it now?

*I don't wish to be presumptuous about your marriage, but I imagine you find yourself in a similar position to mine. After all, if there were no sparks between Flora and you for the first ten years you knew each other, I doubt that too many flew after you and I broke up. Oh, I know she's a good woman and that you have two fine children, but there's no magic in that, is there? There's no special connection that makes the day-to-day bearable, that makes you feel as if you are fulfilling some kind of destiny.*

*Ewan, you and I have always had a destiny, even though events conspired so that we couldn't pursue it. And I have proof of that shared destiny. I have growing inside me our child, the child we feared so many years ago, the child that would have seen us married in 1943. We were foolish not to marry then, or rather, I was foolish to think that a roof of our own was more important than a love of our own.*

Helen holds the letter, her hand trembling too much to be able to continue. She checks the date at the top: September 24, 1958. September 1958. Six months before she was born. She drops the letter and staggers back up the stairs. This is too much. It is all too much. It is the second betrayal of the day, but this one eclipses Duncan's vanishing act.

Before she reaches the top step, Reg swims into her mind. "Daddy," she says softly to the memory of him, smiling and calling her Theda Bara.

Get out of here. Get out of the house. Get away from this madness. She doesn't even close the door as she leaves, just starts jogging up the drive, onto the road, not knowing where she is going. Half a mile down the road, she has to slow down, heaving and coughing, the legacy of twenty-five years of cigarettes being hacked up. But she's glad of these symptoms. They remind her of her own body, her flawed body, that she is alive, that she hasn't disappeared or died. She is still here.

Helen keeps going, half walking, jogging when she can, not stopping until she's in the village, eight kilometres down the road. When an old man smiles at her opposite the post office, she becomes aware that she's still gasping for air, sweat-stained under the arms, her hair drifting around her face. She continues until she comes to the church, with the cemetery stretching out behind it, Annie's grave creating a dark scab near the southern edge.

It is only at the grave site that the confusion in Helen's brain shapes itself into pure rage. "I have been lied to all my life," she says aloud. She thinks of all of Annie's hypocrisies: Her assertion that Helen's acting is just a manifestation of her father's loudmouth showing off. Her insistence on steadiness in one's life. Her edicts regarding chastity when she herself had conceived another man's child, then passed the bastard baby off as her husband's. "How could you?" she asks the shrivelled flowers and fronds that cover the grave. "What did I ever do to you that you could do this to me? How the hell could you do this to all of us?" She grabs a handful of the flowers and slams them onto the grave. She wants to dig the earth with her bare fingers to confront her mother face to face.

She is shaking with anger but when her mind turns to Duncan, she starts to cry. "You've deceived me," she sobs. Gulping air, she tries to steady her breathing, counting breaths, lengthening them. She says out loud, "I've deceived myself. We've all deceived each other. An acting career is one of complete deceit. My life is one long deceit." Her legs feel weak, and she sits on the squat gravestone to the right of Annie's grave. The desire to tear at the clods of earth has been replaced by great sadness, self-loathing and exhaustion. Her breathing returns to normal. All she is aware of is that she would like to lie down, to sleep, wrapped in warm deceptions, never to wake up.

Somehow Helen starts the long walk home. A farmer in his pickup truck gives her a lift, talking about the vicissitudes in the growing and pricing of soybeans the whole way there, for which Helen is grateful. If he notices her swollen face and disarrayed appearance, he says nothing, only adding as she gets out of the truck, "I was sorry to hear about your mother."

Helen enters the silent house, goes to her room and lies on the bed, convinced that her life is effectively over. She is asleep in seconds.

It is dark when Helen wakes up, but with a sliver of light on the horizon. Sunrise. She has slept for more than twelve hours, but still feels exhausted. No, not tired, but empty. She is also ravenous. While she waits for one of the donated casseroles to heat in the microwave, she notices the basement door open, the truth about her own past, about Annie's past, waiting for her. She eats without noticing how good the food is, goes back down the stairs and picks up the letter.

*When I first tried to write you, all I could think of is that we must correct this mistake. Not the mistake of three months ago, but the one I made back in 1943. We belong together, we must be together. I want you to know that I would leave my husband and everything I own, even my children if I had to, to be with you again, to take the path I should have taken long ago. I realize the scandal that would cause, but I know of no way to handle a grave mistake, except to admit it and try to correct it.*

*But I also know you, Ewan, my love. You are a person of much stronger principles than me and although we were restless youngsters together, you never had my sense of adventure. Perhaps it's because you're a man, but I don't think you could ever give all for love. I suspect you could never forgive yourself if you hurt Flora or your children, and I also suspect that you would find it hard to forgive me, for persuading you to do it. Perhaps it's our Presbyterian ancestors, but we feel guilt and shame more sharply than we do other emotions.*

*So I am writing this without much hope, Ewan, but with a desperate need to let you know how I feel. Even without this child, you will always be a part of me, the part I was so careless with, not knowing it was my best part.*

*If you can write or see me, it would help me cope better with the situation I find myself in. With my mother so ill, it would be easy for me to go back home for awhile. I know I have no claim on you, nor do I have the right to ruin your life, the way I have ruined mine. But if I could talk to you, I know it would calm my fevered thoughts, help me get through this.*

*Take care. I hope those ulcers have cleared up. You deserve an easier life than you've had.*

*Yours always,*
*Annie*

Helen puts down the letter to wipe away her tears. So! Not the vixen, not the homewrecker, more than a deceiver, Annie reveals herself at last. Partially. Guilt and shame. My own most common emotional responses, Helen realizes. She could be describing me. A strange mix of emotions is rioting through Helen. My God! Did Reg ever suspect? Did Ewan ever respond? Ah! But Annie never sent the letter. He never knew. Helen feels in her bones how alone and isolated Annie must have felt. And my grandmother died that fall. Before I was born. However did she get through it? She remembers Barbara talking about Annie's breakdown before Helen was born. She suddenly feels a wave of pity for Annie.

While she was caring for Annie after the stroke, Helen often felt sorry for her mother and admired the courage, the will, she applied to the struggle to walk again. Helen had put it down to Annie's innate stubbornness and selfishness. Nobody would stand in her way. Helen now realizes those same qualities probably bolstered Annie through that earlier time. It was her will, her determination that kept Annie going during her pregnancy to bring Helen into a family that wasn't legitimately hers. Helen blinks back a tear. How fearful Annie must have been. The courage. Yes, she deceived to protect herself. But in doing so, she also protected me, Helen thinks. Annie. Not a conventional mother, but a mother nevertheless. Providing what she thought her daughter needed. Never bothering to ask if it happened to be what the daughter thought she needed. She could never have pulled it off if she allowed doubt to seep in. In contemplation lies peril, so she chose rage instead to blot out the path not taken.

Helen considers all the father figures in her life — Reg, John Fitzgerald, Dr. Glickstein. Would things have been different if she'd known her biological father? And who was he, other than a good dancer? Helen sits on the cellar steps and contemplates her new parents, the father she never knew, the mother she hardly knew.

But whenever the word "father" crosses her mind, Reg shoulders into the picture. Reg acquiring Peaches for her, the only child who wanted the dog. Reg standing and clapping the loudest at the school plays. Reg slipping her fifty dollars as she was about to board the plane for London, hissing, "I want you to go down to Tunbridge Wells and see if there's still a pub called The Hound and Hares there. See if Mary Foxton is still the landlord's wife. Don't ask in front of her husband, though. And don't tell your mother." Hearty Reg, playing his role.

"Daddy," she whispers now.

"I am what I've lived," she says aloud. "Whether it's true or not, it's all I've got. The rest of you don't matter. Duncan, you son of a bitch, you missed out on a good woman." Helen knows she doesn't quite believe this yet, but a thin stream of strength bubbles up in her. "I am who I am. I'm sorry I wasn't the daughter you hoped for," she tells Annie, "but I'm more yours than you think." She thinks of the work ahead in trying to sort out the pieces of her life.

*chapter 26*

HELEN HAS SHOWERED, DRESSED AND is drying her hair when she hears a hammering on the kitchen door. For a brief second, as she peers out the window in the door, she thinks it is Duncan, then realizes it is Alistair, with a woman hovering in back of him. Embarrassed, she opens the door.

"G'day, Miss. I hope you don't mind, but the wife and I were worried about you and just thought we should check in." Alistair's smile seems a little strained.

"Oh, please, come in!" Helen stands aside, and Alistair introduces his wife Betty, a solid plump woman with curly hair and a pretty face.

"Like, we know you've been under a strain, what with your mother and all, and I thought maybe I should explain about Duncan ..." Alistair continues.

"My mother died last year," Betty interrupts. "A terrible loss, a mother."

Helen ushers them into the kitchen. "Please have a seat. I just made coffee." The mention of Duncan brings Helen back to his last name. Urquart. Ewan's name. Is this man here in the kitchen a relative? Is he, God forbid, her half-brother? Her legs feel wobbly, her mental state even more so but thankfully her stage training kicks in. Places! Action! She springs around the kitchen, holding out chairs, fetching mugs, milk, a choice of honey or sugar for the coffee, scones and butter tarts left over from the wake. "I do apologize for yesterday. I didn't mean to swear ... even at your brother ..." Helen gestures feebly.

Alistair stirs two heaping spoons of sugar into his mug. "Don't you apologize. I know you were upset, as you have every right to be. Now Betty, here, pointed out that I should try to explain why Duncan is this way. You know, at one time, our families were quite close."

Helen is swept by nausea, but swallows and says, barely audibly, "Were they? How close?"

"My mother once told me that my uncle almost married your mother," he says a little shyly.

Uncle! Relief and anticipation flood through Helen. She has noticed that in the country, everyone around knows everyone else's lineage, that genealogy is a living oral tradition. But. She stops, hesitates, afraid to ask the next question, yet begging for the right answer. "And who is your uncle?"

"Ewan Urquart."

Helen hopes her breathing isn't noticeable. "And your aunt is ... Flora?"

Alistair nods. "Was. She died a few years back. You knew her?"

Helen shakes her head. "Only through my mother. And your uncle, he's dead too, isn't he?"

"Yes. He passed away when I was a teenager."

Helen swallows hard so that her intense curiosity doesn't show. "He must have been a fairly young man."

Betty takes a turn. "Barely over forty. It caused quite a stir around here."

Alistair gives his wife a sharp look. "No need to exaggerate."

Betty stands her ground. "Well, it did cause a stir. I remember it, and I was only about six or seven. Long before I even knew you existed."

"What was the stir? An accident?" Helen tries to sound as casual, as disinterested as possible.

"He took his own life," Alistair announces, his chin just a little higher. "He'd been diagnosed with stomach cancer. There wasn't much they could do for him, so I guess he decided to end it his own way. With his rifle. In the barn."

"Poor Flora," Betty murmurs in benediction.

Helen too, feels a great sadness, a door closing. "Yes, poor woman. When would that have been, Alistair?"

"September 1958. I remember it because that was when my Dad took over the farm and we moved in. Flora and the girls moved to Ottawa."

Helen nods, and is aware of how much her heart is hammering. Tears are threatening to flood her cheeks.

"The farm where I saw you yesterday?"

"The very one."

Once more, Helen's slips into character mode. "More coffee?" Both mugs slide forward for more.

Betty leans across the table. "Anyways, we were going into town to get some groceries and pay the property taxes and I said to Alistair, we must look in on you. See that you're alright. Did your mother ever talk about Ewan?"

"Yes, she did. I think she loved him very much, right to the end. You know when you're old, the past often seems more vivid than the present." Helen considers telling them more but, aware of her fragile state, stops herself.

"Well, a good job she didn't marry him," Betty decides, "Else she would have been in the same boat as poor Flora, widowed young, with little insurance. Had to take work as a housekeeper. She led a hard life, Flora did. The girls did alright, though. One of them is a deputy minister in the government."

"Assistant deputy minister," Alistair corrects.

Helen's heart is tap dancing. *I have half-sisters.* Steadying herself, Helen asks, "What was he like, your Uncle Ewan?"

"Tall, about my height. Smart. Didn't talk a lot, but knew a lot. Always regretted that he was never allowed to continue in school. Told every kid he ever met to stay in school. Well, farmers didn't get much schooling in those days, did they? What you needed to learn was never formally taught. And I guess no one around here had any use for any other kind of learning." Alistair pauses a moment, to bring a picture into focus. "But I remember my mother telling me that he had a kind of curiosity, always teaching himself. He'd buy a new piece of machinery and he'd take it apart, even when there was nothing wrong with it, just so's he could see how it worked. Used to get my grandmother mad, afraid as she was that he'd never be able to put it back together right. But he always did. And he'd read the manual, too. Cover to cover. Even political brochures. 'Got to know what they're thinking,' he'd say." He pauses again, allowing Betty her chance.

"Well, I guess it runs in the family. That's where your brains and your love of books comes from, Alistair."

"You read a lot?" Helen asks.

Alistair is shy, as if a deformed part of his anatomy has been pointed out. "When I get the chance. Better than a lot of that rubbish you see on TV."

"Alistair! Helen's an actress. She works in TV!" An embarrassed Betty smiles brightly at Helen.

"Not much!" Helen assures her. "Not if I can work at anything else!"

"I guess it's hard work, like anything else," Betty sighs, as if she has toiled in television for years. "All those lines!"

"What do you read?" Helen asks gently.

"Anything he can get his hands on!" Betty announces. "There are more books cluttering the family room! And he won't let me get rid of any of them!"

Alistair is annoyed at these revelations. "A lot of those books were Uncle Ewan's. You can't just throw them out! That's about all he left behind. That and 120 acres of stones." Betty is suitably chastised, and Helen pushes a plate of butter tarts toward her. "Some of those books are even valuable. That fella who held the auction at the Muir place last year said that those old maps would fetch a good price."

"Maps?" Helen helps herself to a butter tart.

"Old atlases, I guess you'd call them. Books with maps of each continent and country. For elevation and precipitation, too. Uncle Ewan loved poring over them, tracing with his finger the route from … I don't know, New Delhi to Madras. Could tell you how long it might take you to get there, too." Again he pauses to let a memory flower, then smiles.

"My Aunt Flora used to say, 'Ewan's on holiday' when she'd come into the kitchen and see him studying at the kitchen table. But, oh, he could have some black moods, too, I know. I remember one time when I was a kid and raising a calf in his barn, going in there and finding him drunk as a skunk, yelling at the cows, slapping their haunches and telling them they'd ruined his life." Alistair shakes his head. "But he'd get over it. Guess we all have a bit of Black Celt in us."

I certainly do, Helen silently acknowledges.

"That's probably where Duncan got his travel bug from," Betty adds. "Poor Duncan. "

Helen pulls herself from the image of Ewan. "Why 'poor Duncan'?"

Alistair sits up straighter. "Well, you see, that's what we came here to explain about. It was him who found Uncle Ewan in the barn, rifle between his knees, the top of his head blown off."

Helen shudders. "Duncan found the body?"

"Yup. We were both helping with chores at that time, 'cause we were living just down the road, and it was his turn to do the morning milking. He was hysterical afterwards, in a sort of state of shock. And it was after that he started making stuff up. Not only lying, but inventing stuff that never happened. Like he just didn't want to deal with reality anymore. Never could take any kind of responsibility. We thought he would get over it, but he never did."

"He was with me when my mother had her last stroke. That was certainly real enough," Helen says quietly. "I guess that's why he left in such a hurry."

"Yup, that would be it," nods Alistair. "Just likes to live inside his head."

No wonder I felt an affinity, Helen thinks, remembering her childhood fancies. Aloud she says, "And you think he's back in Malaysia?"

Alistair sits up. "Oh, I don't know about that. He came here because he was in some trouble with the law."

"Over his boat business?"

"What boat business? Only boats Duncan has known are the tramp freighters he's worked on for years. Just never been able to settle down, traipsing all over the world. We were surprised to learn about the wife and kids. If, in fact, he was telling the truth about them."

"Poor things," Betty chirps. "Who'll support them now? We don't even know how to get in touch with them. And whatever else, they're kin. He just leaves it to other people to pick up the pieces."

Helen nods, and they all take a few seconds to acknowledge the sadness of the situation. Helen's anger at Duncan slides into pity and then she smiles. "Well, you can stop worrying about this broken piece. As I say, I hardly knew him. I overreacted, I guess, because of my mother's death. If it's all the same to you, I would rather if you didn't mention this to anyone else. It's embarrassing."

Both Betty and Alistair sit up straighter. "We wouldn't tell a soul," Betty says. "It's a private matter." Helen now feels assured that perhaps only half the county will hear about the grieving actress daughter who was having a fling with mad Duncan Urquart on the night her mother died. Helen changes the subject, asking questions about the farm, their children.

"Are you planning on staying here awhile?" Betty says when they get up to leave.

Helen thinks a moment. "No. I think I'll take a few days break. Go back to Toronto to straighten out some things. Then come back later to deal with the house."

Betty pats Helen's arm. "A break would do you a world of good."

Helen smiles. "Thank you so much for coming by. I felt so silly about yesterday."

Betty pats her again. "Don't you have another thought about it. Or about that good-for-nothing Duncan. You just take care of yourself."

Alistair firmly shakes Helen's hand, and their eyes meet for a moment. There is a greater familiarity there than the circumstances have warranted. Familiarity, from the word "family." This is my cousin, Helen realizes with a shiver. She is looking at the same soft grey eyes she sees in the mirror every morning, but in the face of a stranger. "It's been a pleasure to meet you," she says, strongly pumping their hands, unwilling to let them go. "Thanks again."

Betty, halfway to the car, calls over her shoulder, "Come by the house anytime!"

Helen nods. "I will," and thinks, I may have to. "I'd love to see those old atlases."

\*\*\*

It is midday when Helen stands in front of Annie's grave holding a jar of flowers she has cut from the garden at the house — gladioli, snapdragons, zinnias, cosmos and roses, all in varying shades of pink, Annie's favourite colour. Next to the faded arrangements already heaped on the grave the fresh flowers seem garishly alive.

Helen gently puts them down and remains on her haunches, letting her sense of loss spill over onto the grave. The mother she never knew. Who wanted to be known and loved, but who never had the talent for it. Who never trusted anyone else to keep her secret. "I know now, Mom," Helen whispers. "I know about Ewan, and it's alright."

A gulping sob escapes her, and she quickly stands, looking around to see if anyone else has seen or heard. She is alone in the churchyard except for a student on a lawn tractor, mowing the grass around the church. She leans against the stone next to Annie's plot, aware that there is no more anger left. Only great sadness that Annie never shared her secret. And a great sense of loss that she could never bring herself to tell Helen. Imagined conversations and scenes involving a new closeness to her mother run through Helen's thoughts.

Then it occurs to her that Annie did have a confessor. Night after night, sometimes during the day, Annie had summoned up Ewan. Helen looks ahead and her eyes fall on the tombstone one row behind Annie's. "Ewan Kenneth Urquart, 1920–1958" it reads. "Beloved husband of Flora May MacMillan, 1921–1995." She looks stupidly from Annie's plot back to Ewan's stone. She never stopped wanting to be with him, and now she is! "You clever old thing," she says, smiling.

She squats down again and whispers to her mother, "It did turn out right. If you'd have married him, you'd have been a widow at forty. You never would have lived in Montreal, taken all those trips, or even owned a mink coat, not with the amount of money that farm brings in. You made the right decision, even if you didn't know it. Ah, I know you loved him, but it's hard to keep love alive when times are hard. You could have saved yourself all that rage."

Then she thinks about Duncan coming out of the dark every night, and disappearing back into it. A complete fabrication. And how she fell for it. We all have our illusions, she thinks. We all need people to take us dancing. At least I do. Aloud, she whispers, "Did you really know Ewan, Mom? A man who blamed cows for wrecking his life?"

Helen thinks of Bernie. Is he my friend? My roommate? My dancing partner? The answer comes to her immediately. He is all of these, nurturing as many aspects of me as I will allow him to. Bernie moves closer in her emotional hierarchy.

With this shift, Helen feels a strange comfort in being in the company of her newly discovered parents, now both dead. It is like crawling back into a warm, unmade bed in winter. Comfortable and vaguely indulgent. She belongs to them but not with them. Finally, she belongs. She feels a surge of energy, a sense of how alive she is, how good it is to feel her knees creak as she rises, to feel the breeze stir her hair, to be free to go. "I'm free of all of you," she says to the gravestones, "From now on, I'm on my own, no one's daughter." She thinks, I've finally become Helen Bannerman.

# chapter 27

THE PHONE IS RINGING as Helen opens the door, balancing some groceries on one hip.

"Hello!" she says, a little too loudly.

"Don't be mad at me. I called as soon as I could."

"Bernie! Sorry! I just got in."

"So how you doin', darlin'?"

"Fine! Well, alright. Oh Bernie, so much has happened. I have just the most amazing story to tell you."

"Do tell! I'd give anything to get my mind off the fact that my only child is going off to set up a restaurant in Romania! Romania! I don't even know where that is. Do you?"

"It's somewhere over in Eastern Europe, Bernie. Jed will be fine! It might be a great opportunity. All of those former Soviet countries are starting to thrive."

"Romania's where Gypsies come from, right?"

"I'm not sure. They're called Romany, but I'm not sure they're from Romania."

"He'll probably end up joining the Gypsies."

"Bernie, he's already joined the Gypsies. He'll do okay."

Bernie sighs. "Tell me your story."

"I won't now, because it's long and complicated and sad and confusing." Helen lets the words tumble out.

"Wow! What happened?"

Helen laughs. "I know. It sounds strange. For starters, the man I thought was my father wasn't."

"Wow!" Bernie whistles. "You got any other candidates?"

"Yup, the old beau who visited Annie when she was AWOL. I'll tell you all about it when I get back. Which will be soon. I thought I would take your advice. Take a few days off and go back to Toronto. Come back later to deal with the house and the stuff. There's not too much to sort since my sister took all the good stuff. And I can't see hanging on to the house. But I need some time to think it over."

"You take as long as you need. That house isn't going anywhere anytime soon. C'mon home. It's here where you belong."

Belong. That word again. "Yes, it is," says Helen.

"When are you coming back?"

Helen hasn't really thought this through yet. "Let's say Tuesday. I've got some stuff I'll have to do at the bank Monday. I'll take off early Tuesday."

"Sounds grand. I'll tell the cats. Try to rustle up a good dinner. That gives me a whole day to vacuum, too. Need to start with a shovel, I think."

"Don't go overboard, Bernie. I want things the way they were before. I'll buy us a nice bottle of wine. Courtesy of Annie." Helen pauses, then, "Did my dahlias bloom?"

"Blooms the size of saucers, my dear. And the roses have finally climbed over that trellis in the back."

Helen is suddenly eager to be home. "You know, I've missed all of that, all of you, so much."

"Same here, honey." A pause then, "You really okay? Sort things out between your Momma and you?"

Helen smiles, kicks off her shoes. "Well, I've started, Bernie. I still have some way to go. Might help to talk it over with you."

"I'm all ears, honey."

"Great, but it's not just your ears I'm interested in."

There is a pause before Bernie says quietly, "You mean it this time?"

Helen's turn to hesitate. "Yes, I think I do. I've been in such turmoil, I don't know what I want. But whenever I think about the future, you seem to be in it."

"Well, now, that's the best news I've heard in a long while. I could certainly use a future. We'll talk more when you get back."

"I can't wait to get back," Helen gushes, then realizes she means it.

Bernie chuckles, "Then I'm definitely going to have to vacuum."

Helen laughs. "See you after lunch on Tuesday."

As she makes herself a cup of tea, Helen goes over what she must do before she leaves, even makes a list. Empty the fridge. Take at least one load of old clothes to the Sally Ann when she goes into the bank. Pack up the plants, perhaps taking the ones she doesn't want into St. Andrew's or to Mrs. Forbes. Change the message on the phone. Water the garden. The business — the busy-ness — of day-to-day living. Clean up this kitchen, she adds as she looks around. She picks the brandy bottle up off the sideboard and takes it to the sink. "I won't be drinking this," she says, and she pours the remains down the sink.

Helen doesn't do any of the chores. Instead she takes her tea into the living room where Annie's wheelchair is folded in one corner, and the clock, now alone on the mantel, provides steady evidence that life keeps going on. Take the wheelchair back to the medical supply place, Helen notes mentally, then pulls it to the centre of the room and sits in it, looking out over the river. It's a hazy afternoon, with few birds singing, but a muskrat is carving a slowly widening V as he swims to the opposite bank.

She came home, Helen smiles. She came back to what she knew, and, as best as possible, she corrected her mistakes. Did she know I would find that letter? Is that why she was so upset the day I was down there? No, she realizes, she was impatient with me no matter what I was doing. She never planned on dying. But I'll never know, will I? And it doesn't matter.

Helen takes a sip of tea. Poor Annie. Always trying to control things. To control her own life. And she did, in a way.

Helen sighs. None of it turned out the way Annie thought it would, she realizes. For the first time, Helen feels genuine empathy with her mother. But then, is this how *I* saw *my* life turning out? She saw it through. That's all any of us do.

Helen releases the brake on the wheelchair, pushes herself forward and twirls around the living room. She stops in front of the fireplace then stands, folds the wheelchair and fetches the list from the kitchen counter. "Take the clock to Toronto," she says aloud.